Smooth Talkin' Stranger

ALSO BY LORRAINE HEATH

Hard Lovin' Man

Smooth Talkin' Stranger

LORRAINE HEATH

POCKET **STAR** BOOKS
New York   London   Toronto   Sydney

An *Original* Publication of POCKET BOOKS

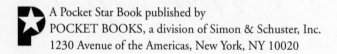 A Pocket Star Book published by
POCKET BOOKS, a division of Simon & Schuster, Inc.
1230 Avenue of the Americas, New York, NY 10020

Copyright © 2004 by Jan Nowasky

ISBN: 0-7394-4160-4

Cover design by Rod Hernandez
Photo © IT Int'l/eStock Photo/PictureQuest

Manufactured in the United States of America

For Laurie,
with fond memories of the beach house days,
for always making us feel welcome,
for being such a special addition to our family.

Smooth Talkin' Stranger

Chapter 1

It had been so long. Too long.

She'd forgotten how hot his mouth would get as he trailed it along her throat, seeking out the sensitive spot just below her ear, nipping her tender flesh, before swirling his tongue along the outer shell, ending the journey with a gentle nibbling of her lobe and endearments murmured in a voice raspy with yearning.

She'd forgotten how slowly he removed her clothes, as though he were awed by the creamy texture of her skin that each released button revealed, as though she were an unexpected gift discovered on Christmas morning to be unwrapped without hurry, the uncovering of what lay inside to be savored as much as the item nestled within.

She'd forgotten how gently demanding he could be as he glided his roughened palms along her ribs, until he cradled her breasts within his hands, his callused fingers kneading and teasing, taunting her with the memories of all the other times he'd stroked her, never in a hurry, taking his time until she was writhing against him.

She released a tiny whimper, and he drew her nearer, blanketing her mouth with his own, his tongue delving deep and sure, plundering, conquering. With his hands, he cupped her bare backside, pressing her hips against his, the unmistakable hard evidence of his longing burning hot against her soft belly.

She wanted to weep for the joy of his desire for her. It had been so long. Too long.

She wound her arms around his neck to keep from melting at his feet, the heat intensifying with each touch, each exploration. She'd forgotten how broad his shoulders were, how his defined muscles quivered as passion took hold. She slid one hand down his strong back, along his hip, until finally she wedged her way between their bodies and wrapped her fingers around him. She'd forgotten how magnificent the velvety length of him felt. Tightening her hold, she stroked him.

His guttural groan echoed through the darkness.

And then she was falling, falling onto the giving softness of the bed that was in direct contrast to the hardened body lying on top of her. Nestled between her thighs where he belonged, he entered her with one solid, powerful thrust that had her crying out in ecstasy.

It had been so long. Too long.

Oh, God. She thought she'd die from the glorious sensations building within her as he pumped his massive body against hers—unmercifully, mercifully. She'd forgotten how beautifully they moved together, their bodies seeking fulfillment, their hearts reaffirming their love.

She was climbing toward the exalted pinnacle of pleasure. It had been too, too long.

And when he carried her swiftly over the precipice, her orgasm rocked her foundation, had her screaming his name right before the tears of wonder engulfed her.

It had been so long. Too long.

Steve hadn't made love to her since he died.

With his face buried in his hands, Hunter Fletcher sat on the edge of his bed, his body drenched in sweat, his muscles still quivering. He'd known she was inebriated. You didn't pick up a woman at a bar and expect her to be stone-cold sober. But he hadn't realized exactly how drunk she was. Not until she'd called out her husband's name with such longing that he realized he'd made one hell of a mistake. By then it had been too late for him. He couldn't have stopped if his life had depended on it. As a matter of fact, stopping at that precise moment probably would have killed him.

With a deep sigh, he plowed his hands through his hair. He'd known she was married, of course. The wedding band nestled up against the engagement ring sporting a diamond too small to glitter had clued him in to her marital status. Which was fine with him. Married women were safer, not looking for commitment. They'd tapped into that pipe dream already, and if they were with him, they'd given up on it. Usually they wanted nothing more than to get back at their husbands, and he was only too happy to oblige.

The disadvantage to preferring married women was that those willing to cheat on their husbands were few and far between, which meant that he spent a good deal of his time living like a monk, so when he did finally find a willing lady, he made the most of their brief time together.

Which usually wasn't a problem. Two willing partners just looking for a quick romp. No names exchanged, no phone numbers memorized, no unrealistic expectations to be met.

Fast, furious, hot, and wild.

It was the way that he liked it. None of that romantic crap women required in order to remain in a relationship for any length of time. Sex. Pure and simple. Animalistic. Nature at its most basic—and in his opinion—finest level.

The woman in his bed right now had certainly

been willing, but he had a feeling she was going to wake up with a mountain of regrets. What he'd delivered was obviously not what she'd intended to order.

He supposed he could hope she would awaken with no memory of what had transpired between them. Then he could lie and tell her that he'd been too drunk to deliver on the promise he'd made at the bar. Although he doubted that *he'd* ever forget this night. Not if he lived to be a thousand.

She'd drawn his attention because she looked incredibly out of place, a woman trying so desperately to appear as though she belonged that it became obvious she didn't. He, on the other hand, was skilled at appearing to belong in places where he didn't. He also had the advantage of being the best at determining who didn't fit in. He'd done it throughout the world—for a covert branch of the CIA that few people knew much about until the war on terrorism escalated.

So figuring out that she didn't really belong at the bar had been simple.

What he'd failed to realize was that she also didn't belong in his bed.

A damned shame. He couldn't remember the last time he'd had sex this intense or satisfying. The woman had incredible legs and a well-toned body that told him she was as physical outside of bed as she was in it. It had crossed his mind—briefly and insanely—that getting to know her outside of bed would be equally rewarding.

He twisted slightly and gazed over his shoulder at her, lying on her side. Spilling in through the uncurtained windows, pale moonlight danced lightly over her bare shoulder, bare back. He was half tempted to nudge aside that sheet bunched at her waist and once again enjoy the sight of her perfectly rounded backside. Removing her clothes had nearly brought him to his knees as he slowly revealed her firm breasts, her flat stomach, her silken skin limned by the moonlight. She'd wanted the darkness; he'd happily obliged, knowing he could use the moon to his advantage.

And use it he had. He'd never relished the sight of a woman's body revealed as much as he had tonight. He'd never taken so much time to get to know a woman. What was it about this one that fascinated him, that urged him not to rush, that caused him to actually care about pleasing her?

After her cry had ceased to echo through his mind, after he was once again able to move his sated limbs, he'd eased off her. She'd rolled over and immediately drifted off to sleep—or passed out. He was hoping for the former.

Honest to God, she hadn't seemed drunk enough that she wouldn't realize she wasn't with her husband. She hadn't seemed drunk at all. Relaxed, sure. Feeling good, definitely. Content to be with him, without a doubt.

His harsh curse seemed out of place within the stillness of his bedroom. He didn't know why it bothered him so much that she'd confused him with someone else. He'd gotten what he wanted: great sex with an attractive woman.

What more did he need?

He shot down the demons that threatened to taunt him with suggestions that he did indeed need much more. He'd shut off his emotions long ago and caged up his heart. It was part of the reason he was so good at what he did. Nothing affected his concentration. Nothing distracted him from his purpose.

Not even a doe-eyed beauty whose hair looked as though it had been spun from moonbeams. He wondered what her bastard of a husband had done that sent her scurrying to the bar in the first place. When Hunter had approached her, she'd appeared vulnerable and hopeful at the same time. Grateful even.

A woman in need of rescue. And he'd found himself wanting to rescue her.

Some rescue.

He wasn't certain why he envied her husband. It went beyond the sex, beyond her physical beauty. Maybe it was the depth of love he'd heard woven through the guy's name when she'd uttered it. Maybe it was the way she'd clutched him as though she never wanted to let him go, clutched him thinking he was her husband.

He contemplated waking her up, driving her back to the bar, helping to get her home—wherever home was. But his survival instincts kicked in. He wasn't a knight in shining armor. Maybe he was even a little drunk himself.

He rolled back on to the bed, draped himself over her with his chest against her back, and pretended what he'd never envisioned with any other woman. He imagined that she was his, that it was his name she'd sent echoing into the night.

Chapter 2

Serena Hamilton awoke with a pounding headache that didn't bother her nearly as much as it should have—probably because her body felt so damned good. Her toes were still curling, her nerve endings still humming in contentment. She thought of that scene in *Gone with the Wind:* Scarlet in bed the morning after Rhett had carried her up the stairs. Good God. Steve had always been talented at bringing her pleasure, but last night he'd been spectacular. He'd picked up a trick or two since the last time . . .

The last time.

The words stabbed into her with painful precision. *The last time.* The last time had, in fact, been the *last* time. Her body stopped humming, her toes uncurled, and her headache threatened to crack open her skull.

No, no, no. It had all been a dream. An incredibly lovely dream. But it had all felt so blessedly real and warm and tactile—not her hands touching her body, but someone else's, not her body pressed against a soft pillow, but pressed against firm muscles and toned limbs. The power of the mind to transform desires into such realistic fantasy was absolutely amazing. But none of her previous dreams had ever been as overpowering.

Slowly she opened her eyes. The sun streamed in through a bare window. Who'd removed her frilly curtains? Who'd left the window naked, without personality, without beauty? Furthermore, who'd changed the size and shape of the window?

With a slow dawning, her fuzzy brain began to gain clarity, and she realized the window wasn't hers. Nor was the wall. God help her. This room wasn't hers either.

Her heart kicked painfully against her ribs. Her throat knotted up, and she couldn't have swallowed even if her mouth hadn't felt as though someone had stuffed cotton into it. Her stomach roiled. She thought she might bring up the frozen strawberry margaritas and cheese-laden nachos she'd feasted on late last night.

Cautiously she shifted her gaze until it slammed into the man sitting in a chair beside the bed. A man whose image hovered at the edges of recognition.

His elbows were planted on jean-clad thighs, his large hands wrapped around a black mug, his deep brown eyes studying her. His denim shirt, only half buttoned, barely revealed a light covering of hair on his chest. At least he was dressed.

Unfortunately, she wasn't. The horror of that realization hit her hard. Inhaling sharply, she clutched the sheet against her chest as though that action could somehow undo the improbable scenario screaming through her mind. She felt as though her thought processes were stumbling along, creating a children's book like the ones she'd read to Riker when he was a baby.

Naked.

Naked in bed.

Naked in bed with a stranger.

A handsome stranger at that, in a dark, elemental sort of way. Locks of his black hair fell forward, not in any sort of style, more like something that simply didn't want to be controlled. He didn't look as though he'd shaved in a couple of days. Five o'clock shadow that more closely resembled forty-eight-hour shadow.

Her first impression was that he wasn't the type she'd want to meet in a deserted alley. All right. Obviously that hadn't been her first impression. Since she was lying in his bed, she had to assume that her first impression had been something entirely different—an attraction that she'd been unable to deny.

"I wasn't sure how you liked your coffee," he said in a deep rumble that implied he knew *different* things about her, her preferences in other areas, aspects of her that she might wish he didn't know.

He cocked his head slightly to the side, and she slid her gaze to four black mugs sitting on the nightstand. She briefly wondered if this man was aware that bright colors existed and could do a great deal to improve one's mood first thing in the morning. She preferred yellows and oranges. Sunshine colors, her son called them.

"Black. With milk. With sugar. With milk and sugar. If you're into cream or you're a tea drinker, you're out of luck."

She thought she detected actual regret in his words. "Milk and sugar," she rasped, as though someone had replaced her vocal cords with fine sandpaper.

Holding the sheet tightly against her upper body, she made a motion to sit up, the soreness between her legs causing her to still. Any hope she had that all she'd done was sleep in his bed vanished.

She struggled to position herself against the headboard without revealing any additional flesh. To his credit, he never dipped his eyes but held hers steadily while he extended the mug toward her. With shaking hands, she took it, careful not to touch him, this man whom she feared she might have touched far too much and way too intimately.

While concentrating on taking a sip of coffee, she heard a slight rattling. Shifting her gaze, she saw him shake a small bottle, spilling a couple of tablets into his cupped hand.

"Figured you could use this, too," he said. "Figure you might have a headache brewing."

Oh, it's not brewing. It's brewed.

Hesitantly, she reached out, hoping he'd understand that she simply wanted him to dump the painkiller on her palm, didn't want to actually touch him. Apparently, he did, because he held his hand over hers and turned it slightly until the tablets tumbled off. She shoved them into her mouth, chased them down with the coffee, and couldn't hold back the grimace this time.

"Tea drinker, huh?"

She almost smiled at his astute observation.

"English Breakfast," she said quietly, thinking it ludicrous that she was hesitant to reveal her morning habits when she'd already apparently revealed a good deal more than that before this morning.

When she lifted her gaze back to him, he was again hunched forward, holding his mug with both hands, watching her, apparently no more willing than she was to discuss why his bed was as rumpled as it was.

"Do you remember much about last night?" he asked.

All right, she was wrong on that point. He *was* willing to discuss it.

"Enough."

"Questions?"

She almost choked on her coffee, holding up a

hand when he shot out of the chair, apparently to come to her rescue.

"I'm sorry. You reminded me of a professor who's just finished a lecture and wants to make sure his students understood all the important points."

He settled back, a corner of his mouth hitching up as though to carry amusement into his eyes. "We didn't do a whole hell of a lot of talking."

"So I gathered." And she wasn't particularly in a mood to discuss anything now. She didn't know how to handle this morning-after crap, especially when she could barely remember the night before. Although she feared her lack of memory might be more of a defense mechanism rather than any sort of true amnesia. To acknowledge the memories would be to admit what she'd done, and she wasn't exactly proud of her actions last night or where she found herself this morning.

She wasn't in the habit of going home with strangers. Hell, she wasn't in the habit of going home with men she knew! Last night had been an aberration, a fluke. One too many margaritas, one too many lonely nights. An incredibly sexy man who even now had her contemplating the advantages of staying in his bed a little longer.

Not an option. She had responsibilities, commitments, obligations. None of which lent themselves well to waking up in a stranger's bed.

She glanced around the room. He must have only recently moved in. Nothing hung on the walls. No photos sat on the dresser. No plants or knickknacks offered a hint to his likes or dislikes. Her clothes were draped over the foot of the bed, a startling reminder that they weren't on her. She inhaled a deep breath. "I need to get home."

He nodded slowly. "You're welcome to use the shower. I set some clean towels—"

"I'm not going to shower. I just want to throw on my clothes and get out of here as quickly as possible."

She thought she saw regret wash over his features, but the emotion was gone so quickly that she couldn't be sure. She almost apologized for seeming ungrateful. Based on the way her body had felt when she'd awoken, she had a feeling she should be thanking him profusely.

"Suit yourself. I'll wait downstairs to drive you back to the bar so you can pick up your car." He jerked a thumb toward the door. "Door locks."

He rose to his full height, and she wondered how—even with too many margaritas in her system—she could have imagined she was with Steve. Steve had been tall, but this man was taller, broader, gave the impression of power waiting to be unleashed.

Carrying himself as though everything was a comfortable fit, he walked out of the room and closed the door.

The firm click echoing between the barren walls snapped her out of her lethargy. She scrambled out of bed, hurried across the room, and threw the lock. Then she pressed herself against the door, seeking some sort of comfort while she trembled uncontrollably. Oh, God, how could she have slept with a stranger?

Steve had died nearly six years ago. In all the time since they'd handed her a folded flag, she'd had not one date.

She laughed mirthlessly. Last night she'd broken with tradition. Instead of curling up with a romance novel while soaking in a tub filled with luxuriant bubbles, surrounded by scented candles, she'd decided to go out on the town. She'd driven to Austin and walked along Sixth Street until she'd finally gathered enough courage to step into a bar. What an idiot.

She'd felt so uncomfortable, so conspicuous, so out of place. She'd thought a margarita would calm her nerves. One drink had led to two, to three, to four. By the time the man had joined her, she'd apparently lost all her inhibitions. What a fool. She could have discovered when it was too late that she'd gone home with a serial murderer, a sexual deviant, a woman beater.

Instead, she'd lucked out. She'd gone home with a man who'd carried her higher than she'd ever flown. The sex had been great—more than great. That was the one memory that she'd completely retained from the night before.

Ironically, the terrific sex only added to her guilt. Because as good as Steve had been, he'd never been *that* good. It felt like a betrayal to his memory to find such joy in another man's body. Part of her wondered if she'd hung onto Steve for so long because she feared discovering that what they'd had together had existed only in her mind.

It had always been hard, so hard, to let another man in. And yet, last night, it had been so incredibly easy—not because of the margaritas she'd downed but because of the man who'd reached across the table and wrapped his hand around hers. The man who'd pressed a kiss to her palm and, with his eyes more than his words, had invited her to go home with him.

Then he'd made her ever so glad that she had.

And now she was assailed with guilt because she'd enjoyed herself. Because she was a mother and a daughter, and she had responsibilities that she'd ignored last night. She hadn't tucked her son into bed. She hadn't made certain that her father was coping with the recent loss of her mother.

Last night she'd been selfish, thinking of only what she'd needed, and last night, she'd desperately needed a man. And by God, she'd certainly found one.

. Now she was in his bedroom when she really needed to be in hers. She didn't want to take her cell phone out of her purse and see how many voicemail messages or missed calls were waiting for her. She'd warned her father that she planned to stay out late. She simply hadn't expected at the time that she'd stay out until the early hours of the morning. She needed to get home.

Wrapping her arms around herself, she crossed the hardwood floor to the bathroom. He was obviously a man of simple tastes. The bathroom was as un-adorned as the bedroom. It contained no evidence that it served any purpose other than its primary function—no potpourri, embroidered hand towels, or carved soaps in decorative dishes. She walked to the sink, gazed in the mirror, and wanted to die from mortification.

"Oh, dear God!"

Alice Cooper on his worst day stared back at her.

Her mascara was smeared around her eyes, reach-ing down to her cheeks, her hair was little more than blond tangled tufts that looked as though it belonged on some creature in a Dr. Seuss book. No wonder he'd been unable to tear his gaze from her face.

She looked as though she'd been resurrected from the dead. Whatever attentions he'd bestowed on her last night had to have been the result of a generous heart, because she was certainly lacking any sort of

sexual appeal this morning—and for all she knew
had been lacking it last night. She'd obviously deluded herself into thinking she'd looked terrific.

Dropping back her head, she audibly sighed and
wondered if crawling out the window and hitching a
ride back to town was a viable option, because she
certainly didn't want to have to face this guy again.
But she didn't know where she was exactly or how far
she was from town.

Her only way of getting home was waiting for her
downstairs. And after he returned her to her minivan, she'd never set eyes on him again. She found
whatever small consolation she could in that fact.

Taking a deep breath, she gathered up her courage.
She had no choice except to face him again. She might
as well do it on her terms.

Hunter stood in his living room, his arm braced
against the floor-to-ceiling plate glass window
that looked out over the lake. The upstairs balcony
that led off his bedroom offered a better view, but
his bedroom was currently occupied. Besides, he'd
convinced himself that the trees at eye level made
this view more tranquil. And right now, he craved
tranquility and absolution. Although he seriously
doubted that either would be forthcoming.

He repeatedly told himself that he hadn't done
anything wrong, anything he should be ashamed of.

He'd spotted an attractive lady at the bar, sitting alone, downing margaritas as though they were lemonades on a hot summer afternoon. He'd sidled up to her, made small talk—for the life of him, he couldn't remember what they'd talked about—invited her back to his place, and shown her a good time.

Still, his actions nagged at him. Probably because she'd looked so appalled when she'd come fully awake and realized she wasn't where she expected to be. Her brown eyes, the most communicative pair he'd ever seen, were practically neon lights flashing every thought running through her pretty little head. She certainly didn't step out on her husband much. If he were a betting man, he'd bet last night was the first time.

For some unfathomable reason, that knowledge pleased him. He didn't want to think of her as running all over creation, hopping into bed with any guy she happened across. He couldn't recall ever feeling this possessive twinge. It was downright irritating.

He glanced at his watch for the twentieth time in as many minutes. If it took her this long when she was just throwing on her clothes, he'd hate to have to wait around on her when she was doing more than that. On the other hand, he couldn't help but believe that in spite of her infidelity, she was a woman worth waiting on.

Hearing footsteps on the stairs, he glanced over his shoulder. She'd done a lot more than toss on her red flowing skirt and white lacy top. And he wished to hell she hadn't, because she made him want to escort her right back up the stairs and offer her a repeat of last night.

All her makeup was gone, although it appeared she'd dabbed something glossy onto her lips. Her short cropped hair was fluffier now, softer looking—like dandelions waiting for a soft breath to blow the petals away. And he was sorely tempted to skim his breath over her curls, along her throat, across her shoulder.

She still looked as though she didn't belong, and he wondered what it would take to make her appear as if she did belong here in his house—a notion that annoyed him for its audacity at passing through his mind.

Lifting a delicate shoulder, she turned her head slightly as though embarrassed. "I decided to shower after all."

He couldn't prevent his grin from forming. He'd figured once she'd caught sight of herself in the mirror that she'd at least want to scrub her face. "I thought you might."

She'd approached and was near enough now that he could see the blush creeping up her cheeks, could smell the scent of his spicy soap on her skin. And he hoped to hell that the fragrance of her perfume remained on his sheets.

"I don't usually wear that much makeup," she said defensively, as though he'd insulted her because he'd seen her less than perfect face this morning. The odd thing was that he'd still been attracted to her—probably because the heat and sweat they'd worked up the night before had been responsible for the smearing.

"Figured you didn't." It was one of the things that had clued him in that she probably wasn't a regular at the bar. She'd reminded him of the way teenage girls looked when they first enter adolescence and started playing around with eyeliner and eye shadow and all the other powdery gunk women dabbed on their face to appeal to the opposite sex.

Now that she was here, ready to go, he found himself loath to take her back to the bar, but he wasn't sure how to entice her into staying. He wasn't in the habit of wanting women to hang around. He had enough complications in his profession. He didn't need the distractions in his personal life.

Still, before he could think through the ramifications, he jerked a thumb over his shoulder. "Did you want to eat breakfast before you go? I boil a mean egg."

Her lips twitched, her eyes sparkled, and he realized that teasing her was a bad idea. It was her smile that had prompted him to invite her out here to begin with.

"No, thanks. I really do need to get home."

Yeah, her husband was probably fit to be tied right about now, because she'd been out all night. Or maybe he was out of town and would be arriving home at any moment. Whatever deviations in her life had allowed her to have the freedom to roam last night were probably drawing to a close. The clock had struck midnight, and he had a feeling she wasn't going to leave a glass slipper behind so he could find her again.

He escorted her out of his house and to his recently purchased black jeep. He opened the passenger door for her, conscious of the fact that they were both taking extra effort not to make eye contact, not to touch. It was a game he'd played countless times: a stranger before, a lover during, a stranger after—as though everything experienced during sex wasn't strong enough or good enough to last into the afterward. Like an exploding star that burned brilliantly and then quickly diminished into blackness.

The unvarnished history of his relationships with women: they always faded into nothing but a distant memory. It was a fact of his life that had never bothered him until this morning.

He settled into the driver's seat, started up the vehicle, and wished to hell that he could think of something appropriate to say to this woman sitting beside him.

Any apology would come out as sounding insincere, because it would be. Knowing he should feel sorry didn't necessarily make him sorry.

Telling her that last night had been the best in his life probably wasn't the way to go either. It had been more than the way their bodies had melded together. He'd felt a connection, a balance that he couldn't explain. As though they'd choreographed their moves before, rehearsed with each other a thousand times, knew the rhythm, and understood the subtle nuances of each other's motions. He'd experienced none of the initial awkwardness he usually did as he tried to determine a woman's particular peculiarities.

He couldn't explain all that he'd felt last night. Sensations that went beyond the physical. He'd never flown so high, so quickly, so intensely, as though every aspect of his being had come into play, had participated.

He told himself that it was only because he'd gone so long without a woman in his bed, but he knew instinctually that it was more than that. That there was something about her that he couldn't explain. And as much as he wanted to pepper her with questions, get to know her better, he knew for his own sake—and hers—the less they knew about each other, the easier it would be to forget that last night had ever happened.

So he drove in silence, finding it strange to contemplate that letting her go was going to be difficult—as though he had any sort of choice in the matter. She was a one-night stand. His life was littered with them.

Yet he couldn't seem to think of her in that inconsequential way, or place her in a comfortable niche that would render her insignificant. In spite of the fact that she'd betrayed her husband and her vows, he felt as though she deserved more respect, more consideration.

With her arms crossed protectively over her chest, she stared out the window. He wondered if she was mulling over excuses to explain her absence. He considered tossing out a few scenarios for her. Quick thinking in dangerous situations was his forte.

Only he hoped she wouldn't find herself in danger, hoped her husband wasn't a man with a destructive temper. Unfortunately Hunter also knew that if he were her husband and discovered she'd been with another man, hell, he'd kill the bastard. The irony in his thinking wasn't totally lost on him—himself being the bastard in need of killing.

He pulled into the parking lot she directed him to and stopped beside the only vehicle remaining. A minivan. He refrained from swearing out loud. She no doubt had kids. He was the last thing she needed in her life. A repeat performance was definitely out of the question.

She darted a quick glance his way. "Uh, thanks for the lift."

She reached for the handle.

"Look," he began. She stopped and gazed back at him. He reached into his shirt pocket and pulled out the folded scrap of paper he'd written on while he'd waited for her downstairs. "If for any reason, you need to get in touch with me . . ."

He extended the paper, aware that he was offering too little, too late. Still, it was more than he'd ever offered to anyone else. "My name and number."

She shook her head. He waved it in front of her. "Just in case. You never know . . ."

Never knew if her husband might figure out she'd been unfaithful and take his wrath out on her and leave her with no place to go. Never knew if she might find herself pregnant and unable to explain her condition or unsure who the father might be. Never knew if she might simply want to cross paths again—although he realized the latter was incredibly unlikely.

He noticed the slight trembling in her fingers as she took his offering, and he couldn't stop himself from uttering, "I'm sorry."

And damn if he didn't discover that he *did* in fact mean the words.

She lifted her gaze and gave him an almost impish grin. "I'm trying to be."

What in the hell did she mean by *that?*

She opened the door.

"Wait," he ordered with the stern voice he'd used to command men.

She stilled and once again looked back at him.

"I know it's none of my business, but what did your husband do that made you go to the bar alone last night, that prompted you to go home with me?"

A deep sadness touched her eyes. "He died."

With the door slamming in her wake, she was out of his jeep and running for her minivan before he could utter an oath. He clambered out of the jeep, barely in time to watch her drive off.

Then he cursed again.

He didn't even know her name.

Chapter 3

"Where in thunderation have you been?"

"Mom! You're home!"

Honeybunch and Lucky yipped, sniffed at her feet, and ducked their noses beneath her skirt.

Serena had barely closed the back door that led into the kitchen when her father, son, and the part-beagle-part-whatever-had-gotten-off-its-leash mutts noticed her arrival. Grimacing, she pressed her fingertips to both temples, her hovering headache threatening to return full force, the odor of scrambled eggs churning her stomach, causing it to threaten revolt. She forced a cheerfulness that she didn't truly feel into her words. "Hello, sweetie. Good morning, Dad."

With her feet, she nudged the dogs aside and walked farther into the kitchen.

"Don't 'good morning' me," her father said. "I've already called the police, the county sheriff, and every hospital in the area—"

"Dad." She held up a hand to stifle his diatribe. She didn't need the scolding this morning, no matter how well-deserved it might be. She'd chastised herself repeatedly on the drive home, and he couldn't say anything to her that she hadn't already said to herself several times over and much more harshly.

Besides she had no intention of explaining last night in front of her son, and she knew her father would eventually confront her and demand to know what she'd been up to. Ten years had passed since she'd moved out from beneath his roof, but whenever she came home for a spell, she was his child again. He pestered her with questions, offered advice that she seldom appreciated, and gave the impression that he didn't know how she managed on her own.

But she had managed for a long time now, and she imagined managing on her own—and alone— would continue for a good while longer. She had the impression that the man she'd spent last night with wasn't the marrying kind.

"I'm a grown woman," she told him, a little more harshly than she'd intended, "fully capable of taking care of myself."

Usually. She had doubts about last night, although admittedly she was safe and sound and not much worse for wear.

She crossed the kitchen where she'd spent so many hours talking with her mother, and once again, felt the sharp pang of recent loss. Maybe it wasn't the loneliness from losing Steve finally catching up with her that had sent her to the bar; maybe it was trying to fulfill her mother's last request: *Get out, Serena. Stop mourning. You're too young not to be looking for another man.*

She wondered if her mother had given similar advice to her father. She'd only been gone two weeks, and already three ladies from the church had hit on Serena's fifty-six-year-old father as though he were God's gift to widows.

Serena wrapped her arms around Riker, bent over, and kissed the top of his head. He smelled earthy, like puppies, hay, and dirt, mixed in with chocolate milk. "Looks like Grandpa is taking good care of you."

Riker tilted up his face to look at her with blue eyes that mirrored his father's. "Yeah, but we were worried."

"I had a little too much to drink. You never drive when you've had too much to drink."

"I know, I know," he grumbled.

His best friend's dad was the chief of police in the small town of Hopeful where she and Riker lived. Hell, *her* best friend was the chief of police. That was part of the problem as well. As happy as she was for Jack, glad that he'd finally trusted love and recently gotten married, she unexpectedly found herself floundering again as she had immediately after Steve had died. She hadn't realized how dependent she'd become on Jack to fulfill the role of a man in her life.

With boys the same age and Steve a common thread between them, she and Jack had drifted into a relationship that closely resembled marriage—always being there for the other, satisfying that second parent role that constantly reared its inconvenient head. It was difficult being a single parent, trying to fulfill all of a child's needs alone, especially when society was set up toward two-parent families. Sometimes she simply needed someone to act as a sounding board, and a man served well when it came to raising a boy.

But now with Jack devoting most of his time to his new family and her mother losing her battle to cancer, Serena felt as though her foundation was in danger of crumbling. She'd always considered herself strong. Right now, she simply felt a soul-deep weariness that sometimes left her too exhausted to even think about getting out of bed.

"So what did you do then?" her dad asked, censure in his voice, bringing her back to the present. "Last night? If you were too drunk to drive?"

"I found a room, slept over." A carefully worded truth if she ever heard one, but she'd never lied to her father. She didn't feel like starting now, although it was incredibly tempting—but the effort required to fabricate a story wasn't worth it.

He narrowed his eyes in suspicion just as he had the night she'd lost her virginity in the bed of Steve's beat-up pickup truck—on a pile of blankets that had smelled like hay and horses. Her father hadn't said anything that night, but his glare had spoken louder than any words could have. She'd felt as though she'd walked through the door with a virgin in a red circle with a slash through it drawn on her forehead. She wasn't sure what to draw and slash on her forehead now. Good mom? Mourning wife? Bereft daughter?

What sort of mother hit the bars and ended up in a stranger's bed? What sort of devoted wife dishonored the memory of her husband as she had? It was strange to be standing here feeling as though she'd betrayed a man who'd been gone so many years—when for so long she'd felt as though he'd betrayed her by dying. Irrational thoughts, every damn one of them.

She patted Riker's head, his shoulders, his back; he was her precious anchor in the storm of life. She bent down and kissed the top of his head again. "I'm sorry, baby."

"For what?"

Tears stung her eyes. "I shouldn't have gone out last night. I shouldn't have left you alone."

"I wasn't alone. I was with Grandpa."

She hugged him more tightly. "I know. But I should have been here."

"Mom, you're hurting me."

She unwound her arms and stepped back. "I just missed you so much."

Damn it. That was part of the problem. Anytime she took time for herself, she felt guilty, as though she was being unfair to Riker, selfishly denying him her presence. It was bad enough that he was denied the presence of a father. She owed him.

"I'm going to take a hot shower, and then you can tell me all about your time with Grandpa." She looked at her dad. "Later we can go through some more of Mother's things."

"You ought to have some breakfast before you head upstairs," her dad groused.

"I'll drink a cup of tea later."

She walked through the house that still carried the lemony scent of the furniture polish her mother had used for more than thirty years to keep everything glowing. The hardwood floor creaked beneath her feet, protesting its age.

Serena had grown up on two thousand acres of land that had been devoted to cattle. Over the years, her father had sold portions of it off to land developers. There was more money in land than in cattle these days, and he'd recognized early on that those who came after him had no interest in becoming a slave to the demands of ranching as he'd been.

She trudged up the stairs to her bedroom, the walls still reflecting the girl she'd been in high school, the girl she'd been when she married Steve the summer she graduated. Pompoms were tacked to the wall. Prom corsages and spirit ribbons were pinned to the bulletin board. Frilly curtains she'd sewn in home ec class adorned the windows.

This room had been her haven. She'd always been able to sit on her bed, knowing after a time, her mother would rap on the door to check on her, knowing that with only a look, her mother would come inside and hold her. Words were seldom needed, love the communicative thread. No matter how old Serena had grown, she'd known her mother would always be there, reaching out to her, comforting her.

Only now her mother was gone.

Tears filled her eyes, blurring everything that surrounded her. She could have told her mother about the mistake she'd made last night. She pressed her hand to mouth. Her mother would have made her feel better about her irresponsibility, her bad decision, her insane behavior. She could hear her mother's wise voice now.

"It's done. Learn from it and move on."

Learn what? That she couldn't stop thinking about the man who'd been sitting beside the bed when she'd awoken this morning? Couldn't seem to shake the dreamlike state he'd carried her into last night? She felt as though he'd branded her with his mouth and hands—and that was an action that until last night had been Steve's domain exclusively.

She'd never kissed anyone other than Steve, had never slept with anyone except Steve.

As old-fashioned as it seemed, she'd always been a one-man woman, a one-boy girl. She had fallen in love with Steve when she was fourteen. Maybe if she'd broadened her horizons when she was younger, she wouldn't find it so difficult to do so now, but every step took her into unfamiliar territory, carried her farther away from Steve, and removed her from her comfort zone.

She'd figured that sooner or later, she would let someone else into her life—the loneliness factor was simply too great to go on forever by herself—but she certainly hadn't taken that initial step toward starting over the way she'd expected.

She reached into her purse and pulled out the slip of paper he'd given her. *Hunter.* Was that his first name, his last? A nickname? For only a moment, she contemplated calling the phone number he'd provided and asking him about his name. But what did it truly matter? She'd never see him again.

She grabbed her robe and walked down the hallway to the bathroom. She set her clothes aside, turned on the shower full force, and as soon as the water began creating steam behind the plastic curtain, she stripped off her clothes and ducked beneath the welcoming spray. She had showered at Hunter's, but she simply felt in need of another cleansing, anything to clear her mind, to vanquish the fog.

She remembered last night a bit more clearly now. There had been something about his eyes, something innately protective about them. She'd felt safe when he'd sat across from her at the booth. Safe and secure, no longer out of place. She'd thought she should have felt uncomfortable with his nearness. She hadn't shown much interest in men—except for Jack, who had failed to notice—since Steve died.

Not that she had many opportunities to meet men in Hopeful. The town boasted a population of nine thousand on a good day when traffic was brisk. She enjoyed the small town atmosphere near Houston. But Austin would always be her home, even though they didn't technically live within the city limits. Lately she'd been contemplating moving back. Now she didn't know if that possibility was wise or not.

Riker was already complaining about missing his friends, and even though she told herself that this was home and children adjusted and she couldn't make her life decisions based on a nine-year-old's social life, she found herself doing exactly that. She'd established her own home-based interior decorating business—Window Dressings—so she would always be available for Riker, could determine her own hours, go on school field trips, and never have to deal with a difficult boss when she wanted to schedule time off to be with her son.

Every decision she'd made since his birth had been made with his welfare in mind. Until last night.

Last night, she'd given in to *her* longings, *her* needs, *her* desires.

She pressed her back to the tiled wall and sank down into the bathtub, wrapped her arms tightly around her drawn up knees, and let the tears fall.

Oh, God, it hurt, it hurt, it hurt. The loneliness she'd struggled so valiantly against when Steve died was back, like a tight rubber band pressing in on her chest, threatening to crush her physically and emotionally.

"Oh, Mom, I miss you," she rasped, her voice echoing around her. Why did people have to die, Goddamn it!

She'd finally adjusted to Steve being gone—no, not adjusted. Accepted. Accepted that he was gone. Now she was trying to accept that her mother was no longer with her.

She hit the side of the tub, felt the pain shoot up her arm. Damn it! She hadn't been ready for either of them to go. Steve had been only twenty-three, her mother had only recently turned fifty. Too young. Too damned young, both of them.

Oh, God, it hurt. The first week after her mother's death, she'd been numb, walking around in a haze.

She'd always heard that people who were truly de-
pressed didn't commit suicide. They were so lethargic
that they didn't want to do anything.

The dangerous moments came when they started
coming out of the depression. When they started
feeling like doing something again. Too often, the
first thing they felt like doing was killing themselves
and without the weight of lethargy, they did just
that.

She supposed in a manner of speaking, she'd reacted the same way. She'd been numb, lethargic for
days. And when she'd finally started coming out of it,
she'd wanted to feel . . . to feel *anything* . . . to feel
alive . . . to feel loved . . . to stop feeling so damned
lonely.

And she'd certainly felt alive last night. Her body
had hummed as it hadn't in years. From the moment
he'd touched her, she'd wanted exactly what he'd offered. And he'd been so good, considerate, and tender. Last night, he'd been exactly what she needed.

She began to shiver as the water grew tepid, and she
was left with no more tears to shed. She forced herself
to her feet, turned off the shower, grabbed a towel,
and began to dry off. Her gaze fell on the love bite on
the curve of her breast. Gingerly she touched it. It
closely matched the one she'd spotted on her neck earlier, when she'd first looked in a mirror this morning.

With the reminder, her legs grew weak and she

settled on the edge of the tub. What if she became pregnant? The thought didn't appall her as it should have. She'd always wanted more children. Of course, she'd always planned to have a husband to go along with them. She had an irrational urge to call Hunter, to hear his voice.

Snap out of it! It wasn't as if she'd ever see him again. She didn't think she'd ever set foot in another bar, might not even set foot out of the house. She needed to stop thinking about him. She got up, finished drying off, pushed the crackly shower curtain back, and climbed out of the tub.

She felt like hell. Too much booze and too many tears simply didn't mix. Her eyelids were in danger of scratching her eyes every time she blinked, her throat was raw.

She slipped on her robe and tightened the sash. Habit had her wiping down the tub, then hanging the towel up to dry before she tossed it in the hamper. Her mother had always worried about mold and mildew.

Serena worked hard to follow her example. Miss Perfect homemaker. Well, she certainly didn't feel perfect anymore.

Chapter 4

"Don't give that one away."

Serena looked at the green evening gown she'd removed from the closet, then at her father sitting on the edge of the quilt-covered bed. The room was a balance of masculinity and femininity. Heavy mahogany furniture: a four-poster bed, a mirrored dresser, a tall bureau, bedside tables holding lamps with fringed shades. Yellow flowers on the wallpaper, yellow lacy curtains in the windows. Decorative doilies that her grandmother had crocheted collected dust on top of the dresser. In clusters on each doily stood an assortment of perfume bottles, given to Mary Barnett by her children, opened but never used.

Here was evidence of a life, gifts appreciated, mementos treasured, a history, moments in time captured. A stranger had but to walk into this room to have a sense of who Mary Barnett had been and what had been important to her.

No such evidence existed within the bedroom of the man she'd slept with last night. As a matter of fact, almost nothing in the rooms she'd seen had revealed a hint to his likes and dislikes. The house had been stark, bare.

And while a part of her argued that he must have only recently moved into the house, something told her that he hadn't. That he led a spartan life.

She didn't think most men were into decorating, but surely this man favored *something,* appreciated some sort of artwork or decoration. She'd seen no photos, no statuettes, no silk greenery. Nothing except furniture. The couch and the couple of chairs in the living room where he'd been gazing out at the lake severely limited the number of people he could have over to visit at one time.

Unlike this house, which had always welcomed people. No matter how many of her friends came to visit, her mother had always managed to find another chair to accommodate them. Something to snack on could always be found on the counter. The refrigerator kept an abundance of drinks cold.

The man this morning could offer nothing more than coffee and a boiled egg. She'd almost been tempted to share an egg with him, to spend a few more minutes in his presence, to become better acquainted with him so she'd at least have memories other than a torrid night spent in his arms. And the memories were certainly there, slowly surfacing, reheating her body—

"Rena?"

She snapped back to the present to find herself still holding the gown, her father still sitting on the bed.

"Where were you?" he asked.

Slightly off-kilter, she smiled. "You know me. Always daydreaming." She lifted the dress slightly. "You said to keep this one, right?"

"Right." Her father tilted his head to the side as though his memories were too heavy. "She wore it on that tropical cruise I took her on for our twenty-fifth anniversary. We danced." He released a gentle scoff. "We didn't dance enough, you know that?"

She saw the tears brimming in his eyes before he looked away. She knew the tears embarrassed him. He was of a generation that didn't give in to emotion. Pretending not to notice what he was trying to hide, she hung the evening gown to the right side of the closet, marking it as something considered and determined not yet ready to be parted with—which so far had been every piece of clothing she'd shown to her dad.

Her mother seldom threw anything away. That was part of the reason Serena had decided to stay and help her father go through some of her mother's things.

"Go through it now, go through it later," her brother, Kevin, had muttered. "Makes no difference to me. I'm not interested in any of it."

A big-time lawyer now, he seemed embarrassed by their family's humble beginnings. Sometimes she wanted to take her mother's cast-iron skillet to her older brother's head.

"Dad, we don't have to go through the closet this afternoon. I plan to stay for a few weeks."

"What about your business?"

There wasn't a lot of demand for decorators in Hopeful, so hers wasn't a lucrative business, but she enjoyed the creative aspect of designing and sewing unique window treatments.

"I don't have any clients waiting for anything right now."

"But if you're here, you can't get clients," he pointed out.

"Dad, the whole point in having my own business is so I can work when I feel like working. I don't plan to become a millionaire by sewing and hanging curtains." She had a few benefits from the Army, and she'd invested Steve's life insurance, so if she lived frugally she didn't have to worry.

"As much as you like reading, I figured you'd open a bookstore. I could float you a loan for that."

She smiled, because her father was always offering to float a loan to her for one thing or another. "I'd love to open a bookstore, but I think it would impinge on my freedom. It's more difficult to get away from a business that has set hours."

"You could move home, go to one of the schools around here, and get yourself a college education. You were always smart, Rena."

"I know, Dad, but I feel like I'm too old for school now."

"Jack went to school. You helped him, and he's older than you."

But she thought Jack had had something to prove. And she didn't have anything to prove, nothing she wanted to do that *required* a college education. Although she knew she'd benefit from the learning, she wanted to do other things with her time.

"I don't want to spend my time studying," she admitted.

"But you liked studying—"

"When I was seventeen. I also liked being a cheerleader and doing cartwheels. But I don't want to do either of those right now."

"You changed, Rena."

"We all change, Dad."

He released what sounded like a burdened sigh. "Let's get back to your mother's things."

Thank goodness. She knew she was being particularly touchy this afternoon, but she wasn't in the mood to have her actions and judgments questioned.

She reached for another dress, a lovely blue one with a swirling skirt. She considered simply moving it to the right side of the closet, but held it aloft instead and raised her brows.

"That can go," her father said gruffly.

She couldn't keep the surprise out of her voice. "Really? Well, that's certainly a first."

"She wore that thing the day the doctor gave her the damned diagnosis," he grumbled as though it were cursed, as though if her mother had worn something else she might have received a clean bill of health.

"I'm sorry, Dad. I know everything brings back memories. Honestly, we can do this another time."

"I'd rather get it done."

"Okay." Carefully she folded the dress and placed it in the box that she planned to drop off at the church later.

"Want to tell me now about the fella that gave you that love bite on your neck?"

She jerked upright so quickly that she almost threw out her back. "Not particularly, no."

Turning away from him, she pulled a frilly blouse out of the closet and held it up for his inspection. He gave a brusque nod. She dropped it into the box.

"He from around here?"

She rolled her eyes. "Yes." She gave him that much in hopes that he'd be satisfied and move on—

"Does he have a name that I'd recognize?"

"Probably not."

"Why don't you give it to me and then we'll know for sure."

With a sigh, she let her shoulders sag. "Dad—"

"I know, I know, you're a grown woman. But if I don't worry about you, then I have to worry about me. What am I going to do without your mother?"

"The same thing I've done without Steve. Take it one day at a time."

He gave her a sad smile. "Your mom and me . . . we had such plans for when I retired. I'm about as close to retirement as a rancher can get. I've sold off my cattle, sold off parcels of my land . . . all too late. I grumbled that entire cruise, worrying about the damn cows. I never took time away. She insisted, though. Our twenty-fifth." He nodded sagely. "I should have danced with her more."

Crossing her arms over her chest, leaning against the door jamb, she decided they were probably done for the day. Every time she tried to help her father sort through things, he ended up drifting into memories.

" 'Bout near killed me to tell her that I was all right with her leaving if she was ready to go. I wasn't, you know. But I knew I never would be, and she was struggling too hard to stay."

She crossed the room, sat beside him on the bed, and wrapped her arms around him. "I know, Dad."

"I should have danced with her more." He patted her hand with his, gnarled and wrinkled from years of labor, but still so strong. "I think Steve would have told you to let him go."

Tears flooded her eyes, her chest tightened. Was that where he'd planned for this conversation to go all along? To offer absolution for what he might be guessing had transpired last night?

It had always been her mother she'd confided in while her father spent the time after dinner sitting in front of the television with the newspaper and a glass of comfort beside him. Southern Comfort. She wondered now if he'd paid more attention that she'd ever realized.

"Dad—"

"You need to dance more, Rena. Don't wait until you're as old as me to realize that, because by then the arthritis makes it hard."

A tiny bubble of laughter escaped, and she hugged him tightly. "Oh, Dad, aren't we a mess?"

"I reckon we are. Take all her clothes to the church. She'd chastise me for waiting until they were out of fashion to do so. You know your mom. Always giving to others more than she ever gave to herself." Stretching, he rose to his feet. "Time to find my grandson and take him fishing."

After watching him amble from the room, she turned to the task at hand. She packed away all her mother's clothes, except for the green evening gown. She decided to leave it hanging in the closet to serve as a reminder to them both that they needed to dance more.

When she was finished packing, she went to her bedroom, sat on the edge of her bed, picked up the phone, and dialed a number she knew from memory. Two rings later—

"Morgan."

"Hi, Jack."

"Hey, gorgeous."

"Is this a bad time to call?"

"No, I'm in the office doing some paperwork. We've had a couple of convenience store robberies."

"In Hopeful?"

"Yeah, I think maybe it's a punk passing through. But you didn't call to discuss police work."

"No, I just wanted to hear a familiar voice. How are you?" In many ways, Hunter reminded her of Jack: tall, broad-shouldered, dark complexion. But Jack's eyes were a startling blue.

"Happily married."

She laughed. He'd married Kelley, his high school English teacher. They had a lot of history that Serena didn't quite understand, but she knew two people who were in love when she saw them. "I'm glad to hear it. How is everyone else?"

"Doing great. How are things there?"

"Dad's doing pretty good." She'd always appreciated that Jack had gotten along so well with her parents, that they'd made him and his son feel so welcomed the first time they'd visited. They'd even invited them to spend time at the family beach house on occasion. "He misses Mom."

"Yeah, I imagine he does. She was a swell lady. If there's anything I can—"

"You already did it, Jack, by being here for the funeral, handling so many of the arrangements. It meant a lot to the family."

"Your family means a lot to me, Serena. When are you going to come home? Jason isn't used to doing things without his buddy. He's missing him."

"I'm not sure when we're coming home. Riker is missing Jason—and you. I think he's always thought of you as the man in his life."

There was a brief silence, and then, "So why'd you really call, Serena?"

She closed her eyes. Jack knew her too, too well. "I did something . . . crazy last night. I went out."

"About damn time."

She rolled her eyes. Jack had been after her for some time to start going out. Every other weekend he took care of Riker so she could have time to herself. And she'd always curled up with a book. "I thought you'd be glad to hear about that."

"You don't sound too thrilled. Didn't it go well?"

"Well, that depends. I did meet someone."

"Good for you."

Because it was Jack, because they'd shared so much, she could reveal the truth.

"I slept with him."

"Was it good?"

"It was great." She released a startled laugh. "Oh, God, Jack, I'd forgotten how good it could be."

"I've been telling you for years, Serena, that you're too young to be spending all your nights at home alone."

"I know. I've just never done this kind of thing before."

"You gonna see him again?"

"I don't know."

"What's stopping you?"

What was stopping her? "I barely know him. I'm having second thoughts about last night."

"So that's the real reason you called."

"Yeah. I certainly can't talk to Dad about this. I've lost touch with all my friends around here. You're the only one I can share this with."

"Did you like him?"

"Yeah, I did."

"Then see him again. Have a summer fling."

"But, Jack, I'm a mother—"

"You're a woman, Serena. A young, attractive woman. Live a little."

"It's different for a woman than it is for a man, Jack."

"Doesn't have to be. Not in this day and time. Go have some fun. You deserve it."

"Maybe I will. Thanks, Jack."

"For what?"

"For always being there."

She hung up the phone and returned to the closet in her parents' bedroom. She skimmed her fingers over the evening gown. It was never an easy process to pack away a life. The hardest part was making sure that one didn't pack away one's own life. She was beginning to realize that she'd deluded herself into thinking that she hadn't done just that six years ago.

She'd always been there for Riker, been there for Jack and Jason. But when was the last time that she'd truly been there for herself?

Last night. Last night, she'd felt like a *woman!* Attractive, desired.

Then this morning, she'd been like her father worrying about the cows. Good Lord. A handsome man had taken her to bed, and instead of savoring the moments when she'd awoken, she'd started feeling guilty.

Jack and her father were telling her the same thing. Get out, have fun. But she needed more than dancing in her life. She *wanted* more than dancing. She wanted to wake up next to a man. She wanted love and passion. She wanted once again to experience the joy of living.

Chapter 5

Sitting at the bar, Hunter noticed her the second she walked through the door. The tension eased out of his body the way it did when he spotted his prey under the cover of darkness and knew that his mission was close to being completed. Only this time, he was hoping his mission was only just beginning.

Her gaze locked with his, and even from this distance, he noted a measure of uncertainty, her gait faltering before she headed across the room. Tonight she didn't look as out of place, probably because she wasn't trying so hard to look as though she belonged.

She wore a plain white blouse, the top buttons undone to reveal her throat and the slightest hint of her breast. Her snug-fitting jeans enhanced her trim figure and clearly revealed long legs that didn't stop. The sensual sway of her tight little butt held him mesmerized until she slid into a booth where shadows formed a canopy of intimacy.

She didn't walk like a woman who realized that

men followed her movements with keen interest. She was sexy as hell, and the fact that she seemed totally unaware of her appeal made her even more attractive to him. Unfortunately, she also drew the attention of several other men in the room, and he figured if he didn't respond to her arrival soon, he'd lose his advantage.

He signaled the bartender. "Another whiskey sour and a frozen strawberry margarita. Make it a schooner."

He took a deep breath and released it slowly, knowing he was probably a fool for feeling as grateful as he did because she'd shown. He wasn't a man who left things to chance, but tonight he'd wagered against fate. If she returned, he'd move forward. If she didn't, he wouldn't look back.

He was grateful that his resolve not to look back wasn't going to be put to the test. He'd fought against his instincts to track her down all day. He possessed the skills. Locating objectives was how he made his living. He figured he could have located her by nightfall. She wouldn't have been trying to hide from him and that would have simplified his task. But he hadn't wanted to go into the *hunter* mentality. He wanted her, but only if the attraction was mutual. Her return led him to believe that it was.

Something about her had struck a resounding chord deep within him, and he'd known getting her out of his system would be difficult. Last night had been a fluke. Obviously she seldom frequented bars.

Still, she'd come back. Now he just had to decide what he was going to do about it. When the bartender returned, Hunter paid the tab, left a generous tip—he was suddenly feeling extremely generous tonight—grabbed the drinks, and strode toward the booth.

When he got there, on the off-chance that he'd misread her, he waited for her to acknowledge him, to give him permission to join her, which she did with a winsome smile that made his gut clench and his protective nature kick in. He set the margarita in front of her and slid onto the bench opposite her, when he would have liked nothing more than to sit beside her, slip his arm around her, and welcome her with a kiss.

She wore far less makeup tonight. Her short blond hair looked softer, not as stiff, gentle curls a man could run his fingers through without worrying about moving them out of place, because it was obvious that their *place* was wherever they happened to be. Her eyes had drawn him in last night, but he preferred tonight's entire package.

"I don't know why I'm here," she said softly, her gaze flickering between his and the frosty schooner he'd set in front of her.

Resting his forearms on the table, he leaned

nearer. "I know why I'm here. I was hoping you'd show."

She lifted her shoulders. "And here I am."

"And here you are."

She concentrated on sipping her margarita, just as she had this morning sipping her coffee, as though she needed time to consider what she wanted to say.

"Do you come here often?" she asked.

"Last night was a first." In more ways than he cared to contemplate. He'd never had trouble getting a lady out of his system. In only one night, she'd managed to burrow so deeply under his skin that he knew any more time in her company would be a big mistake—and here he was tempting himself.

"For me, too," she said.

Nodding, he drank his whiskey sour.

"You figured that out last night, didn't you?"

He set his glass down. "Yep."

"What gave me away?"

He rubbed his jaw. He'd shaved tonight. Gotten a haircut this afternoon. Tonight it seemed their roles were reversed. While she'd been looking to gain someone's attention last night, tonight he'd spruced up in hopes of gaining hers. "Your eyes, mostly."

"Because of all the eye shadow and mascara—"

He shook his head. "Because you looked scared."

"I'm still scared."

"Me, too."

Her eyes widened as though she were surprised by his confession. He was having a difficult time believing he'd revealed his true feelings. He'd spent so many years pretending to be what he wasn't that sometimes he forgot what he was.

"Why are you scared?" she asked softly.

"I don't have a lot to offer, and you strike me as a woman who needs a man who has a lot to offer."

"You're afraid you'll get hurt?"

"It's more that I'm afraid I'll hurt you. Relationships aren't my thing."

"Are you unable to commit? Or unwilling?"

"A little of both, I guess."

"So you're here simply looking for a repeat of last night?"

He wished that was all he was looking for. It would certainly help to keep his life uncomplicated. He avoided answering her question by posing one of his own. "Are you?"

"I don't know what I'm looking for."

Downing his drink, he decided the better part of valor would be to get up and walk out before she realized that regardless of what she might be looking for, he wasn't it. He'd done things he knew she'd never approve of. Hers was a world of apple pie and baseball, a world she enjoyed because men like him did things that no one talked about.

But he had no interest in walking out. She was a

curiosity, a woman who interested him outside of bed.

"What if you hadn't spotted me when you came through the door?" he asked.

She tapped her glass. "I would have left." She looked embarrassed with the admission. "So I guess I do know what I was looking for. I was looking for you. Which seems a bit odd. I don't even know if Hunter is your first name or your last."

"First. And yours would be?"

"Serena."

Serena. He liked it. "It suits you."

"My parents would be glad to know you approve."

He liked the way she teased, the way she carried a note of warmth in her voice when she mentioned her parents. He'd never cared one way or the other whether his approved of anything.

"You drive a minivan. I assume you have kids?"

She gave him a smile so tender that it caused an ache to form in his chest.

"I have a son. Riker. He's nine."

He arched a brow. "Riker? That's an unusual name."

"His dad was a Star Trek geek."

She wrapped so much fondness into the word geek that she left no doubt as to how much she'd loved the man, how much she still did. It was a path that he didn't want to travel, unraveling her history with another man, knowing what she might have shared with her husband, what she would probably never share with Hunter.

He was certain some psychiatrist would label his aversion as some sort of denial, inability to cope . . . who the hell knew or cared? He felt what he felt. That's all there was to it.

He didn't need to analyze it, label it, or dissect it. Probably the reason he avoided people. He didn't want someone to look into his eyes and see the dark man he'd become.

He watched as she drank her margarita, the silence easing between them, her eyes taking on a winsomeness, and he figured she was reliving moments spent with her husband. Damn, he didn't like the man, and he didn't even know him. Didn't want to know him.

"A few doors down is a place with a dance floor. You interested?" he asked.

Abruptly she stopped sipping her drink, and a bubble of laughter floated toward him. The sweet sound would have drawn him in and held him captive if he wasn't working so hard to not be offended that she was laughing at him.

"A private joke?" he asked.

She bobbed her head. "Sort of. More like perfect timing. My dad and I were talking this afternoon and he said that I needed to dance more. And here you suggest dancing." She shook her head slightly, her smile bright. "It just seemed destined or something. I don't know. Fate, I guess. That's part of the reason I came back tonight. Some of the things he said."

"Does he live in Austin?"

"On a ranch outside of Austin, near 35 toward San Marcos."

"You're a country girl, then?" he asked.

"Pretty much. When I was growing up, Austin was just beginning this big population spurt. I hardly recognize it when I come home. And I get disoriented going down 183. The city has changed so much."

Everything within him stilled as he analyzed what she'd said, what she hadn't. "You don't live here?"

"No, I live in Hopeful. It's a little town near Houston. Not many people have heard of it." She trailed her finger along the glass, wiping away its dew as though she needed to collect her thoughts before meeting his gaze. "My mom passed away a couple of weeks ago. I decided to stay for a while and help my dad adjust, settle in. I'm only here for a few weeks."

She'd just thrown him a safety net. He could continue to see her without worrying that she'd expect more than he could give. They might get a bit more involved, but in a short time their relationship—a word he couldn't recall ever using in his association with women—would draw to a natural end. She would go home to her small town, get back to her life there, and he'd return to what he needed to do.

Calm settled over him. They'd go into this arrangement without expectations of any permanence. He'd thought he might have one more night with her, and now it seemed he could have more. He already knew he wanted more.

She didn't make him feel awkward for having the social skills of a corpse. She didn't push or demand. And she was hell in bed. The next time, though, he was determined that she'd realize it was him making her scream and not her dead husband.

"I'm sorry for your loss," he said. The words seemed trivial, and he was certain they couldn't begin to ease her sorrow.

"I appreciate the sentiment. Last night I forgot the sadness for a while."

"Maybe we can make that happen again." Reaching across the table, he took her hand, threaded his fingers through hers. "Do you want to check out that club down the street?"

She gave him a smile that he was coming to recognize as one that signaled she was pleased. It radiated joy, but in a tender way, in a way that made him feel as though he was doing something that she truly liked.

"Give me a minute to finish my drink?"

He nodded, almost saying that he'd give her anything she wanted. But the words sounded too corny, and they weren't completely true. He only had so much to give, and he only had it to give for a short time. He was scheduled to leave on a mission in a few weeks. Despite his skill and caution, there was always a chance he wouldn't come back. The last thing she needed was to suffer another loss.

But he'd give her what he could while they were together, and he'd make certain that when they parted ways, she'd have no hard feelings. They were both going into this knowing it wouldn't last; it was a relationship for the short-term.

And that made it something he could handle without fear of hurting her. He'd hurt enough people; he certainly had no plans to add her to the list.

Without the haze of alcohol clouding her senses, Serena understood now why she'd gone home with him last night. His eyes. A deep, dark chocolate that reminded her of the creamy fudge that she always indulged in whenever her path crossed a fudge shop during vacation. But more than the richness of his eyes was the intensity with which he watched her. As though no one else existed in the room, as though his entire concentration was focused on her, as though she were the only thing of importance in his life.

He wasn't much for idle chitchat. But she had the feeling that she could open him up if she worked at it. She just wasn't certain how much she really wanted to know. The more she knew about him, the more important he would become. He lived here; she lived four hours away. They wouldn't be a world apart, but she'd had a long-distance relationship before, when Steve had been assigned overseas. The separation had almost killed her, but it was like they said—whoever *they* were. *That which doesn't kill you makes you stronger.*

And she had grown stronger. She'd learned to make decisions on her own, decisions that affected all three of them. She'd learned to rely on her own judgment, to be independent. She'd learned lessons she hadn't even realized she'd needed to be taught.

And she was still learning, if the past two days were any indication. She'd certainly not expected to find herself seeking a man for a second night. But this man intrigued her as no one had before him. Not even Jack—even though for a while she'd thought she was falling in love with him.

But Jack's voice didn't send shivers cascading along her spine. His touch didn't send heat swirling through her, didn't cause an ache that demanded attention. While every aspect of the man sitting across from her held her riveted.

She was fairly certain that Hunter had been waiting for her—as though he knew her better than she knew herself. Part of her felt emboldened by her actions, and part of her simply wanted to get to know him better so she wouldn't have to feel guilty about sleeping with a stranger.

She sucked hard on the straw, drawing up the margarita, fighting back a curse as she was hit with a brain freeze.

She didn't want to get drunk tonight, but she thought being a little more relaxed couldn't hurt. She wasn't exactly sure where she was headed with this man. She only knew that she was grateful that she'd come back here, more grateful that he was with her now.

She knew so little about him, and yet she felt that she knew so much. Deep creases had made themselves at home within a rugged face that she thought the elements of nature—wind, rain, sun—might have played a role in shaping. With deeply tanned skin, he gave the appearance of a man whose occupation kept him outdoors a good deal of the time. She was certain he didn't work in an office. She remembered the rasping of his hands over her skin, could feel the coarse texture of his fingers still laced through hers. She could feel the tempered strength in his fingers, could see it in the breadth of his shoulders. His navy blue shirt fit him like a second skin. Not an ounce of fat anywhere to be seen.

She thought about engaging in a little game of twenty questions, but it seemed a little late for that, and she was loath to admit that she'd slept with a man knowing so little about him. Besides, she had a feeling he wouldn't embrace the spirit of the game, would offer up curt answers that might in time irritate her. Better to let their relationship evolve naturally. He'd share with her what he would, when he was ready. And she'd do the same.

She certainly hadn't come here looking for a summer fling, but she had a feeling that she might be headed into one. She was filled with a sense of anticipation, wondering how the night might unfold. Last night had been completely out of character for her. Yet here she was again, tempting him and herself.

At least she thought she was tempting him. He seldom took his eyes off her, and he definitely had the look of a man who was pleased by what was before him. And she certainly liked her view. He exuded confidence. As she'd noted this morning, he was comfortable in his environment, with himself. She wished she could achieve that same level of contentment. Being in the bar was an uneasy fit.

"I got married right out of high school." She didn't know why she felt compelled to blurt that out. "I had a child before I was eighteen. I never really did the single girl scene. I'm not sure how to do it."

"Could have fooled me."

"No, I didn't fool you. Not one bit."

He shrugged. "Just be yourself."

Being herself was soaking in the tub with a good book. She wanted more than that. But now she wanted a good man, to explore possibilities. Besides, she couldn't imagine that Hunter would be content with all she had to offer, when she'd suddenly grown discontent with it. "I'm not explaining myself very well."

He tightened his hold on her hand as he leaned toward her, earnestness in his eyes. "Look, Serena, I have no expectations for tonight. If it ends up being a repeat of last night, great. If not, I'm okay with that, too. I enjoy being with you."

She liked his voice—a deep baritone that wove comfort around the syllables.

"You have simple tastes."

He grinned, a devastatingly handsome grin. "Now how am I supposed to respond to that statement without offending you?"

She cringed, realizing how she must sound, a desperate woman who needed her confidence boosted. "I'm not fishing for compliments. I think I'm trying to redefine myself. I see myself as a widow, a mother . . . neither of which is particularly sexy—"

"Dang, woman, then you must not own a mirror."

His rapid-fire response stunned her. Was she sexy?

She'd never thought of herself in that way. She'd begun to see herself as a harried mother running from scouts to soccer practice to school functions.

She was a businesswoman so focused on selling her product that she never thought about selling herself.

Yet, here she was sitting with a man who she thought could have probably chosen any woman in this bar—but he'd been waiting for her. Flattered, more than she'd been in years, she smiled. "Thank you. I think."

His grin disappeared. "You honestly don't realize how attractive you are, do you?"

"It's been a while since I've felt that way," she admitted.

Holding her gaze, he lifted her hand and pressed a kiss to her fingers. "Trust me. I only go for the pretty ones."

"Did you tell me that last night?"

"I don't remember a lot of what we talked about last night. But I probably said something along the lines of 'Are your eyes hurting? Because they're killing me.'"

Laughing, she shook her head. "No, you wouldn't have used a corny pickup line like that."

"You sure?"

She nodded, not certain why she was as sure as she was. She only knew that she was. Images of last night began to play through her mind like a collage of special moments. "You asked if I was lonely, if I wanted some company. I've held the loneliness at bay for a long time, and last night, it just caught up with me.

But you made me smile and I hadn't smiled in a long time."

"That's not all I did."

His smile was slight, his eyes warm, his voice . . . satisfied, but revealing no cockiness. He took pride in what he'd accomplished—not that she could blame him when she'd been the recipient of his attentions.

No, making her smile wasn't all he'd done. He'd had her writhing in pleasure, screaming in ecstasy. She wished she could be as comfortable with what had transpired between them last night as he was. "No, that's not all you did," she acknowledged.

He kissed her fingers again. "It was mutual."

"Making you smile?"

"Everything." He gave his head a quick nod. "Finish your drink. I'm ready to hold something other than your hand, and a dance floor should provide that opportunity."

And she was ready to be held. She shoved her almost empty glass aside and hoped she was flashing him a seductive smile. "Then let's go."

He stood and took her hand, helping her to her feet, not relinquishing his claim to her as he guided her through the crowded bar. He shoved open the door and led her outside.

The sultry night air descended. Summer was here to stay. She'd always thought Austin was humid until she'd moved closer to the Texas coast. Now, she found Austin humidity pleasant.

They entered the club, still holding hands. She hadn't expected that of him. But then she had to acknowledge that she didn't know him well enough to understand fully what she should expect of him. She wasn't even sure what she expected of this evening either. As he'd suggested, perhaps a repeat of last night. A few too many drinks and heading home with him.

Although truthfully, she didn't know if she could be a one-night stand for two nights in a row. In spite of Jack's encouragement that she should do exactly that.

As they wove through the crowd, heading for the dance floor, where the country music wasn't punctuated with too many conversations, she wondered if he needed more than that as well, more than hungry hands and writhing bodies. If more than a woman was missing from his life, just as more than a man was missing from hers.

She longed for the quiet conversations, the trust, the pouring out of one's hopes and dreams. She had no one to truly share her dreams with. As much as Jack cared for her, he had his own life, his own family, his own dreams.

When she and Hunter reached an empty spot on the dance floor, he took her in his arms, holding her closely. He didn't bother to pretend that their bodies weren't intimately acquainted—even if their hearts and souls were still strangers. She welcomed the opportunity not to pretend either.

Wrapping her arms around his neck, pressing her cheek to his shoulder, listening to the hard pounding of his heart echoing within his chest, she decided that she liked that he was honest, with his body as well as his words.

She must have sensed that last night as well. His hands fit nicely at the small of her back, one turning downward slightly to lay claim to her bottom. Instinctively she knew he wasn't a man who would whisper false promises.

And she needed, wanted that. As much as she needed the physical strength he offered. She felt as though she was wrapped in a cocoon of intimacy.

She remembered now that he'd managed to create the same feelings when he'd approached her table last night.

"Care for some company?" he'd asked.

And being the witty girl about town that she was . . . she'd only nodded.

His smile had been warm, sincere, had drawn her in. His dark eyes had held her captive. When he spoke, his low voice had resonated through her. There was power in the way he moved, but she'd never felt threatened.

She'd felt attraction: hot, burning, immediate. It

was more than his handsome features, his great body. It was the way he made her feel safe.

"What's a nice girl like you doing in a place like this?" he'd asked at one point.

"Trying not to be nice," she'd confessed.

He'd laughed, a low rumble that had increased the intimacy between them and sparked her desire.

"I can help you out there," he'd promised.

And she'd wanted the promise fulfilled. He made her feel attractive, desirable, and in so doing, he'd become irresistible. A man who wanted her when she hadn't felt wanted in a long time.

With his attentions, she'd suddenly felt young again, carefree. She wanted to explore her sexuality, wanted to explore him. She wanted to run her fingers over the outline of muscles visible beneath his shirt. She wanted to press her lips against his lips, taste him. The physical attraction was undeniable, but it was more than that.

It was the same thing he was giving her tonight. Time. Time to test the waters. Time to get comfortable with the journey their bodies wanted to make. Time to allow her heart in—or to protect it if need be.

But she'd been protecting her heart for six years now. She was weary of the numbness, of looking at a man and not daring to see the potential of what they might share.

Hunter managed with his penetrating looks, his sensual touches, his slow journeys to stir to life everything that had died with Steve—a young girl's dreams with all the possibilities that life had to offer. In a heartbeat, she'd grown old. She'd buried her femininity. She'd focused her entire being on her son.

And in one night, Hunter had managed to reawaken all that had lain dormant for so long. More importantly, being with him had made her realize that she'd denied her own needs for far too long. She'd set them aside, pretended that they didn't exist.

Irrational guilt pricked her conscience. Steve was gone. It was long past time to move on, to go forward. But the going forward hurt because it meant leaving him behind.

She kept his memory alive for his son, and in so doing, she'd kept him alive for herself. His son had gone so long without a father, had relied on her to be both parents. But she was tired of being alone, tired of relying on Jack to be the pseudo man in her life. She needed a real man of warm flesh, hot blood, passionate kisses.

"You all right?" Hunter's deep voice rumbled near her ear, while his hands moved comfortingly over her back, drawing her nearer when it was almost impossible for them to be any closer unless they removed their clothes.

She tilted her head back, held his intense dark

gaze, and forced herself to smile, not wanting to disclose the unsettling direction of her thoughts. "It's just been a long while since I danced. Steve wasn't much of a dancer."

It was the wrong thing to say. She felt it immediately. A subtle tightening of the muscles beneath her fingers, a distancing between them that had nothing to do with physical closeness. She thought about how much it would hurt if he suddenly said, "Yeah, neither was Louise, or Margaret, or Mary." If he spoke of any other woman in his life. And she desperately wished she'd stopped with the smile or used her mouth to kiss him rather than to speak.

"I'm sorry," she murmured. "I'm not thinking about—"

"Don't worry about it."

Cupping the back of her head, Hunter guided her face into the comforting nook of his shoulder. She liked being here, liked being within the reassuring circle of his arms. She wanted to leave ghosts and the past behind as the slow country song wove around them. The lyrics told of a man who'd realized too late that he hadn't appreciated his woman—not until she'd fallen in love with another. She could write her own lyrics about a woman who lost her chance at love because she failed to recognize what was right in front of her—a man who made her believe she was attractive, made her feel like a woman.

Jack had never looked at her with desire. They'd never been anything more than friends.

Hunter was lover material. But would he want to be more than that? Could she become involved with a man who didn't? Having only had one man in her life since she was fourteen, she was at a disadvantage. She'd never experienced rejection—except for Jack. And his rejection hadn't come as a blow to her heart. It was more along the lines of disappointment.

When the song ended, Hunter drew her up against his side with his hand clamped firmly, possessively, against her waist, and led her to an empty table along the side of the room. He pulled out a chair for her and after she sat, he lowered his head to hers intimately, whispering as though to share a secret. "I'll be right back with drinks."

She watched him walk away. When the crowd swallowed him up, she turned her attention to the dance floor, where other couples were still dancing. It had been a long time since she'd thought of herself as part of a couple, since she'd had a man's undivided attention. She'd forgotten how much she enjoyed it. The opening of doors, pulling out of a chair, fetching of the drinks. Little things that spoke of togetherness. As her gaze drifted over other men, she was aware that none snagged her interest as Hunter did, and she found the loneliness creeping back in, could hardly wait for him to return to her.

A shadow passed in front of her, and she looked over—realizing she'd offered a welcoming smile a little too soon.

The man was rangy and probably not as tall as his hat made him appear. Although he was nice looking, he didn't appeal to her. She remembered how when she'd first looked up at Hunter last night, she'd been immediately intrigued.

"Hey, darlin', what's a pretty little lady like you doing all alone when we got music playing?"

His words came out slightly slurred, which made her uncomfortable. She was accustomed to crowded playgrounds and amusements parks, not unwanted attention at a nightclub. She suddenly desperately wanted Hunter to return. She glanced over her shoulder.

"Hey, darlin', I'm talkin' to you."

He wrapped his hand around her arm. She jerked free.

"I'm not alone," she said.

He grinned crookedly. "Two chairs, one empty. That's alone for right now. Come on and dance with me."

He leaned down as though to grab her again, and she held up her hand to stave him off. "I'm sorry, but I'm not interested."

"How do you know if you ain't tried it? Come on now, be a good sport and show me a good time."

"The lady's not interested."

The voice resonated with authority. Two glasses appeared on the table before she was even aware Hunter had returned. He angled his body so the other man had to look around him to see her.

"This is between me and her," the man said.

"It might have been, but now it's between you and me."

"I just want a dance."

"What you're going to get is trouble if you don't move on."

Grinning, the man held up his hands in supplication. "All right. All right. I sure as hell don't want no trouble."

He turned, and then his fist was flying back toward—

Before Serena could even issue a warning, Hunter had the man flattened against the wall behind their table, the man's swinging arm wedged behind his back and raised so high that she thought it might pop out of the socket. She'd never seen anyone move as fast with such force and control as Hunter had.

She couldn't hear what was being said, but the man's eyes were bulging and his head was bobbing. Hunter stepped back, and the man swiped his hat from his head. He did appear considerably shorter without it.

"My apologies, ma'am. No insult intended. Y'all have a nice night now, ya hear?"

He walked off and Hunter took his seat.

"Sorry you had to go through that," he said.

She wasn't. She hadn't enjoyed the man's hassling her, but she had to admit to being impressed by Hunter's response to it. This morning she'd had the impression of power leashed. It was obvious that Hunter knew not only how to protect himself, but how to protect her. Seeing him in action was an aphrodisiac. Reaching across the table, she laid her hand over his. "That was the sort of thing I was afraid was going to happen last night while I was alone. What did you say to him?"

"Most of it I can't repeat in front of a lady."

"Give me a hint."

"That he was half a second away from hearing bone snap."

"You would have done it."

He shook his head. "Probably not. With drunks the threat is usually enough."

"But you *could* have done it."

"Sure." He turned his hand over, wrapped his fingers around hers, and stroked his thumb in a circle over her skin. "But I wouldn't have liked doing it."

"What *do* you do for a living?" she asked.

"Right now I'm between jobs."

He said it easily, without any shame or discomfort, but she knew it couldn't be easy for a man when the slow economy caught up with him. No matter how confident a man was, losing a job had to be a blow to his ego. She squeezed his hand in comfort. "I'm sorry. This damn economy. I keep thinking it's going to improve, but I know so many people who have been laid off. If there's anything I can do—"

He pressed his finger against her lips. "You can not worry about it, enjoy your drink, and dance with me again."

She smiled. "Sounds like a plan."

Although she thought she'd enjoy dancing with him more than drinking her margarita. With the straw, she stirred her drink.

"Tell me about your son," he said.

She lifted her gaze to his, saw genuine interest in his eyes. "He's my favorite subject."

"I figured that out earlier."

"You seem good at figuring things out."

"I'm good at reading body language."

An understatement. She'd learned last night that he was extremely skilled at communicating with his body.

"People communicate more with their facial expressions than they do with their words," he added. "Your face lit up earlier when you mentioned Riker."

"He's my pride and joy. He's a good boy, but he wants to grow up too fast."

"Everyone wants to grow up too fast."

"Did you?"

He nodded slowly. "Joined the Army when I was seventeen. Thought I was tough. Discovered I didn't know what tough was."

"You were certainly tough earlier—with that cowboy."

"Can't abide bullies. Especially drunk bullies."

She sensed he had a history there, something he wasn't saying. "Were you the skinny kid who got picked on?"

"In some ways, at some point in our lives, we're all the skinny kid who gets picked on."

"You really think so?"

"Sure. At that point, though, we all make a decision: we can become a bully ourselves, or we can stand up to him, or we invite him to take another kick."

"Sounds like a metaphor for life."

He shrugged and grinned at her. "I get stupidly philosophical when I drink."

"Not stupidly."

His grin vanished. He planted his elbows on the table, leaned toward her, and trailed his finger along her arm. Warm shivers danced over her skin.

"You get relaxed when you drink," he said.

She nodded. "I don't want to get quite as relaxed tonight."

"I'm good with that."

Oh, he was more than good.

"I made you laugh last night," she said.

"I enjoy a woman who makes me laugh." His eyes darkened. "I especially enjoy you." He closed his hand around hers. "Let's dance."

He took her back out to the dance floor for another slow number that had them barely moving. She wasn't certain that they were truly dancing. They were simply holding each other close.

And she did love the way he held her, the way her body fit against his, as though every dip and curve she possessed had been fashioned with him in mind.

When the music increased in tempo, they retired to the table, ordered more drinks, and simply enjoyed each other's presence, as though each were grateful that for tonight at least, neither was alone. When the music slowed, they returned to the dance floor.

After the lights flooded the club, signaling its intent to close, they headed to the parking lot.

"Where are you parked?" he asked.

"Over here. Back row." It had been the only place left by the time she'd arrived. A shadowy place that even the streetlights couldn't reach. But nestled up against his side, with his arm anchored around her waist, she felt no apprehension. She knew she was safe, protected.

She'd come here with expectations of seeing him again, being with him again. He hadn't rushed her home as she'd anticipated he would, but had given her an evening of slow dancing and not quite as many margaritas.

But as she stopped beside the minivan, doubts suddenly assailed her. She didn't know protocol, was suddenly unsure. Did she simply follow him? Did she tell him that she'd follow him? What if he'd decided he didn't want her tonight?

Turning, she lifted her gaze to his, shadowed by the night. "Well—"

He cradled her face between hands she remembered only too well and lowered his mouth to hers. The heat was immediate, the sparks as bright as any fireworks launched on the Fourth of July. His tongue swept through her mouth while his thumbs caressed the corners. Her trembling knees grew weak, and she wondered where she'd find the strength to maneuver the gas pedal and brake. Her body grew hot as sensations swirled through her.

He ended the kiss as abruptly as he'd begun it, his harsh breathing echoing around her, his forehead pressed to hers. "You want to go in my jeep or follow me?"

"I'll follow."

Chapter 6

Serena paid more attention to the road they traveled, trying to memorize a route that was fairly straightforward.

He turned off the road onto a dirt trail that led through trees to the large log house she remembered. She'd warned her father—after she'd tucked Riker into bed—that she might be late again and he shouldn't wait up. Nor should he worry.

Hunter had left the porch light on. He brought his jeep to a halt and she stopped her van behind it. Briefly, she wondered if maybe she should have had another margarita. She wasn't nearly as inebriated tonight, not nearly as relaxed as she'd obviously been last night.

She gathered up her purse and opened the door, not surprised to find him already standing there waiting for her. She wanted to be sophisticated, but she suddenly felt like a country girl brought up on Methodist sermons.

He slipped his arm around her, anchoring her

against his side, his hand cupping her waist. "You all right?"

She wanted to laugh hysterically, but didn't. "Why are you so good at reading me?"

"You're easy to read. If this isn't what you want—"

"It is," she rushed to assure him.

"All right."

She thought she heard relief in his tone, an absence of the gruffness in this voice that she'd come to associate with him. They walked in tandem to the house, up the steps. He relinquished his hold as he unlocked the door and shoved it open.

No alarm system beeped to be turned off. She had a feeling that he didn't need one, could protect himself without any problem. He hadn't left any lights on inside, but moonlight along with the porch light spilled in through the bared windows. With the faint glow of both she could distinguish shadows and shapes as she walked inside. She heard the door close and realized that she was grateful for the darkness. Within it, she could be a woman that she wasn't in the light.

She turned to face him and found herself wrapped in his embrace, his mouth hot and hungry, his hands equally so. She dropped her purse to the floor and wound her arms around his neck, pressing her body against his. Kicking off her shoes shortened her by an inch, but didn't cause him to lose contact. His growl vibrated between them.

He began backing her up, his mouth trailing greedily along her throat while he tugged her shirt out of her jeans.

"Don't leave any marks," she rasped.

"What?"

"On my neck."

His tongue replaced his lips, licking, soothing, and dipping into the V of her shirt. Then he was unbuttoning her shirt as eagerly as she was unbuttoning his. Both shirts fell to the floor as they reached the stairs. He stopped momentarily, slipping one strap of her bra off her shoulder, his lips following the curve of her shoulder and then the lacy edge of her bra, his warm breath wafting over her skin, sending shivers along her spine, leaving dew along her flesh. He closed his mouth over her nipple, his tongue swirling over the lace, and she thought it couldn't feel any more erotic if he were actually touching her skin.

The sensation was heavenly, enticing. She released a tiny whimper and wondered how much longer her legs could support her. He trailed his finger along the top of the lace and nudged it down until nothing kept his questing mouth from suckling her flesh, while his hands sought out the clasp. Then her bra was gone.

He dipped down, slipped an arm beneath her knees, lifted her, and carried her up the stairs, impatience evident in each stride, in the tense muscles of his shoulders beneath her fingers.

Instead of laying her on the bed as she'd expected, he set her beside it, standing, while he knelt before her. He unfastened her jeans, tugged them down. Then his mouth was against her lacy panties as it had been against her bra, teasing, suckling, his tongue stroking, promising to go more deeply. He guided her onto the bed, spread her thighs further—

"I can't do this," she said suddenly, clamping her knees together.

He stilled, his harsh breathing echoing between them, his hands against her outer thighs shaking— much to her surprise.

"Look, if I'm getting too personal here—"

"No, it's not that." Too personal? She'd already slept with him for goodness sakes. How much more personal could it get? Crossing her arms over her chest, she felt like such a fool. "I'm sorry. I can't do any of this."

She surged to her feet, had to put a hand on his shoulder to steady herself so she wouldn't topple over—she'd come up so fast, her balance off. "I need to go home."

He grabbed her hand, halting her retreat, and for the first time, fear swept through her.

"Was I going too fast?" he asked.

He was only silhouette and shadows, but she

heard sincerity in his voice—along with bafflement. She was embarrassed, ashamed, mortified. She'd tried to convince herself that they had something special, but too many doubts remained.

"It's not you," she said quietly. "It's me . . ." She couldn't believe she was using that argument. "I can't do casual sex. I thought I could. After last night . . . but I can't. I know you probably didn't get the impression last night, but I'm a little old-fashioned. I don't even know your full name."

"Fletcher. Hunter Fletcher. And yours would be?"

The moonlight revealed a sadness to his crooked grin that almost made her cry, the temptation increased by the absurdity of his question. She'd thought he was the one holding back, not sharing, and she'd been just as bad. "Serena Hamilton."

He studied her as though he thought he should have known her name. With a sigh, he rose and sat on the edge of the bed. He had yet to release her hand, but she could sense an easing in the tension in him, as though he were accepting that what he'd had with her last night wasn't what he was going to get tonight.

"Do you think you could just lie on the bed and let me hold you?" he asked. "Just for a few minutes?"

It was such a simple request, delivered with such sincerity.

"Will you keep your jeans on?" she asked.

He chuckled. "Yeah."

"I know you must think I'm a nutcase—"

"No, I'm actually not surprised."

"You're not."

"I was surprised you came home with me at all."

"I shouldn't have."

"I'm glad you did, though." He stretched out on the bed and scooted back a bit. "Come here."

She thought about running downstairs and retrieving her shirt—

"Do you want to grab a shirt out of my closet?" he asked.

"How do you always know what I'm thinking?"

"I told you. You're easy to read."

"But it's dark, and we're in shadows."

"I spend a lot of time in the dark, trying to judge things. Come here."

"What do you mean by that?"

"It's not important. Come here," he urged.

Tentatively, she eased onto the bed, rolled onto her side facing him, with her arms crossed over her chest, to provide a little distance from the intimacy. She was surprised and grateful that he didn't immediately put an arm around her.

Releasing a long slow sigh of relief, she felt compelled to tell him, "You're only the second man I've ever had sex with."

Reaching out, he combed his fingers through her

hair. "I've lost count of the number of women I've slept with."

"That doesn't make me feel any better or less cheap."

She heard him swallow.

"You're the first one I've ever invited back."

Three things occurred to her: that she felt special, that she was sad for him, and that he might not be the healthiest of men based on his promiscuity.

"Last night"—she tried to remember—"you used a condom."

"Yes. You can rest easy. I don't have any diseases. I'm particular about the women I keep company with."

"Not too particular if you only see them once."

She could see his smile in the moonlight, and it occurred to her that his room might not warrant curtains after all.

"Not jealous, are you?" he asked.

"Of course not."

Jealous wasn't the right word. She was disappointed. She didn't want to think that if she hadn't shown up tonight, he would have settled for someone else—or that during either night, he'd *settled* for her.

"Have you ever been married?" she asked.

"Nope."

"Been engaged?"

"Nope."

"Been serious—"

"Nope. Seventeen to go."

"Excuse me?"

"I thought we were playing twenty questions here. You really wasted the first three. Since I admitted you've been the only one I've invited back, those three questions you asked should have been a given."

"I didn't think you were truly serious when you said—"

"I was." He kissed her brow, her nose, her chin.

"Why aren't you angry that I said no after getting as far as we did? Most men would think I was a tease—"

"Most men didn't spend last night with you."

"Meaning?"

"I realized too late that maybe I shouldn't have spent last night with you. Since you were willing to come back here tonight, I was hoping maybe I'd misjudged. But I'm glad I didn't."

"I didn't think any man was glad when he didn't get sex."

"Didn't say I was glad that I'm not getting sex. Simply glad that I hadn't misjudged you. I want you," he said quietly, "but the next time, I don't want there to be any ghosts in this bed with us. I didn't know you weren't with me last night until you called out another man's name. I'm not sure you're a hundred percent with me tonight. That hurts."

Her stomach knotted up, her heart fluttered just below her throat. She hadn't realized she'd actually called out for Steve. How unfair to this man that she had. How incredible that he was with her now. "I want to be."

"But you're not."

"Not a hundred percent, no." She tilted her face toward him. "It's not so much because of Steve, though. It's more because I don't know you very well. And yet, I'm terribly attracted to you."

He trailed his fingers along her cheek. "Same goes."

"You *are* a smooth talker," she said, with teasing in her voice.

He laughed, a deep rumble that shook the bed slightly. Turning her hand until her palm was pressed against his chest instead of her own, she felt the laugher travel through him. The sensation filled her with joy. She didn't think he laughed often, but she liked the sound of it.

"I'm not much for smooth talkin'," he said, "but my words are always honest."

"So what do we do about this attraction?" she asked.

"For right now, you probably get dressed and I take you home."

"You don't have to take me, I have my car," she reminded him.

"I know, but I'll follow to make sure you get there all right."

She liked that idea, that he was willing to see her safely home. He rolled away from her.

"Want me to get your clothes?" he asked.

"No, I'll get them."

"Feel free to turn on the lights."

"No, thanks."

"I'll be down in a couple of minutes," he said as though he understood that she wanted to get dressed with some measure of privacy.

She found her bra hanging over the banister, her shirt on the floor. As she slipped into her shirt and stuffed her bra into her jeans pocket, she walked to the window. Through the trees, she could see moonlight reflected off the lake. She shouldn't have come here tonight, and yet she was glad she had.

She knew Hunter a little better, and she'd reaffirmed that sex wasn't something she could take lightly—even if she had last night. Why had it been so easy to fall in love at fourteen? On second thought, at fourteen, everything had been easy—except math.

She crossed her arms over her chest. Now she weighed every decision she made, determined possible consequences, and worried that she was making a wrong choice. Where was the fun in that?

She turned at the sound of approaching footsteps. He'd obviously opted to find a shirt upstairs instead of waiting to retrieve the one that had been lying on the floor beside hers, the one she'd folded and set on the couch.

"It's not too late to change your mind," he said with a quick nod toward the stairs. "About staying."

It was tempting. He was tempting. But staying was a short-term solution to her long-time problem.

She crossed over to him, raised up on her toes, wound her arms around his neck, scraped her fingers up into his hair, and kissed him—deeply, thoroughly. With only a hint of passion. She didn't want to start a seduction, but neither did she want him to think that she wasn't grateful for the evening he'd given her. Leaning back, she stroked her fingers along the side of his face. "Thank you for tonight. But it's best if I don't stay."

He kept his promise and followed her home. To her surprise, he got out of his jeep and walked her up the steps of the porch, as though tonight had been a planned date.

They stood beneath the porch light that her father had left on, and she found it strange that she thought this was the most uncomfortable part of the evening. She wondered how he would end it. With a caress, a kiss—

"Good night," he finally said.

He began to walk off.

"Hunter?"

He stopped and looked back over his shoulder.

"Do you fish?" she asked quickly, before her courage deserted her.

"What?"

"My dad has a pond that he keeps stocked with fish. Now that you know the way, I thought tomorrow, maybe you'd like to come out here, have a picnic, fish—"

"What time?"

"Noon?"

He returned to her and gave her a soul-searing, heart-melting kiss that made her debate the wisdom of not spending the night with him.

But the truth was that even as his kiss stole her breath, it couldn't pilfer her thoughts, and she knew she needed more than kisses, she needed an opportunity for a relationship to grow. He eased back, rubbed his thumb over her damp, swollen lips, and quietly said, "Tomorrow."

Then he was gone, into the darkness, as though he'd never been there.

Chapter 7

The sound of unexpected gunfire reverberated around him. The air echoed the screams of frantic men, and even in the darkness, he could clearly envision the face—always the same face hidden beneath a layer of grime, eyes noticeably visible, as the soldier tried to appear brave, even as he knew death was approaching.

Another crack of weapons fire had Hunter bolting upright in bed, his body bathed in sweat, the damp sheets pooled around his waist. Breathing harshly, he sought to calm his erratic heart.

Heavy storm clouds prevented the moonlight and distant starlight from spilling in through the windows. What did it say about a man and his phobias when he couldn't sleep in absolute darkness? Perhaps that he'd already done it one time too many.

He had nothing to fear in the darkness. As a man, he knew that. As a boy, he'd been terrified of the darkness that engulfed him whenever his father shoved him in the closet and closed the door—as though he were tired of having to deal with his child. Out of sight, out of mind. Whenever one of his father's moods hit, the nearest closet sufficed: the one in the hallway, the one in Hunter's bedroom, the one in his parents' bedroom. The last was the worst, because of the sounds he'd hear: his father's fist laying into his mother, her cries, the squeaking bedsprings. And he could do nothing to stop his father from hurting his mother.

But the noise had never been as bad as the silence. It had arrived abruptly one night. His mother's screams had simply stopped. The eerie quiet had terrified him. And then he'd heard his father crying.

That night a policeman had opened the closet door. It wasn't until Hunter was much older that he'd come to understand the truth: his parents were drug addicts, drug dealers. And in a drug-induced rage, his father had killed his mother.

Hunter had been passed from one foster home to another. Until he was seventeen. Then he'd enlisted in the Army. He'd been a good soldier, followed orders. Then the CIA had recruited him.

His missions varied. Because of his dark coloring, he was often sent to infiltrate terrorist cells. Gather what information he could. Sometimes he and his team members were sent to neutralize a threat—in any way necessary. Under the cover of darkness, while most people slept, they slipped in, they carried out their mission, they slipped out. They generated no headlines. They were never interviewed. Their existence had been whispered about, but never confirmed until the escalating war on terrorism forced the CIA to reveal that it had been rebuilding a paramilitary network of spies.

Hunter thought of himself as more of a soldier than a spy.

He untangled the sheet from around his legs, threw it back, climbed out of bed, and walked to the window. Lightning flashed. The volley of thunder soon following reminded him of his dream, was probably responsible for the nightmare returning after so many months in hiding. One failed mission that had resulted in his capture. And he couldn't let go of it.

Raising his arms and bracing them on either side of the window, he dropped his head, his chin almost touching his chest, each breath he took echoing loudly around him. He shouldn't have brought the woman home, but having done so, he should have buried himself so deeply within her that he could forget the unpleasant side of his profession. The part no one ever talked about.

Serena Hamilton. She'd been responsible for releasing the nightmares as well. She'd given him her name, and in so doing, she'd unleashed the demons.

He told himself it was simply coincidence. She'd called out for Steve in the throes of passion. Her last name was Hamilton. Once he'd met a Steve Hamilton. A young kid taking on a man's job. Not that Hunter had been that much older.

"You ever been to Austin, man?"

"No."

"I grew up near there. It's paradise. I used to work at this bar. Best margaritas. Man, I could sure use one right now."

The mission to rescue the Badger—Hunter's code name because of his ability to burrow his way into enemy strongholds—had been rapidly going south. He'd been captured ten days earlier, his mission compromised when another agent had sold information to a foreign government. Hunter's captors hadn't been merciful. He'd expected to die in that dark cell, had actually prayed for death—and he wasn't a praying man.

Instead a rescue operation had been ordered. The men knew nothing about him except for his code name. They somehow managed to get him out of his cell, but it didn't appear that any of them were going to get out of the complex.

Coincidence. Her husband couldn't have been that Hamilton, the young team member who'd been shot, the man left in Hunter's care because Hunter was too weak from his ordeal to aid in the reconnaissance while the others rapidly scouted out the escape route.

"Matches . . . pocket," the man had rasped.

Hunter had found a matchbook. Hamilton had closed his hand around it and whispered, "Paradise."

It wasn't until days later that Hunter had discovered the matchbook in his own pocket. For the Paradise Lounge. Not a single match missing. He couldn't figure out why it had been so important to the young man. Unless it was the date written within a heart on the inside cover.

Six years had passed since that horrendous night. That was too much time for Serena to still be mourning, to be calling out for her husband while in another's bed. The names might be the same. But the men couldn't be.

Because if they were, then it would mean that Serena had loved her husband more than Hunter thought it humanly possible to love anyone.

He couldn't chance it, couldn't risk seeing her again—no matter how much he wanted to. No, she'd get the message when he didn't show up for the picnic tomorrow. She'd understand then that she was nothing more than a one-night stand. That he'd changed his mind.

Better to cause her a little disappointment now than to have her learn the truth. She'd slept with the man who was responsible for her husband's death.

Chapter 8

"Mom, do you think Grandpa is going to get rid of his horses, too?"

"Not for a while, sweetie." Inside the barn, Serena tugged on the cinch before patting the mare's withers. The pond was at the edge of the property, and while the terrain was bumpy, it wasn't impossible for a truck to traverse. Still, she preferred riding a horse. Riker did as well, so it worked out for both of them.

"He got rid of the cows," Riker pointed out.

"I know." She gave him a brave smile, trying not to let him see all the doubts surfacing because it was two o'clock and Hunter had yet to show. She didn't want to acknowledge the possibility that if she wasn't putting out, then he'd decided he wasn't putting in an appearance.

She wanted their time together to mean more to him than sex. An idiotic, unrealistic notion when the whole basis of their relationship was a chemical reaction that resulted in a firestorm sparked by little more than a look followed by a touch. She'd tossed and turned all night because she hadn't given in, hadn't accepted the physical release her body knew he could have provided.

As a result, she was grumpy, tense, and in need of a man. *Desperately* in need of a man. Damn him for resurrecting all the sexual desires she thought she'd buried. She felt as though they'd been hovering near the surface waiting for a chance to escape, and Hunter Fletcher had granted them freedom.

Now that they were free, they wanted to make up for lost time, which caused her to run hot one minute, lukewarm the next, but never cold. Every part of her body seemed to be vying for attention. She didn't think her nipples had relaxed since Hunter had kissed her good night. It was irritating. She was irritated. Why hadn't he returned as he'd promised he would?

Today she sharply felt what she hadn't yesterday: cheap. She fluctuated between devastation and burning anger. She thought about his final kiss. Had she detected remorse in it, regret, apology? A good-bye instead of a good night?

She felt foolish. Foolish for going to the bar that first time, more foolish for returning a second time. Foolish for being grateful she'd had another evening with him. Foolish for inviting him to come out here. Foolish for obviously being more interested in him than he was in her.

She'd actually been humming in the kitchen while she'd prepared the picnic. Now she was hungry, Riker was hungry. She had a headache hovering because she'd expected to eat long before now. She was tired and ill-tempered and had decided she wasn't cut out for nightlife.

She needed to meet a single father at a PTA meeting. Someone who went to bed shortly after his children did. Not someone who partied until the bars closed. She was too old for this. And just as quickly as that thought came, the realization followed that she was really too young to be thinking she was too old.

She wanted to retreat to the comfort of her bed. But she'd promised Riker a picnic and a fishing trip. She never went back on her word . . . unlike some people who would remain nameless. She wished she had remained nameless as well.

Names exchanged had obviously shifted the relationship, scared him off. That surprised her. He didn't strike her as a man who frightened easily, even though he'd admitted to being scared. But then he'd also admitted that he wasn't interested in a relationship. Had he been serious when he'd said that he'd never shown interest in a woman twice?

Was he like the lightning that had come with the storm in the early hours of the morning? Only striking once, but leaving destruction in its wake?

She'd never before experienced the sting of rejection. She wondered how women managed to keep dating when relationships didn't work out.

She'd punched Hunter's phone number out four times already—all but the last number. She couldn't make herself press that final digit, the one that would complete the call and cause the phone to ring at his end.

Her calling him spoke of a desperation that she didn't want to acknowledge—not even to herself. Besides, relationships consisted of more than just the physical aspects, and while he might excel in that area, he left a lot to be desired in other areas.

He wasn't dependable. He made appointments and didn't keep them. He was—

"Mom, who are you talking to?"

She jerked her attention back to Riker. "What?"

"I keep hearing you cursing, like maybe you're mad. Did I do something?"

This time she gave him an honest, open smile and ruffled his blond hair. "Oh, no, sweetie. You didn't do anything wrong. I'm just running things through my mind. Are you ready to go?"

"I've been ready forever."

Hardly forever, although in his young mind it probably felt that they'd been waiting that long.

While Riker grabbed the reins to his horse, she took the reins to hers and turned toward the open doorway. Clad in jeans and a plain gray work shirt, a man stood just inside the doorway. She hadn't heard his arrival, and she was irritated at the gladness that his presence caused to sweep through her when only moments before she'd been absolutely furious with him.

"Who's that?" Riker asked.

"A friend." Although a *friend* wouldn't have kept her waiting without calling. An acquaintance possibly. Someone who didn't care. She handed the reins off to Riker. "You wait here."

"Why?"

"Because I said."

He rolled his eyes, and she cursed the unreasonable statement that she'd sworn before she had a child that she'd never say. While growing up, she'd always thought it was a condescending statement, always wanted to know the real reason behind things her mother had told her to do. Strange how now that she was a parent, she found those three little words were appropriate more times than she'd ever realized they would be.

With her boots kicking up the straw and dust, she marched through the barn, aware that her hands were balling into fists and her stomach was knotting more tightly with each stride that brought her closer to the man who had yet to move from the doorway. When she finally reached him, she refused to be amiable. Instead she simply said with as flat a voice as she could muster, "I didn't think you were coming."

"I wasn't."

The anger spiked and disappointment roared in. She didn't know whether to ask why he'd decided not to come or why he had. She crossed her arms over her chest. "I see."

"No, you probably don't."

"Then explain it."

"It's like I said last night. Relationships aren't exactly my thing. It occurred to me that some of the things I said might have given you the impression I wanted more than I did. I'm not looking for anything permanent—"

"Did I say something that made you think *I* was?"

His eyes widened at that, as though the tartness in her voice as well as the words might have taken him by surprise.

An easy smile spread across his face. "No, you didn't. I just figured a woman with a kid—"

"I have a son. I have a child. I do not have a kid. A goat has a kid."

His smile vanished. "You're mad. That's the very reason that I decided not to come. Because if a guy sees a woman more than once, she starts to get demanding, has expectations—"

"Then why did you bother to come at all?"

"Because I couldn't stay away."

His obvious displeasure at the confession would have pleased her if she weren't so angry at him. "Took you long enough to figure that out."

"As a general rule, I have a great deal of self-control."

"So I'm supposed to be flattered that you battled with yourself for only two hours before losing the good fight?"

A corner of his mouth hitched up again. "That's right. I've never lost the battle before."

Now she was not only flattered, but hit with a strange sort of self-satisfaction. It was an odd feeling to know that she was . . . irresistible. But it hardly made up for his behavior today.

"And what do you expect now that you're here?"

"I was sorta hoping that you'd cut me some slack and forgive me for being late."

"I see." With her arms still crossed, she slowly walked around him. He did have a fine butt. When she was facing him again, she said, "I don't see any flowers."

He angled his head. "What?"

"When a man is seeking forgiveness, he usually brings flowers. Since you make it a habit not to see a woman more than once, am I to assume that you're not familiar with this ritual?"

He chuckled low. "I've never given a woman flowers."

"How about a box of chocolates?"

"Nope."

"For future reference, a box of chocolates goes a long way with me."

"You're assuming a lot there, thinking that there's going to be a future when I can't even get a warm hello out of you."

"I'm hurt, Hunter. Last night, you told me that I'd hurt you. Well, now *I'm* hurt, because you didn't care enough to—"

"I did care, damn it. That's the reason I fought not to come. Because I know I could hurt you."

"Have you ever hit a woman?"

"Hell, no!"

"Then how are you going to hurt me?"

"By not being what you need."

She lifted her shoulders with a hapless shrug. "How do you know what I need? I don't know what I need. A relationship takes time to build and it's more than what happens between the sheets. I haven't asked for a commitment. I didn't ask for you to do anything more than go on a picnic. If you don't want to be here, then save us both some grief and just leave."

She watched the muscles in his throat work as he swallowed.

"I do want to be here, Serena. And I apologize for showing up late."

She felt the anger subsiding. "You could have told me you had a flat tire."

"I told you last night that my words would always be honest."

"Even if you know they'll make me angry?"

He slowly nodded. "I like you too much not to be honest with you."

"I like you, too. I'm glad you came." The dark expression on her face slowly faded, and was replaced by an impish smile. "Do you know how to ride a horse?"

Hunter slid his gaze past her to where Riker still waited with the horses. Her son had begun shifting from foot to foot, rocking his body back and forth, a sure sign that his impatience to be underway was escalating. She was surprised he hadn't started to pester her yet. Though he did know her well enough to know when she was angry, so he'd probably decided keeping his distance was his best strategy until she cooled down.

"I think I can manage," Hunter said.

"Riker, come here," she called out.

She watched him approach with obvious apprehension, as though he were on his way to the first day of school. He'd had her to himself for so long, and she wondered how he'd react to sharing her for the afternoon. The only time he'd ever even hinted that he wanted a father was when he and Jason had cooked up a scheme for her and Jack to marry.

And she was getting way ahead of herself here. Marriage wasn't even remotely on the horizon. As a matter of fact, she wasn't certain she'd see Hunter beyond this afternoon.

With his faint eyebrows puckered, his mouth set in a mulish twist, Riker stopped before her.

"Riker, this is Mr. Fletcher. He's going to go fishing with us."

"How come?"

"Because I invited him to join us."

"Why?"

She wished she'd prepared him for this moment earlier. She should have expected that he'd be inquisitive about a change to his expected routine, especially when it involved a stranger.

"Because I thought it would be fun to have someone go with us."

"Grandpa could go with us."

"Grandpa took you fishing yesterday."

"But Grandpa likes fishing. He'd go every day—"

"Riker, I wanted to take a friend so I invited Mr. Fletcher to join us. Okay?"

Riker lifted a shoulder. "Okay. Has he got kids?"

Hunter cleared his throat, and Serena wondered if he was expecting her to correct her son for using a word she'd lambasted Hunter for using.

"I don't think so." She cast a glance at Hunter, wondering if he did have children. Based on what he'd said last night, she'd assumed he didn't . . . but what did she really know about him? Just because he'd never married didn't mean that he didn't have children. "Do you have children?"

"No, I don't," he admitted.

So she'd guessed correctly. What she knew about him was a series of guesses. What she absolutely knew about him she could stick on the head of a pin. And yet, here she was, once again, grateful to have his company.

"You like kids?" Riker asked.

"Riker, of course he does," Serena answered quickly, wondering what would possess him to ask such a question. Did he have a fear that he wouldn't be liked? Or perhaps he was simply not comfortable with her introducing a new man into his life. After all, this occasion was a first. And she realized that it shouldn't be a new experience for him, that men in her life shouldn't be so rare that neither of them knew how to respond. "Everyone likes children. Why don't you get a horse for Mr. Fletcher while I introduce him to Grandpa?"

"Actually I met your dad when I drove up. He told me where to find you."

She didn't like hearing *that*, would have preferred he hadn't had to face her father alone. Sometimes her father took his protective stance a bit far. "I hope he didn't give you the third degree."

"On the contrary. He went out of his way to make me feel welcome. Even went so far as to show me his membership card for the NRA."

The National Rifle Association. All right, so her father *was* a little on the overprotective side. She should have warned Hunter to expect it.

"I'm surprised he didn't show you his rifles," she said, hoping he wasn't offended by her father's protective demonstration.

"He offered to."

"Mom, I'm starving," Riker said with a feigned gasp and cough, his hands wrapped around his throat. She'd never been able to determine why he thought either action was a sign of hunger.

"All right. Hurry along then and fetch another horse."

As soon as Riker was outside of hearing distance, she turned back to Hunter. "My dad may not look it, but he's as sharp as barbed wire and old enough not to be afraid to speak his mind. Since I don't usually have men stopping by to visit me, he's probably figured out you're the one I was with the other night." She tapped the mark Hunter had left on her throat.

"Ah," he said with a slow nod. "That's the reason you warned me not to leave any marks."

"Exactly. I hope my dad didn't say anything that made you uncomfortable."

"He wanted to know if my intentions were honorable."

"And what did you tell him?"

"That I'd let him know when I figured it out."

She laughed softly. "He must have loved that."

"Actually, that's when he acquainted me with his NRA membership."

Yes, she could see her father doing that. But she was glad to realize that Hunter didn't seem bothered by her father's inquisition or his response.

She didn't know what to make of this man who was standing before her when he didn't want to be, whose words were honest—although she was left with the impression that he wasn't revealing everything.

He intrigued her. She'd seen him handle a drunk without hesitation. And yet here he was, constantly backing off from her. The one thing she did know was that as long as they could talk honestly with each other maybe a chance existed that they'd be more than lovers.

She smiled with the thought, but knew she was getting ahead of herself. They needed to survive the picnic first.

Chapter 9

⌒

It was the middle of June with temperatures threatening to hit triple digits, and yet Hunter felt as though he'd found paradise beneath the shade of the towering tree with the breeze blowing off the large pond cooling him. The idyllic scene was one Norman Rockwell would have painted.

A quilt that he was fairly certain had actually been stitched by hand was beneath him. A wicker picnic basket was beside him. A boy with a fishing pole sat at the edge of a pond with a brown and white spotted beagle sitting at his feet. Horses were tethered off to the side, munching on the brush, occasionally dipping their heads to drink from the pond.

And a woman sat beside Hunter, her arms wrapped around her long legs, her chin resting on her drawn-up knees. Her jeans were stretched taut across her hips and thighs. She was wearing a tight little red tank top that dipped down to offer a glimpse of what lay beneath the fabric. For the most part she watched the boy. But every now and then her gaze would drift over to him and she'd smile before turning her attention back to the boy.

He thought he could stay here forever. It was what he'd been looking for when he'd bought his house near the lake. He'd thought the house, the land, and the lake were enough. He'd thought that was paradise. Only now was he discovering that he'd been mistaken.

He was stretched out on his side, his full stomach making him lethargic. He'd followed two chicken salad sandwiches with brownies chock full of nuts. He'd topped the meal off with a bright red apple that he wouldn't have been surprised to discover that Serena had actually polished. The boy had eaten a container of strawberries coated in sugar, and fed most of his sandwich to the dog.

"Did you grow up around here?" she suddenly asked, bringing him back to the moment.

"No, I grew up around Houston."

"Do you know where Hopeful is?" she asked.

"Been through there a time or two when going somewhere else."

"That's where Riker and I live now. I didn't know if you remembered me mentioning that last night."

"I'm pretty good at remembering things."

She tilted her face, placed her cheek on her knee, and smiled at him. He liked her smile, the warmth and sincerity of it. His life was filled with deceptions, and he didn't want that with her. He wanted the honesty he kept alluding to. More, he wanted her with an intensity that was almost frightening.

Reaching out, he wrapped his hand around her booted ankle, though he really wanted to place his hand against her rear end. Ease up and over her, lay her down on the quilt. Kiss those soft lips, have her wrap those long legs of hers around him.

But she had the little chaperone with her, and he didn't know how long the kid was going to be content to fish. Hunter hadn't seen him catch anything yet. He couldn't imagine that the boy would keep at it for much longer.

"You haven't lived here long," she said, her voice rising slightly, as though she couldn't quite determine if she was stating a fact or asking a question.

"I bought the house five years ago."

Her eyes widened at that. "You haven't decorated it much."

"It's shelter." He shrugged, moving his hand up her calf and back down to her ankle, wishing the legs of her jeans weren't so straight that he couldn't slip his hand inside. He liked the silkiness of her skin. A shame she hadn't worn shorts.

He'd enjoyed watching her ride the horse. She sat a horse well, had obviously grown up riding.

She settled down beside him until she was on her side as he was. The tank top shifted, stretched, revealed the barest hint of black lace. She was killing him, because if she was a creature of habit, her panties matched the black lace of that bra.

"Surely, you need more than that," she said.

He did. He needed her clothes off so he could feast on the perfection of her body, which he'd only seen in moonlight. And that had been a spectacular viewing.

He took her hand, remembering the feel of her fingers dancing over his skin. He rubbed his thumb along the pads of her palm. "I don't spend much time there," he confessed.

"When you *are* working, what do you do?"

He'd known that question would come up sooner or later. "I'm a consultant."

"What do you consult people about?"

"Security."

"I've been thinking about getting a home security system. Jack promised to—"

"Who's Jack?" he interrupted, surprised by the hard edge he heard in his voice. He didn't bother to correct her assumption that he was in home security rather than national security. Who he really worked for and what he really did wasn't something that he was allowed to disclose.

"Jack Morgan is my neighbor, my friend. My best friend actually. A by-product of his son, Jason, and Riker being best friends. They do everything together."

"So you and Jack do everything together."

She smiled. "Not everything. We do even less together since he got married last Christmas."

He couldn't explain the relief that washed through him. He formed an immediate impression of this Jack, and it wasn't very flattering. If he'd never put a move on Serena, then he was obviously a man without taste in women. If Serena hadn't been attracted to the guy, then he was probably a loser. Like she'd said, they hung out together because of their sons. A person didn't always have control of who his neighbors were. That was part of the reason that Hunter had bought a good deal of the land surrounding his house—so he wouldn't have to deal with neighbors.

"You must have an understanding boss if he's letting you spend the summer here," he said.

She laughed lightly and flopped onto her back. "I'm my own boss. I have a small business. I design and create window treatments." She turned her head to the side and looked at him. "I could do yours."

He shook his head. "Window treatments? What do you treat them with?"

She laughed harder. It was a magical sound that wrapped around his heart.

"You know. Curtains, blinds, draperies. Your windows could use a little personality."

"If I put something on the windows, I couldn't see the lake."

"I could do something creative that wouldn't obstruct the view."

He rolled onto his stomach until their sides were touching. "How did you get into doing people's windows?"

"I had some time on my hands. I wanted to do something that was flexible. I didn't want Riker in day care. Not that there's anything wrong with day care. I'm just a little overprotective. I guess I take after my father. But I sew the curtains at home and hire a handyman to hang them for me. Brings in enough income to get us by." She blushed. "If you have trouble finding work, I could probably offer you some odd jobs—"

"It's not necessary." He knew he should probably disabuse her of the notion that he was unemployed, but he'd promised honest words and so far he hadn't actually lied to her. He'd only said he was between jobs. Which was true. He was taking a few weeks off before he went on his next mission. He'd only been off a couple of days and so far, his vacation wasn't going at all as he'd expected, because he hadn't anticipated Serena.

One night with her hadn't been enough. Two nights had only left him wanting more. And it wasn't because last night had gotten cut short. Although he'd certainly been disappointed. Especially now that he was getting to know her a little better.

"I guess it would be kind of a long commute," she said. "If you worked for me."

"Yeah, but the worst part would be that you'd discover that I'm not much of a handyman."

"Is that the reason that you haven't hung anything on your walls?"

"No, the reason that I haven't hung anything is that I don't have anything to hang."

"What sort of art do you like?"

"I like pictures of naked women."

"Oh!" She sat up and slapped at his shoulder. "You're teasing me now."

He shook his head. "Not really."

"How can I get to know you if you don't tell me what you like and don't like?"

"What's to know? I've got you figured out."

"You do not."

"Sure I do." He pushed himself up to a sitting position. "You're a single mother with an inquisitive son who is fairly well behaved. You had certain things you wanted to accomplish, and that required that you go into business for yourself, so you did. You're a considerate daughter. You don't make a habit of picking up men at bars. You're hell in bed."

She got to her feet and started walking. He didn't know if she was walking away from him, or trying to walk away from what they'd been discussing. He didn't know if she was pleased or upset because he'd pegged her. He stood up and quickly fell into step beside her.

"I knew everything about Steve," she said. "Everything. I knew his family, his dreams, his favorite shows, movies, and music." She glanced over at him. "I mean, I knew everything before we were ever completely intimate. With you, I feel like I'm peddling backwards, and it's odd. We didn't build up to anything. I feel like I should know everything there is to know about you, and I don't know anything. Except that *you're* hell in bed."

He grinned at her repetition. "If you only know one thing about a guy, that's a good thing to know, don't you think?"

Laughing, she stopped walking and faced him. "That's such a guy thing to say. I've never been a short-term type of girl. I don't think you're a long-term kind of guy. I don't know what to make of us."

Us. He'd never been an "us" before, and he hadn't come out here expecting to end up in that category. Two little letters, placed side by side, creating such immense expectations. He didn't quite know what to do about them, about her.

But when she looked at him as she was now—with trusting eyes filled with so much warmth, humor, and kindness—he almost believed that he could leave his solitary life behind. That maybe he could let her hang curtains on his windows, nail pictures to his walls. That he could possess a photograph in which he wasn't the only person reflected in a glossy image.

She opened up possibilities that he'd long ago closed the door on. She made him want—

"Mom?"

Hunter was crouched, his arm half an inch from knocking the kid into the next county before he even realized he'd moved.

Serena responded almost as quickly, snatching her startled son back, folding her arms across his bony chest, surprise evident in her eyes, alarm reflected in the kid's. Both were fairly gasping, as though Hunter's actions had sucked the air right out of them.

He slowly unfolded his body to his full height, held out his hands in as nonthreatening a pose as possible, and took a step back. "I'm sorry. I didn't hear him approach."

Hell, he *hadn't* heard him. How could he not have heard a kid get that close? Children weren't prone to stealth or silence—even when they were trying to be quiet. This kid even had a damned dog hovering at his ankles. How had Hunter not even heard the dog?

He'd been distracted, unfocused—no, he'd been focused. But he'd been focused on her, on the possibilities. Not on his surroundings, not on the dangers—

The dangers? He was on a damned picnic. The

only danger he faced would come from an anthill. He'd been too long searching for the enemy. Trying to keep his country safe until he, himself, was no longer safe. He took another step back. "I should go."

The kid broke free of his mother's hold and when she reached for him again, he eluded her as easily as the wind.

"Do you know karate?" the kid asked, bouncing on the balls of his feet, hopping around like a hyperactive boxer in the ring. "It looked like you were gonna karate-chop me."

Making grunting noises, he cut his hands through the air. "Were you? Were you going to karate-chop me?"

"You took me by surprise—"

"But you know karate? Right?"

"I know some self-defense moves, yeah."

"Can you teach me?" The boy tentatively moved closer, eagerness in his voice, interest in his blue eyes.

Hunter wasn't much into hero worship, but he couldn't understand why he desperately didn't want to disappoint this kid. He shifted his gaze to Serena. Her inviting warmth was gone. Now her eyes held wariness, concern. Could she trust him? Even he no longer knew the answer to that question.

He knew he should leave, but he couldn't quite force himself to take another step back. He wanted to repair the damage, and he wasn't exactly certain how to do that. His father hadn't been a model parent. "I could show you a couple of moves. But it's up to your mom."

The boy turned to her, his small hands clasping her arm. "Please, Mom? It'd be awesome. Jason won't believe it when I tell him. Please."

She shook her head. "I don't think we should impose on Mr. Fletcher."

"Ah, Mom—"

"We've been out here a long time, Riker. We need to get back to Grandpa."

"Ah, Mom, I know you're worried, but I won't get hurt." He snapped his head around to look at Hunter. "Tell her I'll be safe."

He wondered how often the kid had to convince his mom to let him do things. "He won't get hurt."

"There, Mom, see?" He started jumping up and down as though if he could just be at eye-level with her, he could convince her more easily. "Please?"

"All right," she said, nodding jerkily. "Put your fishing equipment away first."

"Cool!" The kid pointed his finger at Hunter. "Don't move an inch. I'll be right back." He raced toward the pond, the dog pouncing along behind him.

Serena folded her arms across her chest. "You were going to hit him."

"But I didn't." Which he considered to be one of the lamest answers he'd ever given.

"Where did you learn karate?"

It wasn't karate exactly, but he didn't think she was particularly interested in the details of his actions. "I told you I was in the army a while back. Special Forces."

"But you're not in the army now."

"No."

She seemed relieved. "Steve was in the army. He was killed on a mission that the government won't talk about."

Well, that information confirmed his suspicions regarding the identity of her husband.

"I couldn't go through that again," she said, before she smiled hesitantly. "The worry. The not knowing. I'm glad you're not in the army anymore."

And he had a feeling she was telling him that if he was, this picnic would be their last. A little voice inside him urged him to come clean, but he'd been groomed to hold everything confidential. A need-to-know basis only.

As much as he was coming to like Serena, he wasn't authorized to disclose any information about himself. It was a part of his life, his profession that he'd come to accept. So he told her only what he could. "I'm glad, too."

• • •

Special Forces.

Serena wasn't surprised to learn that Hunter had been part of the army's elite group. She'd suspected he had some special military training after watching him handle the drunk last night.

When he'd turned on Riker, his eyes had clearly indicated that it had been with intent to harm. His reactions were quick, his reflexes quicker, because he'd reacted instantaneously, but he'd also stopped before anyone was hurt. Once her pounding heart had slowed to normal and she'd been able to begin thinking clearly again, she knew that Riker had never been in any real danger.

She stood with her back against the tree and one boot heel hooked over a bit of peeling bark, watching as Hunter spoke to Riker. He showed more patience than she'd expected him to. He crouched so they were closer to eye level whenever he wanted to speak with Riker. Although she couldn't hear the words, his deep voice was an audible rumble. She was hit with an incredible longing for all the moments when Riker hadn't had a father's devotion.

He had Jack in his life—but never *only* Jack. When Jack gave attention to Riker, he was also giving attention to Jason. The same applied when she gave attention to Jason: she was also giving it to Riker—so Jason never had a mother only. At least not until Jack had married Kelley.

Now the Morgans were a family. And Serena and Riker were back to having only each other.

Of course, Riker had his grandfather's devotion. But that wasn't the same as a father's.

Riker needed a man in his life, a father figure, who was his and his alone. And she was beginning to realize that she wanted a husband again. She missed the giving part of marriage as much as the receiving part. Having someone who needed her as much as she did him.

She didn't know why all these thoughts were suddenly blooming like bluebonnets in spring. She hadn't invited Hunter out here because she'd been considering him for the long-term. She just wanted to get to know him better so she wouldn't feel so guilty if she slept with him again. And she did want to sleep with him again. She wanted to discover if he was as good as her memory of him had built him up to be.

She had a feeling he was better.

She watched as he demonstrated some moves that seemed more like well-choreographed dance steps instead of martial arts techniques. Slow, fluid stretches, bunched muscles. A move to the side. A rapid kick. Good Lord, Hunter was flexible, controlled, and limber. She hadn't expected him to be so limber. She had visions of him demonstrating these moves in the bedroom. Wrapping himself around her, his muscles tightening.

She never found herself getting all hot and bothered when she watched a Jackie Chan movie with the boys. But then Hunter wasn't Jackie Chan.

He was a long drink of water on a hot afternoon. A wall of hard muscle . . .

Suddenly Riker was running over to her. "Did you see me, Mom, did you see me?"

"I was watching." Watching Hunter much more than she'd been watching Riker, but she didn't need to confess that little fact.

Riker kicked his leg out to the side, then did two quick punches in front of him. "Wait until I show Jason." He took a step, released two more quick punches. "Awesome."

She didn't know what he considered to be so awesome. Had to be a guy thing. Riker was skipping, hopping, jumping and twisting in the air, doing things that she knew Hunter hadn't shown him.

Hunter approached, and even with his hands buried in the front pockets of his jeans, he walked with confidence, his strides long and sure. She wanted to draw him up against herself, slide her arms around him, and slip her hands into his back pockets. She wanted to kiss him. But she'd never kissed a man in front of Riker, didn't know how her son would react.

"You're his new hero," she said.

He looked uncomfortable with her assessment, shifted his gaze over to Riker. "He's a quick study."

"I have to confess that those actions he's demonstrating look like something from the movies to me," she said.

He shrugged, a corner of his mouth hitching up into a grin. "I tried to show him something a bit more useful as a defense strategy but he wanted quick and flashy."

"He's wanted to take karate for a while, but there aren't any schools in Hopeful. I appreciate you giving him some of your time."

"It was the least that I could do after scaring you."

"You didn't scare me. You startled me. I've never seen anyone move that quickly."

"You were no slouch in the fast-moving department."

"A mother's instincts."

She glanced around. It would be a while before darkness settled in, but evening would soon be approaching, bringing on one of the sunsets she so enjoyed watching. "We should probably head back in before my dad sends out a posse."

Chapter 10

Considering the fact that her father was standing on the front porch with his arms crossed over his chest when they arrived, Serena was fairly certain that her earlier joke about him sending out a posse wasn't far from the truth. Maybe she'd inherited her overprotective streak from him rather than her mother as she'd often suspected. She was surprised that he didn't follow them into the barn to assist with unsaddling the horses.

"Can I show Grandpa my karate moves?" Riker asked, as soon as he'd dismounted.

"When you've finished seeing to your horse," Serena said.

"Ah, Mom!"

"Riker, if you want the joy of riding you have to accept the responsibility—"

"I know, I know, I know."

He led his horse into the appropriate stall. She looked over at Hunter. "Do you know what to do?"

"Yeah, but I'll take care of your saddle. I'll see to

your horse as well if there's something you need to be doing—like telling your father that he can lock his guns back up."

"It's insane, isn't it? You move away from home, you live your own life, take care of your own business . . . but the second you come home, you're a child again, living under their roof, with a curfew, and a hundred questions to be answered anytime you walk out the door. No matter how old you get, they're always wanting to be parents, seeming not to realize that you manage quite well on your own when they aren't around. Do you find it to be that way when you go home?"

An emotion jumped into his eyes that she couldn't quite identify—longing, loss, remorse. It disappeared with a single blink.

"The only ones who chatter at me are the squirrels out at the lake."

"What about your parents?"

"Long gone." He edged past her and began to remove her saddle.

"I'm sorry," she said quietly.

"Nothing to be sorry for." He hoisted the saddle and dropped it over the railing separating the two stalls.

"How did they die?"

"It's a long story. Leave it at that."

She crossed her arms over her chest, not really

wanting to leave it at *that,* but deciding she had no choice except to respect his request.

"Mom, I'm done. Can I go show Grandpa my karate moves now?" Riker asked.

She'd almost forgotten he was still in the barn, was grateful that Hunter hadn't reacted as he had before. She nodded. "Go ahead."

"Yeehaw!"

He raced out of the barn, stirring up the dust motes.

"Where would I find some oats for the horses?" Hunter asked.

She pointed behind her. "There's a room at the back of the barn."

He started to walk past her . . . stopped. His profile was to her, and she could see the muscle in his jaw clenching and unclenching.

"I wouldn't hurt your son." He shifted his gaze over to her. "Ever."

"I know. I also know that I'm overprotective, but nothing in my life is more important than Riker. If you don't have children then you probably can't understand . . ." She didn't know how to explain. "You'd lay down your life for them without hesitation, you'd do anything to protect them. When they're sick, you feel bad. You simply want them to be happy. And you want nothing—and I mean nothing—to hurt them—emotionally or physically."

"Not in my family. My old man was a drunk. When he was feeling generous, he beat me. When he wasn't, he locked me in the closet."

Horror swept through her as realization dawned. "Is that the reason you don't want curtains on your windows?"

He shifted his gaze over to her. "Maybe. I don't like feeling closed in. Don't look so sad, Serena. Things weren't all that bad. When I was eight, I started the foster home circuit."

She didn't know what to say, had a feeling he was making light of his tragedy and that things had in fact not only been all that bad, but much worse. She ached for him, ached for what he must have endured. And where was his mother during all this time, why hadn't she protected him?

Shaking his head, he looked away. "I can't believe I told you that. I've never told anyone."

He took a step away from her. Reaching out, she wrapped her hand around his arm. He stilled. She didn't know why he'd shared that small part of his past with her, but she wanted him to know that his trust was well placed.

She moved in front of him, touched her palm to his cheek, raised up on her toes, and pressed her lips to his. His arms came around her, and he crushed her against his hard body, one hand holding her in place while the other became entangled in her hair, angling her head while his mouth slashed across hers as he deepened the kiss.

He was hot and hungry, quiet and mysterious.

"Mom? Mom? Mom!"

She pulled back, dizzy and weak, disoriented. Lord help her, this man could turn her into mush before she knew what was happening. She blinked hard, trying to focus. "Riker?"

"Grandpa said *he's* supposed to stay for supper." He pointed toward Hunter as though he'd discovered an unwelcome critter in the stall.

Serena nodded. "Okay."

Riker walked up to her and tugged on her hand. "I'll help you with your horse."

That was a first, a little possessiveness on his part. She looked over her shoulder at Hunter. "You'll stay for supper?"

"Yeah."

She couldn't stop herself from smiling. They'd survived the picnic. Now if they could just survive her father.

It was another Norman Rockwell moment, sitting on a bench swing on the front porch. Hunter felt a peacefulness descend around him that he hadn't felt in a long time. Following a dinner of grilled fajitas, he and Serena had come out here while her father and son had gone inside to watch television, the dogs with them.

Hunter wasn't exactly sure why he'd revealed what he had to Serena in the barn. He wasn't proud of his family background. He'd stopped short of telling her the worst of it. God bless Texas and the death penalty.

Fighting off the oppressive memories, he stretched his arm along the back of the bench and began toying with her slight curls, the muscles in his leg flexing and relaxing, causing the swing to sway lazily. Maybe he'd add a swing to the deck at the back of his house. But he didn't think he'd feel the same sense of contentment sitting there alone as he felt sitting here with her.

"I enjoyed today," he said quietly.

She looked inordinately pleased. "Did you?"

"I did."

"I'm glad. You're always welcome to come back."

He wanted to ask her to come home with him. Spend time on his back porch. Curl up in his bed. She didn't even have to have sex with him. Just press her back to his chest, her bottom to his stomach.

"I'd like to get your phone number before I leave."

She popped up like a kid's jack-in-the-box. "I'll get my business card. It has my cell phone on it, and I always keep it on."

He hadn't meant to send her scurrying into the house, leaving him alone out here. He could see the horses scampering around the corral, where he'd taken them once they were brushed down and fed.

He heard the door open, glanced over his shoulder, and was disappointed to see that it wasn't the person he was hoping for.

"Are you gonna sleep over?" Riker asked.

Hunter had a feeling the question was innocent, one the kid might ask his best friend—two buddies spending the night together, not in the way Hunter would like to sleep with the boy's mom. "No, I'm not."

"When are you leaving?"

"When I'm finished visiting with your mother."

"Are you going to marry her?"

With a sigh, Hunter lifted his arm off the back of the swing, bent forward, and braced his elbows on his thighs. "Think you could close that door and step out here a little farther?"

He didn't want Serena's father listening in on this conversation, although he wouldn't have put it past the old man to have sent the boy out to do a little intelligence gathering. The kid did as Hunter had asked and crossed the porch to stand in front of him.

"Right now, I'm just getting to know your mom. We're becoming friends," Hunter explained.

"Jason's dad got married. It sucks."

Hunter wasn't sure if the kid was supposed to say sucks, if Hunter should correct him or reprimand him or let it go.

"Why does it suck?"

"Because now his dad won't marry my mom. I wanted him to be my dad, too. Dads do stuff that moms don't."

"Like what?"

"Like go to baseball games. Jason's dad took him to a baseball game."

"Your mom would probably take you if you asked her."

"Nah, we're in mourning because Grandma died. We're not supposed to have fun right now."

He didn't say it with any sort of resentment or sadness, simply acceptance. Hunter wondered if Serena had given much thought to what her son was going to be missing out on while they stayed here this summer. As much fun as fishing with Grandpa might be, Hunter had a feeling the kid would rather be back home playing with his friends.

Serena returned outside. "Sorry it took so long. Riker, honey, what are you doing out here?"

The boy just shrugged.

"We were talking guy stuff," Hunter said.

"Oh, what kind of guy stuff?" she asked.

"Baseball, mostly. As a matter of fact, I was just about to tell Riker that I was thinking of going to watch a Round Rock Express game. I was wondering if the two of you wanted to go with me."

Even in the evening shadows, he could see the kid

perk right up and expected him to start bouncing at any minute.

"Really?" Riker asked. "When?"

"I don't know. I'd have to check their schedule. How about if I call your mom to let her know when the next game is?"

"Cool! You won't forget, right?"

"I won't forget."

"Awesome!"

The kid disappeared into the house as though his mission had been accomplished.

"You didn't just get manipulated, did you?" Serena asked, as she sat on the bench seat, a little closer to him than she was before.

"I'm not sure."

"If you don't want to go to a baseball game—"

"No, I do." And he was surprised to find that he meant it. "The question is—do you want to go?"

"I think it would be fun." She handed him her card. "Here you go. So you can call me with the details."

He put his arm around her. "Here's a detail. I like you, Serena. I like you lot."

He kissed her, enjoying the way her body came to rest against his, as though it belonged there. It was a heady thought, to think that maybe he'd met a woman who would finally be with him for more than one night.

Chapter 11

Because Serena considered the minivan safer than his jeep, which she feared might roll over, Hunter drove her vehicle through Austin, Pflugerville, and into Round Rock for the Thursday night game between the Round Rock Express and the Frisco Rough Riders. At Serena's suggestion, he'd purchased tickets for the grassy knoll, which seemed a little far from the action to him, once they were situated on a quilt, but the kid seemed thrilled with the location, had his glove on, and was crouched as though he expected someone to hit a ball right to him.

And Hunter figured that was all that mattered. That the kid was happy.

Riker glanced over his shoulder. "Mom, can I have a hot dog?"

"Sure." She started to get up.

"I'll go with you," Hunter said.

She stilled. "I don't want to leave Riker here by himself."

Hunter glanced around. "Why not?"

"He's too young."

"For what?"

"To be left by himself at a place like this."

He couldn't see the harm in it, but then he'd been on his own since he was eight, and parenting wasn't exactly his thing. "Okay, why don't I get the hot dogs then? You want one?"

"Yes, please. Mustard only for me and Riker. A couple of soft drinks, whatever they have."

He headed up the knoll and made his way to the concession stand. He'd gone to sporting events a time or two, but it was very different going with a woman and her kid. Serena kept a close watch on Riker, as though she thought someone might touch him and he'd disappear in a poof of smoke.

He moved up to the window, ordered the dogs and drinks, caught sight of the bags of cotton candy hanging down, and trusting his instincts, ordered two of those. Then cursed his instincts when the order was delivered and he discovered that carting stuff around for three people was a little more in-volved than doing it for one.

But wending his way through the crowds with a great deal of care, he made it back to the grassy knoll without dropping anything. Serena's smile of pleas-ure made the food reconnaissance worth it.

Riker removed his glove and grabbed a hot dog. "Thanks."

"You're welcome."

"There is just something about a ballpark hot dog," Serena said.

She was wearing a red visor that matched her red tank top. White shorts that hugged that little butt of hers and left a lot of her leg exposed for viewing. His interest in going to the game had jumped up several notches when he'd seen how she was dressed. He definitely liked the scenery up here on the knoll.

She bit into the hot dog and looked as though she was experiencing rapture. He had to look away just so he could eat without leaning over to kiss her. He wasn't much into kissing in public—but then he'd never been with a woman he wanted to kiss in public.

"Did you play baseball when you were a kid?" Riker asked.

"No, I didn't play any sports."

"I want to play Little League next year," Riker said. "I couldn't this year, on account of Grandma"— he stole a glance at Serena, as though he thought he might have said something he shouldn't—"you know."

"We were spending a lot of time up here with Grandma, weren't we, sport?" She rubbed his shoulder, but Hunter was left with the impression she would have preferred to ruffle his hair—except he was wearing an Astros ball cap. "It wouldn't have been fair to the team because you would have missed too many games."

"I know."

"Next year," she said.

"Yeah, next year. I'm going to be the pitcher," he told Hunter. "Jason is the catcher."

"That's the way they do it in the backyard. He hasn't played on a team yet. A coach might decide differently, Riker. You have to be prepared for that."

The boy nodded, sipping his drink, but Hunter figured his mother's words were going in one ear and out the other. Some things only experience could truly teach.

"You could be a coach, couldn't you?"

It took Hunter a second to realize that Riker was asking him, and not his mom.

"I don't know enough about the game to coach," Hunter said.

The kid looked at him as though he'd just announced that he'd forgotten his name.

"I mean, I know the basic rules. Three strikes and you're out, but I wouldn't know when to tell a batter to bunt or when he should steal a base or when he should stay put."

"I could teach you all that. Dads should know all that, so they can be coaches."

Yeah, maybe dads should, but he wasn't planning to be a dad.

"Riker, why don't you turn around and watch the game now?" Serena suggested, a pink that matched the shade of the cotton candy creeping onto her cheeks that Hunter didn't think was the result of the early evening warmth.

Once Riker had put his glove back on and turned to watch the game, Serena leaned toward Hunter and whispered, "I'm sorry. He's been a little obsessed with having a dad since Jack got married." Her gaze darted over to the bags of pink fluff. "Just two bags of cotton candy?"

"I'm not much into sweets."

"How did you know I was?"

"Lucky guess."

She opened a bag and reached around Riker. "Here you go. You need to be sure and thank Mr. Fletcher."

The kid glanced over his shoulder. "Thanks." Then the glove was off again and the candy was disappearing.

"I've always been a sucker for cotton candy," Serena said as she opened her own bag. She pinched off a bit and then looked at him. "Are you sure you don't want any?"

He thought the look she gave him could have melted the sugar she was holding in her hand. His gaze darted between her eyes and the bit of fluff she held between her finger and thumb.

"Sure, why not?" he said.

She placed the candy against his lips, he parted them, and before he could even bite, it had all melted away. She licked her fingers. "What do you think?"

That it was suddenly too damned hot out here.

"It has potential."

She laughed and held the open bag toward him. "Help yourself."

Only he wasn't interested in feeding it to himself.

"Mom, can I go over there, down by the fence line to watch?"

"No, let's just stay up here."

"You don't have to go with me."

"No, Riker, there are too many people here tonight."

The boy's shoulders sagged forward as he returned his attention to the game.

"He'd probably be okay—" Hunter began, before she stopped him with a shake of her head.

"I'd worry too much. If I looked away, he'd be gone."

"He seems obedient—"

"Oh, I don't think he'd run off. I worry that someone might take him. There are people like that. You hear about it all the time."

"It seems a little paranoid—"

"That's my style: paranoid protectiveness."

She didn't seem offended or angry that he'd

questioned her, but was simply letting him know that she wasn't going to change her approach on his say-so.

So their parenting styles would definitely differ. Parenting styles? When had he ever considered a parenting style?

He'd never contemplated becoming a parent. Kids were a distraction. You had to worry about what they ate, what time they went to bed, what sports they played, and whether or not you could allow them to walk away from you.

And he certainly wasn't thinking about becoming a parent now. It was a responsibility he didn't need or want.

"Are you all right?" she asked. "You look like the hot dog might not be agreeing with you."

Something wasn't agreeing with him, but it wasn't what he'd eaten. He took a deep breath. "I'm fine."

"It was really nice of you to arrange tonight. It means a lot to Riker. Means a lot to me that you included him."

"Seemed only fair. It was his suggestion."

"You don't take compliments well."

Mainly because he wasn't used to receiving them. At least not in situations like this, from a lovely woman who was praising him for something other than his bedroom skills.

"You were young when he was born. Did you ever make it to college?"

"No. I'd planned to go, but I was too busy after Riker was born. How about you? Did you go to college?"

"Experience was my education."

She smiled at that. "The instructor can sometimes be unforgiving."

She had that right.

"Yeah, but you seldom forget the lessons," he said.

"It just seems that too often the test is the lesson."

There was a crack of a bat, the roar of the crowd, he heard Riker yelling, Serena looked up, released a tiny squeal, and covered her head. Ah, the baseball.

A couple of young men and several kids were suddenly scrambling onto the quilt. Hunter hated to do it, but it was headed for his hand and he was the tallest of the lot. He had to take it.

The impact stung his hand, but by the time the ball had traveled this distance, it had lost some of its velocity. He was vaguely aware of some yells and clapping.

"Good catch, man," one of the guys said before heading back to where he was sitting. The kids who'd come over scattered away, except for Riker who—with a wide grin on his face—was looking at him.

"Wow! Did you see that, Mom? He just caught it. No glove or nothing."

"I saw it. Very impressive."

Riker bobbed his head. "You could be a coach. Honest."

"That was just being in the right place at the right time." Hunter tossed the ball into Riker's glove. "Here you go, kid."

"Awesome! Thanks." He turned back around and Hunter heard the *thud, thud, thud* as the boy lobbed the ball into his glove.

"That was some catch," Serena said as she straightened her visor.

"How would you know? You didn't see it."

She wrinkled her cute little nose. "I'm not much into baseballs flying toward me. I didn't think they'd reach all the way out here."

"Where did you think home run balls were going to go?"

"I wasn't expecting the farm league to hit many home runs."

"These are all young kids who still dream of making the major leagues. They're going to whack that ball if they get a chance."

"What do you know about dreams?"

That until this moment he'd never had a single one come true. But he wasn't going to share that with her. Instead he leaned toward her and whispered, "Most of my dreams involve you with very little clothing on."

If she were offended, she didn't let on. As a matter of fact, based on the blush creeping into her cheeks and the way she kept pressing her lips into a tight line every time the corners of her mouth started to curl up, he thought maybe she was pleased by his words.

It was dark by the time Hunter pulled the minivan in front of her father's house. Serena felt good about the evening. Content. Riker was still excited about the fact that he'd come home with a home run baseball.

Riker pulled open the side door. "I'm going to show Grandpa my ball."

"Riker," Serena admonished as she stepped out of the van. "Thank Mr. Fletcher for taking you first."

"Thanks, it was great."

"You're welcome."

Hunter was standing beside her, his voice a gentle purr in the night. Riker bounded up the steps and into the house, the door slamming behind him.

"Did you want to come in for a cup of coffee?" Serena asked.

"Nah, it's late. I should head out."

"Thank you for tonight. It was really nice. Special." *Kiss me,* she thought. *Just kiss me.*

She'd wanted him to kiss her during the game. Not that baseball allowed for a lot of "kiss me" moments. Unlike football. The excitement around touchdowns lent itself to hot, steamy kisses more than a base hit did.

"So does it count as a date when your son is with us?" he asked.

"I think so."

He reached up and removed her visor. "Thank you for going with me."

The kiss was slow and leisurely. He wrapped his arms around her and drew her against him until she was flattened against his chest. Even the hot, sultry night couldn't compete with the heat of his kiss.

It poured into her, through her. It made her feel giddy and drunk. Maybe it wasn't the margaritas that first night that had inebriated her. Maybe it was this. The touch of his lips against hers, the stroke of his tongue, the way he suckled and thrust and latched onto her mouth as though it were a lifeline.

Whenever he kissed her, she felt as though he was giving everything he had to give, holding nothing back. He communicated with his kiss more than he ever did with words. She felt treasured, appreciated, beautiful.

She felt that this moment was theirs, that no one could ever take it away from them. That she'd been waiting for him.

He drew back from the kiss and pressed his forehead against hers. "Is there any chance after you put your son to bed that you and I could sneak away for a little late night dancing?"

She knew he wanted more than dancing. His arms were looped around her, his hands hooked at her lower back, keeping their bodies touching. Why deny what she so desperately wanted?

"I'm all sticky," she said. "I'd need to shower—"

"I have a shower at my place."

"Let me put Riker to bed, gather up a few things, and let my dad know that I'm going to be out for a while."

Chapter 12

Hunter had never considered himself a coward, but he'd contemplated waiting in the jeep or on the porch. But in the end, he'd accepted her invitation to wait inside.

Which of course meant waiting with her father.

"Have a little Southern Comfort," her father said, setting a glass on the little table beside him.

"Thank you, sir."

Her father sat in a recliner, popped up the foot rest, and settled back. Hunter took the glass he'd been offered, took a swallow, and nearly coughed. Straight Southern Comfort.

"Too strong?" Larry asked.

"No, sir, it's just fine, thank you."

Larry glanced over at him, and Hunter had a feeling he was being scrutinized from the top of his head to the heels of his shoes.

"Rena said you're going to go out and *watch* the lake?"

The question wasn't as innocent as it sounded,

and Hunter knew it. The old man made it sound like he couldn't figure out why anyone would look at a lake or even suggest doing so. It rang more along the lines of, "You're gonna do *what?*"

"Yes, sir, I have a very nice view of the lake and when the moon is out, as it is tonight, it's a pretty sight. I thought Serena might enjoy"—he cleared his throat—"looking at it."

Nodding, her father narrowed one eye and Hunter wondered if he was practicing looking down the barrel of a rifle.

"She's a grown girl, my daughter."

"Yes, sir." *She most definitely is that.*

"Too old for me to be telling her what to do."

Thank God. Hunter was beginning to wonder if they should send fathers with daughters in to do their interrogations.

"But I don't want to see her get hurt."

"Neither do I."

"You ever been married, son?"

"No, sir."

"You ever contemplate it?"

"Not until recently, no."

The old man narrowed his eye again.

Hunter heard footsteps, glanced over his shoulder.

Serena had come down the stairs between the living room and kitchen. "Riker is ready for bed. He wondered if you'd like to come up and say good night."

Hunter had never gotten out of a chair so quickly. If the choice was between a father or a boy, he was going with the boy. "I'd like that."

He excused himself, crossed the room, and followed Serena up the stairs. Photos lined the wall. Her as a baby, a gapped-toothed child, a young girl, a young woman. In every picture she looked happy.

"I'm sorry if my dad was interrogating you," she said in a low voice.

"I've had worse."

"I was afraid he might have run you off," she said as she reached the top of the stairs and turned to face him.

"I'm not in the habit of running."

She stopped in front of him. "Even when you're scared?"

"Especially when I'm scared."

She smiled and led him into a room on the left. The boy was sitting against the headboard, wearing his glove, and tossing the ball into it. His beagle was curled at the foot of his bed.

Hunter suddenly wasn't sure why he was in this room or what he was supposed to do. He didn't think it was his place to yell at the kid to go to sleep. That had pretty much been his experience with bedtime routine: "Go to sleep!" Lights out. Then darkness and loneliness and wishing someone were there. Even if it was only a spotted beagle.

Reaching out, he petted the dog only because it was something to do.

"He likes you," Riker said.

As though to demonstrate his master's astuteness, the beagle licked Hunter's hand.

"I like him, too."

"Do you have any dogs?"

"No. It wouldn't be fair to the dog. I travel a lot."

"I pet sit."

"Riker, that's in Hopeful, not here." She glanced over at Hunter. "He takes care of the neighbors' pets when they go out of town."

"Ah, so there's another resourceful entrepreneur in the family," Hunter said.

"What's that mean?" Riker asked.

"Someone who has a business."

"If you moved to Hopeful, you could get a dog and I could take care of it when you're out of town," Riker said.

"Riker, I thought you just wanted to thank Mr. Fletcher again and tell him good night. Not try to talk him into moving to Hopeful."

"But if you moved to Hopeful," the boy said, his imploring eyes on Hunter like prison searchlights, "we could go to more ball games and you could teach me more karate."

He suddenly sat up straight, as though someone jerked him upright. "I know! You could be an entrepreneur, too. You could have a business. Kick-Butt Karate!"

Hunter grinned. He'd thought the father was bad. Shoot! This kid was going to have his life planned out before the lights went out.

Laughing, Serena placed her hands on her son's shoulders and eased him back down. She brought the covers up, patting him here and there, lovingly, tenderly. Something Hunter imagined she'd done a thousand times.

"There are several flaws in your plan," she told Riker.

"Like what?"

"Well, first of all, I don't think a business should have 'butt' in its name, and you don't need to be saying it."

Hunter found it interesting that she hadn't mentioned that Riker didn't need to be encouraging Hunter to move to Hopeful.

The boy looked back at him. "We'll come up with another name."

"Riker, it's time for you to say good night," she told him.

"Ah, Mom—"

"Ah, Riker."

The kid rolled his eyes and turned onto his side. "Good night."

"Good night," Hunter said. But it seemed lacking and he thought there was something else he should say.

He watched as Serena bent down and kissed her son's head. "Good night. Sweet dreams."

That was it. Sweet dreams.

He followed Serena out of the room. She turned off the light as they entered the hallway and a night-light glowed near the boy's bed.

"You can wait here or go visit with my dad while I get a couple of things," she whispered.

"I'll wait."

He watched her disappear into a room down the hallway, then he glanced back into the room where the boy was sleeping. He was still wearing his baseball glove. The dog had curled up to nestle against the boy's stomach.

And for the first time in his life, Hunter had a clear sense of how important his job was. He wanted this boy to always be able to sleep with sweet dreams.

Serena sat on the passenger side trying to relax, trying not to feel as though she was doing something she shouldn't. She wouldn't have this problem if she was in Hopeful. She could hire a babysitter, she wouldn't have her father issuing a warning to be careful as she headed out the door.

Be careful? It was a little late for that.

Somewhere along the way, she'd thrown caution

to the wind. She knew she couldn't stay here forever, but while she was here, what was wrong with enjoying herself, enjoying the man beside her? She'd anticipated that they'd have another night together.

In a small canvas tote, she'd placed a toothbrush, a fresh set of clothes. In her purse she was carting around an unopened pack of birth control pills. She'd called her doctor in Hopeful and asked that a prescription be called in here. Now she was just waiting for the arrival of her period—which should be any day now—so she could begin the countdown for when she should begin taking them.

So having sex on a regular basis was a possibility that she'd accepted. And having accepted it, she needed to stop feeling guilty that she was on the verge of having it. It would simply be much easier not to feel guilty if her father didn't suspect.

"I don't think Dad bought the gazing at the lake excuse," she finally said.

"We will gaze at the lake, so you told him the truth." Hunter reached across and squeezed her hand. "Relax, Serena. If you change your mind once we get out there, I'll be content that you're just with me."

She smiled with gratification. Sometimes he said the most unexpected, sweetest things. But she had no plans to chicken out this time.

Hunter pulled the jeep to a stop. He hadn't left any lights on because he hadn't realized he'd be out this late. But he knew every inch of his property, his house. He got out of the jeep, walked around, and opened her door. When she stepped out, he opened the door, took her in his arms, and kissed her.

He'd go slowly tonight. He wouldn't rush her. He wouldn't give her any reasons to begin doubting that she should be here. He'd court her, enjoy her, show her that they could have more than hot and heavy sex.

But as her mouth moved against his, he knew his restraint would be tested. She tasted so good, felt so good. He couldn't determine why she was so different from all the women who'd come before her.

Maybe because there was an innocence to her. Strange to imagine that a woman who'd been married, who had a child, could harbor any sort of innocence. But it was there. The small town feel of a country girl. She may have grown up near Austin, but there was nothing big city about her.

And he liked that. Liked it a lot. And it didn't hurt any that she was sexy as hell.

Pulling away from her, he reached into the jeep, grabbed her bag, and closed the door. Without a word, he slipped his arm around her and guided her to the house. Once inside, he closed the door, locked it, and kissed her again, delivering a promise he intended to keep.

He loved the way she toed off her shoes, just as she had the first and last night that she was here. As though that were her signal—let's get it on. She wasn't wearing heels tonight so she lost very little of her height.

"Shower?" she whispered when he broke off the kiss to get a better angle.

"Right, shower."

He began backing her across the living room, an intimate dance, their lips locked, their hands exploring through their clothes.

They passed by the couch, with the large window spilling moonlight over it, and he thought, There. Why not just make love to her there?

Because she wanted a shower. The downstairs bathroom was closer. Shower there, then the couch. Then he remembered his plan to take it slowly. Not to rush her.

What an idiotic plan.

But it was in place, so he'd carry through on it. He dipped down, lifted her into his arms, and headed up the stairs.

She settled her head into the nook of his shoulder. "Do you always carry women up the stairs?"

"Only you."

"Really?"

He heard the doubt in her voice, wondered why it mattered that she didn't believe him, wondered why she didn't.

"It just seems right," he said.

"Right?"

"To carry you."

He reached the top of the stairs, strode into his bedroom, momentarily considered taking a detour by the bed, but went on through into the bathroom. He lowered her to the floor and switched on the light.

The light was harsh, and he wished he'd kept it off, but once his eyes adjusted, he thought he might run through the house and turn on every light. Her lips were swollen, coated in dew. Her skin was flushed. Her eyes were sultry.

He kept finding himself distracted from his objective. Get her showered.

He walked around her, opened the door to the walk-in shower, and turned on the water. The visor was gone, and her shoes, but otherwise she was dressed as she'd been for the ball game.

She held his gaze as she reached down and slipped off one sock, tossed it aside, and then did the same with the other. Very slowly, she unsnapped and unzipped her shorts. She wiggled out of them. She was wearing skimpy white lacy underwear.

Oh, yeah.

Serena had never considered herself much of a seductress, but standing here now, watching his nostrils flare, his eyes darken, she felt powerful and in control. It was a heady notion. The knuckles of his hand gripping the door were turning white.

She thought she needed some sort of bump and grind music as she grabbed the hem of her tank and eased it up, a quarter of an inch by a quarter of an inch. She was in no hurry. Up, up. He was mesmerized. She didn't think he was even blinking.

She pulled the top over her head, surprised by her brazenness. And excited by it.

He'd said carrying her up the stairs had seemed right. Standing here now, slowly undressing for him seemed right as well. Over the pounding of the shower, she could hear his breathing grow ragged.

She removed her bra, then wiggled out of her panties. He could have been a statue he stood so still as she walked around him and stepped into the shower. The warm water pelting her felt good after an evening in the humid night air.

"Are you going to join me?" she asked.

She might have laughed at the speed with which he tore off his clothes, except that as he stood revealed before her, she realized that she'd never seen him completely naked in the light. Or if she had that first night, she had no memory of it.

And she certainly thought she would have remembered gazing on magnificence such as his. His defined muscles rippled with his movements, and every aspect of his body—every aspect—looked rock hard.

She remembered touching him and how glorious

it had felt. But she didn't remember the sight of him. Now, she knew she'd never forget it.

He stepped into the shower, swung the door shut, and wrapped his arms around her.

"I told myself I was going to go slow," he said, "but I just can't seem to accomplish that where you're concerned."

"I'm glad."

It did seem to her that everything with them was like a freight train rushing past. But as long as it didn't crash, wasn't headed for disaster, she was content to be here in his arms.

The feel of soapy hands traveling over her skin was as sensual as anything she'd ever experienced. He didn't rush as he lathered her up, then used his hands to direct the flow of water. When the soap was rinsed away, he trailed his mouth over the places where the soap had been.

She'd never in her life enjoyed a shower more. Taking the soap, she lathered her hands before moving them over his body. Unlike hers while he'd washed her, his hands didn't remain still. He caressed and squeezed. He skimmed and cradled. It was as though he couldn't get enough of her.

When all the day's grime was gone, he knelt before her. The water continued to pour over her body, rained down on his uplifted face. With his large hands, he cupped her backside before he pressed his mouth between her thighs.

She braced her hands on his shoulders while he stroked her intimately with his tongue. Spirals of pleasure shot through her.

She dropped her head back and let the sensations build as he skillfully plundered. She had the impression of a warrior laying claim to all he intended to conquer. She thought no words would ever be able to adequately describe what she felt right now. A tensing, an easing. An increasing, a lessening.

Each sweep of his tongue carried her higher, before she dropped just a fraction. Her legs weakened, she began to quiver . . .

The water sluiced off her, his fingers dug into her hips, his mouth worked its magic, every sensation built until everything demanded release . . .

And then she shattered with a cry that echoed between the shower walls.

She was vaguely aware of the shower door opening, his movements as he grabbed his discarded jeans, searched through his wallet . . .

He donned the condom, eased her down, and guided her until she'd enveloped his sturdy length. She didn't know where she found the strength, thought she might melt into a pool of nothing, but she somehow managed to hang on, to wrap her arms around him as he pumped himself into her, his body tensing, his arms closing tightly around her as he made a final thrust, his guttural groan following in the echo of her cry.

He continued to spasm as his harsh breathing filled her ears. She could feel the rapid pounding of his heart as the water rained down. She laid her head on his shoulder, content to remain here forever.

Lying in bed with Serena nestled up against his side, and the moon spilling in through the window, Hunter was still trying to figure out what had happened in the shower.

The sex part he understood. That was no mystery.

But the rest of it . . . the possessiveness he'd felt, the joy because he'd brought her such pleasure . . . it had almost eclipsed his own sexual satisfaction. He'd always been determined that a lady left his bed content but he'd never found as much satisfaction as he did in Serena's cries, had never felt that everything he'd done was exclusively for her.

That he'd benefited as well was a bonus.

But all he'd truly cared about was pleasing her. He couldn't stop himself from grinning. He'd never had it so great. With his hands wet, the condom had been a damned nuisance, and he'd been tempted to forego it but the last thing he needed was the responsibility of a kid . . . it was one thing to take someone else's son to a ball game, but to have his own son?

What did he know about fathering?

Except that he'd probably be lousy at it, although he probably wouldn't be around enough to make much of a difference. And the last thing Serena or her children needed was a father who wouldn't be around much.

She released a little sigh and stretched along the length of his body like a contented cat.

"Feeling good?" he asked.

"More like great."

"You're welcome to come and take a shower at my place anytime you want."

"It's a long drive from Hopeful."

He'd known going in that whatever they'd have was temporary. That didn't mean that he had to like it now. "When are you leaving?"

"I'm not sure yet." She tapped her finger against his chest. "We have showers in Hopeful." She lifted herself onto her elbow. "Is there any chance that you might visit Hopeful . . . sometime?"

He threaded his fingers through hers. "Hadn't planned on it, but then lately I find myself doing a lot of things I hadn't planned on."

She lowered her head and circled his nipple with her tongue. He swallowed and groaned at the same time. She was certainly a touching kind of woman, and he found that he really liked that aspect of her. Hell, there wasn't much about her that he didn't like.

"I find myself doing the same," she said. Another lick. A swirl. "Things I hadn't planned. Things I wouldn't have thought I'd do."

A gentle bite.

What was she talking about? He couldn't concentrate when she was teasing him like that.

"I can't believe how quickly I've come to care for you," she said.

"Same goes."

A flick of her tongue. With his free hand, he clutched the sheet. He'd never realized so little could accomplish so much. It was the anticipation, he supposed, that had him ready, near to bursting.

When she finally got around to touching him with her hands—if she ever did—he didn't know if he'd be able to hold back.

She trailed her mouth along his ribs. Sweet torture.

Her hand had started to play, her fingers skimming up and down the inside of his thigh.

He was so close to the edge that he couldn't stand not going over. He reached out to the nightstand, located an unopened packet, ripped into it while she continued to torment him. He sheathed himself, and with a quick move that caused her to gasp, he flipped her onto her back.

"Enough of the torture," he growled. He grabbed her hands, held them above her head, and entered her.

Now it was his turn to torment, holding her hands in place, and using his mouth to kiss, suckle, caress. He knew he probably wasn't being as gentle as he needed to be, that his rough beard might abrade her skin, his mouth might leave the mark she'd warned him not to, but he wanted her with a fierceness that he'd never before felt.

He rocked against her, her cries of pleasure urging him on. He knew exactly when she peaked, felt her entire body curling around him, didn't remember releasing her hands, only knew that they were clutching him as he raced to join her at the finish line.

Never in his life had he been so aware of a woman. Never in his life had a woman terrified him as this one did.

"Four in one night," Serena murmured, her heart thudding. They were both sprawled over the bed, only their hands and feet touching, as though their bodies recognized that they needed a break from the intimacy. "That's a record for me."

"Same goes."

She wanted to laugh. It was as though anything that hinted at emotional intimacy was something he couldn't acknowledge with words he'd chosen himself.

"That surprises me," she said. "You get those condoms on like you're on an assembly line."

"I sure as hell don't want to get you pregnant."

Her thudding heart pounded even harder. She turned her head to the side and studied the profile of the man lying beside her. She'd come to like that his windows had no curtains. That the moonlight allowed her to see him in shadows, not clearly, but enough so she knew his eyes were closed.

His breathing was slowing, and she wondered if he was on the verge of going to sleep. She'd been close to doing the same until a few seconds ago.

"Would that be so awful?" she asked.

"What?"

"If I got pregnant?"

"Disaster."

All the beautiful sensations of the night suddenly turned ugly. What was she doing here with this man she barely knew? They'd had a picnic, he'd taken her son to a baseball game, she'd begun to feel a bond building . . .

He turned his head, and she saw his eyes open.

"That's not what you wanted to hear, is it?"

"I just don't know why you'd think it would be a disaster."

With a sigh he sat up. "I'm not looking for marriage. I'm not going to move to Hopeful and open up the Kick-Butt Karate School. I thought you understood that anything with me was temporary."

She pushed herself to a sitting position. "I did understand that. I'm not looking for anything permanent."

Only she realized that she had begun to think in terms of permanence. Of spending more time near Austin, of having him visit in Hopeful, of inviting him to spend a weekend at the family beach house.

"I'm just not sure that I'd label my getting pregnant as a disaster."

"Well, having been the result of an unplanned one, trust me, I know from experience that they are." He got off the bed and she saw him in silhouette walking past the window as he made his way to the bathroom. He flicked the switch and harsh light poured into the bedroom. He came back and tossed her clothes onto the bed. "Get dressed and I'll take you home."

Session over, mission accomplished. She decided it was a good thing that he hadn't decorated his house with knickknacks because right now she wanted to pick something up and throw it at him.

He walked back into the bathroom. She kicked off the sheets that had become entangled around her legs and snatched up her panties with trembling fingers. She jerked them on. Ignoring her bra, she grabbed her tank top and put it on. She had clean clothes in a bag downstairs, but she wasn't going to take time to retrieve them. Get dressed, get out.

If she wasn't so far from town, she'd call a cab. Damn him for making her feel cheap. She scrambled off the bed, strode to the bathroom, and staggered to a stop. She'd expected to see him getting dressed. Instead she found him hunched over the sink, his arms braced, his head bent. She could see the dampness on his face, but she hadn't heard the water being turned on.

"He used to beat the holy crap out of her," he said quietly. "Blamed her because she and her 'accident' kept him from doing what he wanted in life."

"And what was that?" she asked.

"Who the hell knows?"

"Riker was unplanned," she said quietly. "But we never considered him a disaster. I don't think you were the reason your father beat your mother. He might have used that as an excuse, but it wasn't the reason."

He lifted his head to capture her gaze in the mirror. "But it wasn't easy either, was it?"

"No, but marriage and children never are. That doesn't mean they're to be avoided."

"Well, since I'm religious about using protection, it's not a problem we'll have to deal with." Turning from the mirror, he grinned. "You should have put your shorts on, because that little outfit sure is sexy."

The smile he gave her was one that would have had her melting at his feet only moments ago. Now she simply shook her head. "You're right. It's time for me to go home."

She walked out of the room, went to the bed, and retrieved her shorts. She'd just finished putting them on when he came up behind her and wrapped his arms around her. He pressed his mouth to the side of her throat. "Don't leave mad."

"I'm not mad."

"You're hurt."

She raised her shoulder. "You're right. A baby isn't a reason to get married, and it wasn't the reason I got married before."

She turned within his arms. He'd put on his jeans, but not a shirt. She flattened her palms against his bare chest and lifted her gaze to his. She didn't want to bring Steve into the picture, but she also needed to be up-front with Hunter. "What I have with you is so different from anything I've ever had before." She released a self-conscious laugh. "I'm not even sure that I can say that I have something with you."

He arched a brow in question.

"Other than sex. That I definitely have. It's not enough for me. Even for the short-term."

"It's all I can offer."

She nodded, having finally figured that part out. "Yeah, I know."

And that realization made her sadder than she'd been in a good long time.

• • •

The silence was deafening. As Hunter drove her home, he'd never realized how loud quiet could be.

The silence had never bothered him before, not even after that first night. But now he knew he'd hurt her, and he'd never meant to do that.

He pulled up in front of the house, not surprised to see the porch light on, but surprised to see lights flickering behind the curtains at the window.

"It's almost two o'clock. Don't tell me your father is still up."

"He probably fell asleep watching TV."

He got out of the jeep, went around, and opened the door for her. She was halfway out when he blurted, "If I hurt you, I'm sorry."

She gave him a sad sort of smile. "We keep moving fast and then we have to slow down."

"You said earlier that what we have is different from anything you've ever had before. It's different from anything I've ever had either. I've never considered myself a coward, but I have to admit that you scare me, lady."

"Why would I scare you?"

"I'm not what you're looking for, but I can't seem to retreat."

"I'm not sure if I'm supposed to be flattered."

"You are." He didn't think she'd welcome the kind of heat-seeking kiss that he wanted to give her, so he simply leaned forward and kissed her forehead. "I'll call you."

"I'm not sure you should."

He watched her walk up the steps with her little bag in tow, and it occurred to him that maybe she'd planned to stay the entire night. He did best when he just kept his mouth shut.

He climbed into his jeep and headed home—to his quiet house on the lonely stretch of land.

Chapter 13

For the next month Serena threw herself into getting her mother's things in order, because she was more than ready to return to Hopeful. But then she caught a slight virus that left her tired and nauseous. And it seemed to want to hang around.

Until she finally decided that maybe it was more than a virus.

A watched pot might never boil, but a watched home pregnancy test obviously wasn't shy about revealing its results.

Serena stared at the pink line that appeared beneath the pink control line. This was so not good. The words were what she knew she should be thinking, what she repeated in her mind because of the words she and Hunter had exchanged their last night together, but they held no real emotion.

She sank down onto the edge of the bathtub and tried to feel alarmed, panicked. Instead she felt almost happy. Granted, getting pregnant had certainly not been in her plans, and she knew it hadn't been in Hunter's plans either.

But still she was carrying his child. She placed her hand over her stomach. Flat. No change there, but then it was too early for there to be any. The only evidence she had was a missing period—which she'd tried to attribute to the stress of losing her mother—and breasts that were more tender at this time of the month than usual. Being more tired than usual and nauseous. And the little pink line.

Before she spoke with Hunter, she'd visit the family doctor and have a test run there. If the results came back as she expected that they would, she'd go see Hunter. He wasn't going to be thrilled, but he was the baby's father and she thought he had a right to know.

Then they could deal with the situation together.

He stepped out of his house before she'd opened the door to her van. She was irritated by the gladness that swept through her at the sight of him. Four weeks had passed since she'd last seen him. He'd said he'd call, but he hadn't. Of course, he might have changed his mind after she told him not to call.

She was wishing that she'd called him with the news but she'd felt that she needed to tell him in person. He had a right to know. She believed that with all her heart.

Her hands were trembling as she opened the door and climbed out of the van.

"Hey," he said.

As far as greetings went, she wasn't too impressed. "Hi."

She decided she wasn't one to talk. Hers wasn't much better.

"I wasn't expecting you," he said.

"I didn't think you were, but I needed to talk with you." She crossed her arms over her chest in a defensive posture. It suddenly occurred to her that he might have a woman inside the house. That maybe he'd moved on to someone else.

"Is everything all right?" he asked.

She nodded, shook her head, pressed a hand to her mouth, and fought to blink back the tears that had suddenly sprung forward as though released by a collapsing dam. He was off the front porch and had her in his arms before she had a chance to gain control of herself.

Oh, God, he smelled so good, felt so warm and sturdy. She hadn't thought she was bothered by the fact that he hadn't contacted her, hadn't realized she was bothered by her condition, had thought she was mature enough that she could handle it—even if she had to handle it alone.

"What happened?" he asked. "Is it Riker? Your dad?"

She shook her head. "I'm sorry. I'm so sorry. I know this isn't what you wanted."

He leaned back until he was looking into her eyes, but his arms remained firm around her. "What is it, babe? What's wrong?"

Babe. Why did the endearment have to hurt so much? Why did he show concern now when he hadn't in weeks?

"I'm pregnant." The words exploded out of her mouth before she could stop them, before she could think of a way to soften their impact.

He released her and moved back as though she'd just announced she had Ebola. With his brow furrowed, he focused his gaze on her stomach as though he thought if he stared hard enough he could see the embryo growing inside her. "Are you sure?"

She nodded jerkily, wiped away her tears, and took a deep breath. She was regaining some of her equilibrium. "I did a home pregnancy test—"

"Those aren't always accurate."

"I went to the doctor to confirm the diagnosis." She nodded again. "I'm pregnant."

He took another step back, walked to the right, strode back to the left. Stopped in front of her. Now he was the one nodding. "You make the arrangements. I'll pay for the abortion."

She staggered backward as though he'd punched

her in the gut, when in reality he'd stabbed her through the heart. "I'm not getting an abortion."

"Then why did you come out here?"

"Because you're the father and I thought you had the right to know."

"I used a condom every time."

"Fine. Then that relieves you of all responsibility, doesn't it? Sorry if I put a crimp in your day."

She spun on her heel and headed to the van.

"Serena, wait."

There was authority in his voice that she couldn't have ignored if she wanted to. And damn it, she wanted to. She stopped but she didn't turn around.

"Are you sure—"

"I swear to God that if you ask me if I'm sure if it's yours that I am going to get into this van and drive it right over you—several times."

Although she hadn't been married when she'd discovered she was pregnant with Riker, she'd felt joy. Steve had felt joy. They were both scared to death, but they were also happy. Even though they'd been incredibly young. And here she was, older, carrying the child of a man who obviously preferred not to be bothered.

"I wasn't going to ask that. I was just wondering if there could have been a mistake made with either of the tests—"

"Oh, a mistake was made," she said, spinning

around to glare at him. "There was definitely a mistake made. And I'm the one who made it."

She jerked open the door to the van, clambered in, started the ignition, threw the gear into reverse, and floored the gas pedal. He didn't move, didn't come after her, didn't try to stop her. And that hurt. Hurt more than she wanted to admit.

She was old enough to know better, old enough not to be caught in this situation. And yet here she was, where she had never in her life expected to be again.

She was twenty-seven years old, wondering how she was going to explain it to her father when she couldn't even explain it to herself. And what was she going to tell Riker?

She drove fast and furiously until she spotted the flashing blue and red lights in her rearview mirror. With a curse, she slowed down and pulled over to the side of the road. She reached into her glove compartment for her car registration and proof of insurance. Searching for everything through a film of tears, she fumbled around in her purse until she located her wallet and pulled out her license.

And where were the damn tissues? She hadn't even realized that she'd started crying again. She nearly jumped out of her skin when she heard a rapping on her window. She powered it down and handed over the essentials.

The officer took them, his eyes hard on her. "Are you all right, ma'am?"

Ma'am? They were probably the same age. Did she look as old as she suddenly felt?

"I'm just fine, Officer. Thanks for asking."

Because Hunter hadn't asked. Hadn't asked how she was feeling, hadn't asked if she was scared, hadn't asked how she'd manage. He'd just offered to pay for the damned abortion that had never crossed her mind to even consider.

"You were going eighty in a fifty-five—"

"Officer, just issue the ticket."

The officer removed his sunglasses. "Ma'am, I have to tell you that you don't look as though you're all right."

She swiped at her tears. "I just had some disappointing news, but I'll be fine."

And she would be. She'd faced harder moments in her life. She'd get through this, be the stronger for it. Learn from it, because for a heartbeat, for a single heartbeat, she'd actually contemplated that if Hunter asked, she might consider marrying him. Although she didn't know him well, she'd felt that connection from the beginning.

Only the connection had turned out to be lust or horniness or hormones gone wild. But there had certainly been nothing substantial there.

"Ma'am, is there someone I should contact?"

She shook her head. "I'll sit here until I've calmed down and I promise not to go over the speed limit again."

"I'm going to let you off with a warning this time, ma'am."

Oh, God, the damn tears were starting up again, because of his kindness. "Thank you."

He handed the information back to her. "Whatever it is, ma'am, it's probably not as bad as it seems right now. Things usually aren't."

She nodded. "Thank you, Officer."

"You take care, now, hear?"

She bobbed her head, threw everything into the glove compartment, and took several deep breaths. She placed her hand on her stomach. He was right. Things weren't that bad. She was going to be an unmarried mother, but then again she was an unmarried mother now.

Gossip would no doubt run rampant through her father's church congregation and among his friends. It would be tossed about in Hopeful. But eventually her notoriety would diminish. If she lived in a larger town, no one would care. It was only in small towns that people still raised eyebrows over unwed mothers. So she'd raise a few eyebrows. She also intended to raise this child.

She eased the van onto the road, checked in the rearview mirror, and wished she wasn't disappointed to discover no jeep raising a cloud of dust behind her. How many times was she going to let his reticence disappoint her?

She decided to take a detour before returning to her father's house. She turned onto the lane that led into the cemetery where her mother had been laid to rest. She came to a stop, got out, and walked to the grave where the earth was still raw, where the grass had not yet reclaimed the dirt. There wasn't a head-stone, just a small little temporary marker.

Wishing she'd brought some fresh flowers, she knelt on the ground. "Oh, Mom, you were so under-standing when I got pregnant with Riker. I don't know what you'd feel now. I'm not even sure what I feel. Disappointment in Hunter. Disappointment in myself. Embarrassment for getting caught. And a sort of gladness, because I wanted more children. I thought I'd have three or four by now. It'll be hard, I know that. I wish you were here, Mom. I wish you were here to tell me that everything will be all right."

She felt so alone. Her father, bless him, was a good man, but some things a daughter could only share with her mother or with the man she loved. Some things she should be able to say to a man she'd slept with.

"I've never been so angry in my whole life. I should have expected his reaction. He was honest from the beginning. He didn't want a relationship.

"But there was just something about him, Mom. I wanted to spend time with him, get to know him. And it wasn't simply because he was sexy as sin. You would have called him eye candy.

"I liked the way I felt when I was with him. I stopped feeling old. I started feeling attractive. I liked the way he treated Riker and Riker sure took a shine to him.

"He's a good man, Mom. He just has this irrational prejudice against relationships. I guess I can't blame him. He didn't have it easy growing up.

"I was lucky. I had you and Dad. I'm hoping this one is a girl. I know you always wanted a granddaughter."

She released a slow, calming sigh and felt contentment ease through her. She suddenly felt stronger than she had in a long time. "I can do this, Mom. I'm going to be fine. I'm too much like you. You were so strong fighting the cancer. I'm going to be strong now. I'm facing a battle. I'm going to bring a new little life into the world. I want this baby, Mom. I really do.

"We're going to be just fine."

Chapter 14

She was going to have his kid. Hunter stood at the edge of the lake, wondering how the water could look so calm when his life had gone to hell.

He was going to be a father. And he'd never been so terrified in his entire life. What if he turned out to be like his old man? Bitter and abusive. Then what?

Serena would kick his butt.

She wouldn't be like his mother. Cowering, believing she deserved what his old man had dished out. Just as he'd always wondered what he'd done wrong to anger his father. He'd always thought if he could have just figured out what he did that made his father angry—he'd stop doing it. He hadn't wanted to be bad. He'd just never understood why being an "accident" had meant that he couldn't be loved.

Only now did he realize that being an "accident" had nothing to do with his old man's treatment of him. Hunter wasn't angry because Serena was pregnant. He didn't hate the kid growing inside of her. He didn't hate her.

What he felt—to his utter astonishment—was joy.

He was going to have a kid. And it didn't matter that he didn't know the first thing about raising a kid. He could learn. Serena could teach him. He could figure out how to coach baseball. He could adapt his life.

He could be a father. He'd be nothing like his old man. He'd never strike his kid—no matter how angry he got. He knew that. Deep within himself. He'd never lash out at an innocent person. He'd never shut his kid in a dark closet.

His old man hadn't been mean because of anything Hunter had done. His old man had simply been rotten—to the core. Drugs and violence. He'd blamed his kid because he hadn't been man enough to shoulder the burden for his actions.

Well, Hunter had never had a problem with shouldering responsibility. Although he doubted that Serena would believe that after his reaction this morning.

Serena. He released a deep sigh. She was having his kid. He wondered if she knew yet if it was going to be a boy or a girl.

Of course, she didn't know. Pregnancy tests didn't reveal that—did they? No, of course they didn't.

He dropped his head back and stared at the blue sky until the sunlight almost blinded him. Her news changed everything. He'd offered to pay for an abortion because he'd assumed she'd want one, and he hadn't wanted her to know that the very thought of her not wanting his child was tearing his guts out.

He should have known her better than that. He knew what she wanted—and he'd been afraid to offer it, afraid of hurting her. And in the not offering, he'd caused her more pain.

He'd handled the situation poorly. For someone who was quick thinking on his feet in dangerous situations, he certainly hadn't used his skills this afternoon. He'd been in shock. Stunned.

He knew condoms weren't a hundred percent, but they'd never let him down before. He supposed if they were going to fail, he was grateful that they'd failed with Serena Hamilton.

She was one tough lady and sexy as hell.

The woman had left here ready to spit nails. Not that he blamed her. He'd seen that she was protective and sensitive where Riker was concerned. It seemed she was going to grant the same feelings to his child. A warm knot of contentment settled into his chest. He couldn't have asked for a better mother for his child if he'd gone out searching for one.

Or a better woman to be his wife. She wasn't afraid of him. She challenged him—in bed and out. He wanted her. Not just for a night—but for every night.

Of course, he didn't think he'd given her the impression that those were his feelings. He wasn't even sure that he'd realized those were his feelings until this moment. Or if they'd been hovering near the surface, he'd refused to acknowledge them.

But now that he had, he planned to do something about it. He wanted her as his wife. He wanted her kids in his life. He was going to have to do some bridge mending. And pretty damned quick.

The sun had set by the time he pulled his jeep to a stop in front of her father's house. After showering and shaving, he'd put on a pair of dress slacks and a shirt that was dressy enough without a tie that he thought it would make a statement that he cared. He'd contemplated a tie, but didn't want to give her something she could strangle him with if her mood hadn't improved since she'd barreled off his property—and he had no reason to believe anything had happened to improve it.

Taking a deep breath, he reached across to the passenger side and grabbed the bouquet of assorted flowers and the box of Whitman's Sampler he'd picked up at a grocery store he'd passed on the way here. He climbed out of his jeep and walked up the steps to the porch. He could see faint, flickering light reflected through the windows and figured everyone was watching something on the television.

He rapped on the door, waited a couple of heartbeats, and rapped again. He couldn't recall being this nervous when he was on a mission. Perhaps because the only thing he stood to lose then was his life, and until this moment, he hadn't placed much value on that.

The door swung open, and Larry Barnett stood there, an imposing sentinel with his graying hair and his suspicious glare. "Well, son, haven't seen you in a while."

His voice was sharp-edged enough to slice through a tough steak.

"I was out of town."

"This place you went to . . . out in the boonies was it? No telephones to speak of?"

"I was preoccupied."

"Uh-huh. I get the impression that you weren't the only one."

Hunter was losing patience fast. "Are you going to invite me in?"

"I was given orders not to."

Hunter grimaced. He'd known getting back on her good side wasn't going to be easy, but he'd thought she'd at least offer him the opportunity to try. He held up the flowers, hoping he appeared to be what he was: remorseful and hopeful.

"Rena, he brought flowers," her father called out over his shoulder.

"I don't care. I don't want to see him."

Barnett shrugged. "She's like her mother that way.

Get on her bad side and it's hard to get back on her good. Know what I mean?"

Not really, but the hints were stacking up. Based on the fact that her father hadn't greeted him at the door with a shotgun, Hunter was beginning to also realize that she hadn't broken the news to Barnett. The old man no doubt thought they'd simply had a *little* misunderstanding. Instead it was one hell of a whopper.

"I really need to talk to your daughter," Hunter said.

"Rena, he really needs to talk to you," Barnett called over his shoulder.

"I don't want to talk to him. He did his talking this afternoon."

Barnett furrowed his brow as though some bit of information was new to him. "She says—"

"I heard what she said."

Barnett's brow furrowed more deeply. "You spoke this afternoon?"

"Yeah."

"Not here."

"No, she came to my place."

"This is more than her being in a tiff because you haven't called in nearly a month."

"I think so, yeah."

"You know, son, I gotta tell you that I'm confused as all get-out. You've been here a couple of times, seem like a pleasant enough fella. Now it seems to me that you've done something to hurt my little girl, and I'm beginning to think it's about more than simply not phoning."

Barnett stood there as though he expected Hunter to reveal what the problem was.

"I take it she's watching TV," Hunter said instead.

"TV's on. I don't know that she's watching it."

Hunter thrust the flowers and chocolates toward the old man. "Will you at least give these to her?"

Barnett took them. "The flowers are kind of pitiful looking, aren't they?"

"They were the best that the grocery store had this time of evening."

Barnett grinned. "Bought a couple of grocery store bouquets myself through the years. You can always tell which fellas are in trouble with their ladies. It's always the ones holding a bouquet of flowers at the check-out line."

"Glad you find the situation humorous."

"Oh, I don't find it humorous at all. Not if you've made my Rena unhappy."

At his age, Hunter hadn't expected to be dealing with fathers at the door if he had more than a casual interest in a woman. When had he decided his interest was more than casual? The answer hit him smack in the face. The night he'd returned to the bar.

"Will you just give her the flowers?"

"Sure thing. You might try again tomorrow. Give her a chance to cool down."

Hunter nodded. "I'll consider it."

He turned on his heel, strode off the porch, and jerked open the door to his jeep. He was halfway inside when his gaze fell on the towering trees on either side of the house. Her bedroom was on the second floor.

An old turn-of-century farmhouse. With the skills he possessed, breaking in undetected would be child's play.

The flowers looked like rejects from the florist, a few of the leaves crushed, a couple of the stems broken as though someone had been clutching them too hard. Still, Serena put them into a vase of water because she couldn't simply let them die without giving them a fighting chance.

She added a little sugar to the water because she thought that was a secret her mother had used to revitalize flowers. Or was that something she'd done at Christmas to keep the tree from drying out too quickly?

Fighting back the tears that she'd been holding at bay for most of the evening, she placed the vase on the table and returned to the living room where her father and Riker were watching a Harry Potter movie for the umpteenth time. Her emotions were already on a roller-coaster thrill ride, and she was less than six weeks pregnant.

She was certain that it was hormones that had her weeping over silly flowers and not the brutal rejection she and her unborn child had received that afternoon. What had it taken Hunter? Five whole hours to get out here with an apology?

Well to hell with him. He could rot for all she cared.

Her father's leather recliner squeaked as he shifted around and leaned toward where she was sitting on the couch. "I felt a little sorry for the fella."

"You shouldn't. He doesn't deserve you feeling sorry for him."

"He looked like he'd been put through the wringer."

She held up a hand. "Don't get involved, Dad. There are things here that you don't understand."

"Do I need to be getting out my shotgun?"

More like his hunting knife. Castrate the fella because she sure didn't want to marry him. Not that the thought hadn't danced through her head a time or two since she'd taken the home pregnancy test.

"No, Dad, you don't need to get out your gun."

She watched the images on the television change, but if asked, she couldn't have revealed the plot or the characters' names—other than Harry. She wished she felt like reading—but she didn't.

Everything seemed as though it required more energy than she had to give at the moment. Not a good
sign when she knew the next several months—the
next several years—were going to require an inordi-
nate amount of energy.

When the movie was over, she said good night to
her father and went up the stairs with Riker. She
tucked him into bed.

She sat on the edge of the bed and feathered her
fingers through Riker's blond hair, wondering if this
child she was now carrying would be fair or dark.
Dark probably. People might not even realize that
Riker and this child were siblings.

What would people in Hopeful think? She'd gone
away for a few weeks during the summer and returned pregnant. Perhaps she should come up with
some sort of exciting story when the beautician at
Shear Pleasures who usually cut her hair asked what
was new in her life.

Although in a few months, everyone would know
what was new in her life without asking. She'd been a
blimp when she'd carried Riker, waddling around,
constantly searching for balance.

She couldn't decide whether to tell her father
about her condition before she left for Hopeful or
spare him a few months' worry and tell him when she
could not longer hide the fact.

"Why are you sad, Mom?"

She shook her head. "I'm not. I'm just tired."

"When are we going home?"

"I think it's about time. I'm going to talk to Grandpa about it tomorrow."

"Good. I love Grandpa, but I miss Jason and my other friends."

"I know you do. You've been really good about staying on to help Grandpa. I'm proud of you and I love you."

"Are you sure you're not sad?"

She forced herself to smile. "I'm sure. Good night, sweetie."

She kissed the top of his head before rising to her feet and heading to the door. She switched off the light and walked down the hallway to her own bedroom.

She turned on the light, closed the door, and suddenly found herself pressed up against a hard body, a hand held firmly over her mouth, and her breath backing up into her lungs with such force that it was painful.

"Don't scream," he whispered near her ear. "It's me."

She brought her heel down hard on his instep.

"Damn it!" He released her and stepped back. "What did you do that for?"

She spun on him. "How did you get in here?"

"The kitchen."

She stared at him. "What?"

"The door to the kitchen was unlocked. I walked right in. I even watched you watching television for a while."

She crossed her arms over her chest, feeling equally violated and incensed. "You did not."

"You were watching that movie where the kid flies around on a broom."

"What right did you have—"

"I wanted to talk to you, and you wouldn't come outside," he hissed as though he were the one who'd been treated unfairly.

"So you just invited yourself in?"

"Look, Serena, I know I reacted badly this afternoon—"

"Ya *think?*"

She turned her back on him. The stairs were off from the kitchen, not visible from the living room. He could have gotten in just as he'd said. But regardless of how he'd gotten in, he'd had no right to intrude, and certainly no right to come into her bedroom. She was seething. "You nearly gave me a heart attack."

"Then we're even, because you nearly gave me one this afternoon."

She spun around. "No, we're not even. This isn't a contest of who can outdo whom." She pointed to the door. "Get out. Get the hell out, before I call for my father."

He leaned against the closed door. "If you were going to do that, you would have already done it. Besides, I don't think you're quite ready for him to know why I'm here. He doesn't know yet, does he?"

"I was under the mistaken impression that the baby's father should be the first to know. That he might give a damn."

He took a step toward her. "I do give a damn."

"You have a strange way of showing it." She skirted around her bed, putting more distance between them. She did not want him near, did not want him touching her, did not want him tempering her anger.

"If I'd asked you to marry me, what would you have said?"

"No."

He held up both hands as though he'd made some profound point. "Exactly. So I figured if you weren't there looking for marriage, you were there to get money for an abortion."

She shook her head in frustration. "You're an amazing idiot."

"Yeah, I am."

He grinned, and she wished he hadn't agreed with her so quickly because it made him seem vulnerable.

"So why won't you marry me?" he asked. "I'm fairly good-looking."

She stared openmouthed. Of all the conceited—

Holding her gaze, he took a step toward her. "I've got a nice bit of property."

Another step. "A good paying job."

"I thought you were unemployed."

"No, I said I was between jobs and you jumped to the conclusion that I wasn't working."

"And you didn't think to correct me?"

"It's complicated."

"I don't see how it could possibly be."

He took another step. "I'm good in bed."

With his hand, he cradled her face. "Maybe you've forgotten that last one since I haven't given you any reminders lately."

"None of the reasons you've offered are reasons to get married."

"Maybe not, but they'd make the marriage more tolerable."

"Tolerable? Marriage isn't supposed to be tolerable. It's supposed to be joyous. Something you anticipate. Something you're glad that you're part of."

"Look, you want to get married or not?"

"Not."

"Why not?"

"I've spent a total of four evenings with you. You don't marry someone you've only spent four evenings with."

"A buddy of mine married a woman he spent only

three evenings with. Of course, she was a stripper he met in Vegas."

She arched a brow. "Comparing me to a stripper isn't the way you want to go here." Then she blinked. "You have a buddy? You see, I assumed you had no friends whatsoever. I know almost nothing about you except that you work for some sort of security company—that apparently pays well, even though you didn't correct my earlier assumption that you were unemployed. It's as if you play all these games. And you leave for long periods of time." She hated to admit it, but she couldn't see any reason to deny it. "I went by your house three times in the last month."

"I was out of town investigating some security concerns."

"So you travel a lot with your job."

"Yeah. As a matter of fact, I don't really live here. The house is just a place I come to when I need some time away."

"A vacation home?"

"I guess you could call it that."

"Where do you live?"

"I have a place in Virginia, but I don't stay there much either."

"I don't suppose you could string all these facts together so they make sense?"

"Probably not." He took a step toward her. "But

here's the thing. If you're having my kid, we're getting married."

"I'm not having a *kid*. I'm having a child. And no, we are not getting married."

"I want it on record that it's my kid."

"I can do that without us getting married."

Or at least she thought she could. She hadn't really checked into all the ramifications of having a child and not being married.

He began pacing. "You don't understand. There are things that might be denied this kid if we're not married. Things that might be denied you. It'll be more difficult to provide for you if we're not married."

"I'm not going to marry you."

"Look, you don't have to live with me. You don't even have to take my name. But everything will be a lot simpler if we're married."

"Marriage isn't something that I go into lightly, or as a temporary fix to an unexpected situation."

"What would it take for you to marry me?"

"I'd have to get to know you better."

"Better? You've been in bed with me twice without any clothes on. How much better can you get to know me?"

Oh, she wished she hadn't moved beyond his reach because it had put him beyond hers and right now, she wanted to flatten the palm of her hand against the side of his face with enough force that they'd hear the crack in Hopeful.

"I'm not talking physically. I'm talking in here." She tapped her chest. "Your heart, your soul. Yes, you're attractive. Yes, there is definitely an attraction between us. Until today, I thought you were a decent guy. But from the moment I stepped out of my van this afternoon, you've been a jerk. I'm not marrying a jerk."

"But you're carrying the jerk's *kid*. And yeah, I know only goats have kids, but that's a hang-up that you're going to have to get over because in my world, kids are kids."

"You're bossy. Domineering. Why would I want to marry *that?*"

"That?" He stepped back as though she had hit him. "You see me as a *that?*"

The damn tears started up again, because he sounded truly hurt.

"Hunter, I can't marry a man with whom I have no relationship. You go out of town for a month, and you don't even let me know. You don't call me when you get back. Even though the last words you said to me before today were 'I'll call you.' "

"And you said that you didn't think it'd be a good idea. Besides I'd been home only thirty minutes before you drove up."

"So you say."

"I don't lie, Serena."

She felt a deep sadness. "I don't know you well enough to even know that much about you. Hunter, our getting married could prove to be a disaster."

"Or the best thing that's ever happened to either of us."

Chapter 15

She plopped down onto the bed as though he'd pulled the rug out from beneath her feet. He was feeling a little as though he'd pulled it out from beneath his.

Hunter wasn't sure where that sentiment had come from, but he knew without a doubt that it would probably prove true for him. He could only hope the same could be said for her.

He welcomed the challenge, because he had a feeling she'd be worth it. And the one thing he'd never shied away from was a challenge. The more difficult it seemed, the more he welcomed it. Of course, always before, failure could lead to his death or worse.

Failure here would lead to hurting her, her son, their child. He'd never felt so much was at risk. But he stood to gain so much.

He knelt down on one knee, because he didn't want to be towering over her, didn't want to be in a position of authority. He took her hand, surprised to discover that she was trembling.

"Take a minute to stop being angry with me because of what I said this afternoon," he said quietly. "And listen with an open heart to what I have to say."

Her gaze focused on his, she nodded.

He swallowed hard. He'd never expected to tell anyone what he was about to tell her, and he wasn't quite certain how far he could go, how much he could say. He had to convince her that he was decent, that he was worth the risk. And he didn't have a lot of time to do it.

"The security company you think I work for?"

She nodded again.

"It deals with national security."

"National security," she repeated, shaking her head.

He tightened his fingers around hers. "Serena, I work for the CIA."

She blinked, furrowed her brow, opened her mouth, and closed it. "CIA?"

He nodded. "SOG. Special Operations Group. I'm involved with covert activities, and that, babe, is all I can tell you. All I'll ever be able to tell you. When I go out of town, I can't tell you where I'm going, what I'll be doing, or how long I'll be gone."

"Don't take this wrong, Hunter, but it sounds like BS."

"I know. That's the reason I didn't mention it before or go into any details. Mostly because I can't say much about it, but also because I know it sounds like a piece of fiction."

"You work for the CIA?" she asked, as though needing to confirm in her mind what he'd just told her.

He reached into his back hip pocket and withdrew what looked like a wallet. He opened it. "I work for the CIA."

With trembling fingers she took the wallet and stared at the CIA seal. It certainly looked real. She lifted her gaze to his. "Is what you do dangerous?"

"Yes, but I have a relatively good life insurance policy—"

"I don't care about any damned life insurance. I care about you—"

"But not enough to marry me."

She lowered her gaze to their joined hands. "This is too much, too fast. Everything is so overwhelming."

He cupped her face and tilted it slightly until he could hold her gaze. "There has never been a woman in my life who I've thought about once she left my bed. Except for you. I don't know why I can't get you out of my system. Those probably aren't the sweetest words you've ever heard, but they're honest words. I'll always give you honest words, Serena.

"Marry me, for the sake of this child, if nothing else. And if at any moment, you decide something better is waiting for you up the road, all you have to do is tell me that—and I'll sign the divorce papers without an argument. I'll provide whatever child support you want, and I'll show no hard feelings."

She smiled slightly. "I don't think I've ever heard you string so many words together at one time."

"Because I want this more than I've ever wanted anything in my life. I can't explain it. I never thought I'd get married, never thought I'd have kids. I know we've gone about it ass-backwards, but I'll do whatever it takes to make it work."

To have a family. He liked her, liked the way he felt when he was with her. Hadn't particularly liked the way he'd missed her while he was gone.

"I'm scared, Hunter," she rasped. "Afraid of making a wrong decision, getting married for the wrong reasons. Give me a couple of days to think about it."

"All right. Think about this while you're at it."

He eased up a little and planted his mouth on hers, welcoming her back into his life the way he'd been considering when he'd first caught sight of her that afternoon when she'd driven up—before she'd blindsided him with her surprising news. Before he'd responded like an idiot.

She tasted as good as he remembered, her mouth was as inviting as he'd hoped it would be. She sighed, and he eased her down onto the bed, his body half over hers, his knee between her thighs. Her hands were in his hair, his were in hers.

Right here, he thought, was a damned good reason to get married. All it took was a little touch and they were both kindling ready to start a bonfire. The kiss was hot and hungry, as though they were both starving. He liked that. He liked it a lot.

He even considered moving beyond the kiss, taking her here and now, on this bed that so strongly carried her scent, in this room that he'd explored while he'd waited for her to arrive. The last thing he'd decided that a small-town girl from central Texas would want was to bring a child into this world when she wasn't married to its father. Everywhere he'd looked, he'd seen evidence of her old-fashioned values.

She might talk big about having all these reasons for not marrying him, but he had a feeling that she was as scared as he was, that when it came down to it, she'd put this child first. And that was all that mattered to him.

Because when it came down to it, he'd put the mother of his child first.

Serena welcomed the heat of his kiss, the sturdiness of his body over hers, the strength in his hands holding her head in place. She didn't know if he would be the best thing that had ever happened to her, but she was beginning to think that he might be the best thing that had happened in a good long while.

Lying here beneath him, she almost thought he

had the power to convince her to seek out a Justice of the Peace this very evening.

He rose up, his eyes heated, his breathing heavy. "Think on that," he repeated.

The box springs squeaked and jiggled as he pushed himself off her and the bed. She could do little more than nod, her nerve endings having risen to the surface and become electrified. She was tempted to crawl under the covers and invite him to join her—if she were in her own house, she might have done just that.

With things still to be said, to be discussed, Hunter spun on his heel, crossed the room, jerked open the door, and stepped into the hallway. She caught a flash of her father walking by.

"What the hell?" her father asked, and she wondered if Hunter had heard him approaching and had deliberately chosen that moment to make his exit.

"Hi, Larry," Hunter said, as though he'd just dropped by for lemonade. "See you tomorrow."

Serena scrambled off the bed, just as her father poked his head into her room, his brow furrowed so deeply that she figured he could have planted seeds in it.

"What was that all about?" her father asked. "What was he doing in here? How in the hell did he get in here?"

"He said the kitchen door was unlocked."

Her father gazed into the hallway before looking back at her. "So he just came inside without an invite?"

She nodded. "I have a feeling he does that a lot— as part of his profession." A profession she really didn't want to think about.

"Why didn't you holler for me?"

"He just wanted to talk."

Her father's gaze darted over to the bed, the quilt that wasn't as rumpled as she found herself wishing it might be. "So did you two kiss and make up?"

"I'm not sure what we've done, Dad."

He stepped farther into her room. "Rena, what's going on?"

The damned tears sprung to her eyes. "Oh, Dad, I'm pregnant."

He spread his arms wide, and she rushed into the comforting strength of his embrace. He folded his arms around her, and she realized that she'd been hoping these actions were the ones Hunter would have exhibited when she'd first told him the news.

But he wasn't her father. He was Hunter Fletcher, and she was going to have to accept that if she was going to even consider accepting the proposal he'd made earlier.

"Now, then, girl, it isn't as bad as all that," her father murmured. "I've been hoping for another grandchild."

Her tears flowed in earnest then. She was fairly certain he hadn't been hoping for one under these circumstances.

"We'll work something out," he said.

Swiping the tears from her eyes, she leaned back. "No, Dad, this is my problem. Mine and Hunter's. We'll work it out. I just need you to be available when I need a hug."

"What's his idea of working it out?"

"He asked me to marry him."

"And you said?"

"That I'd think about it. Don't say anything to Riker yet."

"Of course not. I won't say anything to anybody. That's your news to share."

She stepped out of his embrace, and with a big sigh, sat on the edge of her bed. She'd come home to help him deal with the loss of her mother and here she was, the one needing him.

"I really miss Mom right now," she said.

"She'd tell you to trust your heart."

"I know." And as much as Serena trusted her heart, she wondered if she could trust Hunter Fletcher.

She'd expected him to make himself scarce. Instead he was knocking on the door at nine o'clock the next morning.

Shaved, his hair giving the appearance that it had actually been styled—even though the front locks looked as though they were threatening to fall back over his brow—a button-down shirt, Dockers, polished shoes. The breeze brought the tangy scent of men's cologne through the narrow opening of the door. She'd never seen him this dressed up, and looking past him, she thought that even his jeep appeared to have been washed and waxed.

"Thought we'd go look for rings," he said.

She blinked at him, while she ran last night's scenario through her mind. She hadn't accepted any of his proposals. She'd only promised to consider them. "That's a little premature, don't you think?"

He shrugged. "I can always return them if we don't use them, but since rings need to be sized, I figured we could get a head start on the process."

She looked down at the rings that still adorned her left hand. A promise ring that had never been replaced by an engagement ring because a hasty wedding had been needed. And now here she was again with time nipping at her heels.

"Look," he said. "I figure we drive into Austin, hit a mall, look in some jewelry stores, catch some lunch, hit a movie, have some dinner . . . you said you don't know me. How are you going to get to know me if you don't spend more time with me?"

"Shopping for a ring?"

"It's something we'll need to do if you say yes, so we're killing two birds with one stone. Finding a ring, getting to know me."

She laughed at the absurdity of it. "You make it sound so absolutely unenticing. An obligation you obviously would prefer not to do. Come on in while I get ready."

She opened the door wider and when he stepped inside said, "Dad and Riker are in the kitchen finishing up their breakfast if you want some coffee."

"Nah, I'll just wait here."

"I told Dad about the baby," she said quietly.

"Then I'll definitely just stay here. The man has guns, after all."

Smiling brightly, suddenly so glad that he was here, she went into the kitchen to let her dad know that she was going out for the day. Then she hurried up the stairs to her room to get ready to go out.

Getting ready didn't entail changing clothes so much as it did removing her rings. She stood at the mirrored dresser where the jewelry box from her youth rested in the center. She opened it and the ballerina—tilting to one side, the spring that supported her having lost some of its spring—turned slowly as music tinkled. Her senior ring and Steve's senior ring resided within this box. Steve's wedding band was in her jewelry box in Hopeful. And eventually she would move the rings she now wore on her finger to that box as well.

But for now, she needed to put them in a place of safekeeping. She didn't want to remove them in a jewelry store as she placed another wedding band on her finger to test its size. She'd known this moment would come someday—the removing of her wedding ring. She'd known it would be hard.

But she hadn't expected it to feel . . . right. As though the time had arrived to finally say good-bye. With great care, tears stinging her eyes, she eased the rings off her finger. Then she pressed them to her lips and whispered, "Thank you, Steve. The years were too few, but they were the best."

She placed the rings on the worn velvet of the box and closed the lid. "Good-bye, my love."

With a deep breath, she headed for the stairs at the bottom of which another man waited for her.

Chapter 16

As Hunter walked through the mall holding Serena's hand, he couldn't stop himself from constantly rubbing her bare finger. She'd removed her rings, which to him signaled two things: the serious possibility that she was willing to put another man's ring on her finger and the real probability that she was putting the mourning of her husband aside.

He needed both to be true in order to go into this relationship the way he intended, with a total commitment. Of course, it occurred to him that if he kept rubbing her finger the way that he was that he was going to remove her skin and she wouldn't be able to try on any rings.

She was a slow walker, looking in windows, stepping closer to look something over. Her eyes would light up when her gaze fell on something that appealed to her. He could actually see her mentally shaking her head, telling herself no, urging her feet to move when she saw something that she really liked that, for some reason, she didn't want to purchase.

"We can go in and look around," he told her at one point when she'd stopped at a gewgaw store. A junk store really—judging by all the different things in the window that seemed to have no rhyme or reason or pattern to their display.

She shook her head. "I just like to window shop. I would like to browse through a bookstore if we have time."

"We have all day."

She seemed pleased by his answer and it pleased him to think that he might have made her happy.

They finally reached a jewelry store. Her palm grew damp against his, or maybe it was his growing damp against hers. They looked at each other, and he thought they probably resembled two kids who'd gotten into trouble doing something they shouldn't have.

Come to think of it, the truth wasn't that far off.

Looking into her brown eyes, he thought about that first night when she'd had too much to drink. Even then, though, there had been trust in those eyes. He'd been determined not to let her down that night. To give her stars and comets and supernovas. He thought he'd managed to give those to her. In addition, somewhere along the way he'd given her a child.

That he hadn't counted on.

But it was a notion he was growing comfortable

with, an idea that was beginning to sound better by the minute. He hadn't wanted to disappoint her that night when she was little more than a stranger. She was much more than that now, and he definitely had no plans to disappoint her.

He took a deep breath, recognizing that they might be taking the first step toward the last step. "Should we walk in together?"

"We're just going to look, right?"

Suddenly she looked frightened, unsure. Hopeful, anticipatory.

Just as she had that first night.

Holding her gaze, he lifted her hand to his lips, pressed a kiss into the center of her palm. And took her into the store.

Serena had planned to go along, to play the game, to pretend that he might actually place a ring on her finger . . . and then he'd given her the look that he'd given her that first night.

Trust me.

When he'd kissed her palm, she'd thought she might turn to mush right there in the middle of the mall and had totally surrendered.

He did, however, have the most atrocious taste in jewelry. She kept directing him toward the plain gold bands, he kept asking the sales clerk to bring out the biggest, gaudiest rings she'd ever laid eyes on. Her

gaze did keep straying to one ring with a marquise diamond in its center and three diamonds on two sides
of the wedding band that would eventually enclose
the diamond engagement ring. She thought it was
elegant.

But it wasn't something she was going to say that
she wanted. She didn't want him spending a lot of
money on something that might be returned.

It was different when a person was shopping for
rings with someone whom she loved. But when you
were shopping on the off-chance that he could convince you to marry him . . . the excitement was
lacking.

A diamond meant forever. She and Hunter hadn't
spoken about forever. They'd simply barked about
now. About what they were going to do for the short
term—if anything. Get to know each other. It was
insane. She was insane. Insane to even be here in this
jewelry store entertaining the notion that she might
be getting married again.

It was an insult to couples everywhere who started
out hoping for forever—even though it didn't always
work.

They were here looking at rings because of a
maybe, a temporary, a let's see how it goes.

"That one looks really nice on you," said the clerk,
whose name tag read "Gerald."

She tugged it off. "It's cheap."

Hunter released a sigh that left no doubt in her mind that he was growing impatient with the game. Fine. If he didn't have the patience for this, then how would he have the patience for house-hunting or PTA meetings or nights when she was too tired for sex.

"Okay," Hunter said. "I don't call four thousand cheap, but if you do"—he nodded toward Gerald— "what have you got that costs a little more?"

She shook her head. "I'm not talking about its expense. I'm referring to the way it looks. It's not me, Hunter."

"All right then, which one is you?"

"You tell me."

He stared at her as though she'd just rattled off a complicated math equation that even a genius would need a calculator to solve.

She leaned toward Gerald. "Could you give us a minute?"

"Certainly. You're shopping for something that's going to last you a lifetime. I'm not going to rush you."

He closed the glass case, locked it up, and took the key with him as he hastened to the other end of the counter.

"This is pointless, Hunter. We don't know each other. You don't know my taste in things. I don't know yours."

"That's what today is about. Getting to know each other."

He sounded like a young boy who'd just been told that the kid with the baseball was going home and taking the ball with him.

"It takes more than a day—"

"I know that. It takes a whole slew of days strung together. I'm not being naïve here. We have to start somewhere, so we start with the ring." Turning, he signaled for Gerald.

Gerald hurried over. "Yes, sir."

Hunter tapped on the glass. "That one right there in the corner, that's the one she wants."

"Excellent choice. Very sophisticated." He unlocked the glass case and removed the ring.

Serena stared as he set the ring she had indeed taken an interest in on the glass countertop.

"I believe we're in luck, because I think it's your size," Gerald said as he took the ring off the velvet finger that had been used to display it. "Yes, indeedy, it's a five. Would you like to try it on?"

She looked at Hunter, looked at the ring, looked at Gerald. Hunter took the ring from Gerald, took her hand, and slid the ring into place. A perfect fit.

And it did look as elegant as she'd known it would. It was the kind of ring that she'd always felt guilty for wanting. A ring Steve never could have afforded. A ring she never would have asked for.

"It's too much," she whispered.

"We'll take it," Hunter said.

She snapped her attention to Hunter. "You can't purchase it."

"Sure I can."

"What if—"

"We'll worry about the what-ifs later. It's the one you want and it fits. We'll take it."

"Excellent decision," Gerald said, his smile beaming as brightly as any jewel in the case. "And, may I assume that you'll want a ring for the groom?"

"We will," Hunter said, and Serena knew what was coming before he uttered the fateful words with a challenge evident in his eyes. "Now, you tell me which one I want."

It wasn't the one he would have chosen had he been the one doing the choosing. But he figured admitting that might get Serena to thinking that she didn't know him well enough to marry him, and he wasn't willing to risk that.

The ring she'd selected was smooth. Simple. He'd liked one that had some etching in it. He'd just thought it looked a little more masculine, but in the end, to him, a ring was a ring. The only piece of jewelry he'd ever worn was a watch, and he didn't consider it jewelry. In his business it was a tool. So he'd never really worn jewelry.

Of course, at the moment, Serena wasn't either. The rings he'd purchased were to be used maybe, just in case, if they decided to get married. Correction. If she decided to marry him, because he'd already decided that he wanted to marry her.

She sat across from him now at a white cloth-covered table beside a large window that looked out over the lake. The sun would be setting soon, the scene would be spectacular. He'd considered taking her to his place, allowing her to watch the sunset from there, but he figured today that they needed lots of neutral territory. Places where she wouldn't feel threatened or pressured.

The waiter had lit the candle in the center of the table before he'd taken their order. Hunter had ordered a Riesling wine. He never had been a wine drinker but he thought it would lend an air of elegance to the evening that he thought was probably needed when a man was going to make a formal proposal of marriage. Serena was barely sipping it.

"I don't drink when I'm pregnant," she'd said in a low voice, a blush on her cheeks. "But a few sips probably won't hurt."

He didn't want her drunk, but he did want her a little more relaxed, a little more receptive.

"What did your father say when you told him about your condition?" he asked.

She turned her attention away from the sunset. "He offered to get out his guns."

"I appreciate that you dissuaded him from taking that course of action."

"It's the twenty-first century. I don't think people do shotgun weddings—"

Her cell phone ringing had her digging into her purse to retrieve it. He'd planned for a nice romantic evening—

"Hi, Jack."

Great. Hunter signaled the waiter to come over and ordered himself bourbon on the rocks. He was trying not to listen, but based on her beaming smile and her "That's wonderful! When? I'm so happy for you," along with all the other gushing, he assumed the news was good.

His drink had been delivered and he'd downed it by the time she finally closed up the cell phone and slipped it back into her purse.

"That was Jack," she said.

"So I gathered. Good news."

"Kelley is pregnant. Their baby is due about six weeks before mine. How ironic. Riker was born six weeks before Jason."

He didn't miss the fact that she'd referred to this kid she was carrying as hers. He felt a possessiveness kick into him that he wasn't totally prepared to deal with.

"Ours," he said.

"What?"

"Their baby is due six months before *ours.*"

"That's what I said."

"No, you said 'mine.' "

She shook her head. "I don't think so. I don't think of this baby as only mine."

"You don't think of it as ours either. You said, and I quote, 'Their baby is due about six weeks before *mine.*' Meaning *yours* when you should have said *ours,* meaning *ours.*"

She stared at him. "What are you talking about?"

"Hell, if I know." He was babbling like an idiot, doing some sort of comedic routine.

"Do you always argue over inconsequential things?" she asked.

"This isn't arguing."

"What do you call it?"

"Discussing, trying to make a point."

"The point being?"

"It's our baby."

He looked out the window and glared at the setting sun because he didn't want to glare at her. You didn't ask a woman to marry you with anger ringing in your voice or fury burning in your eyes.

"You see, this is the very reason why we can't get married."

He snapped his head around, not having any luck at not glaring. "What is?"

"I don't know you well enough to know you're not angry. To me, you look angry."

"I'm not angry. I'll admit I'm a little ticked off." He released a deep, calming breath. "I brought you here for a reason."

He reached inside his jacket, took out seventeen toothpicks he'd brought from home, and set them before her.

"What are these?" she asked.

"Remember that second night when you started playing twenty questions?"

She looked at him suspiciously. "Yeah."

"Well, you have seventeen questions left. I figure you giving me a toothpick when you ask a question would make it easier to keep track of how many questions you have remaining."

She picked one up, turned it one way, then another, examining it. "Why is there a black mark on the end?"

"If you don't ask all your questions tonight, you can hold onto them until later. And I don't have to suspect you of slipping in any unauthorized toothpicks."

She smiled as though he were some sort of genius. "They're nonexpiring, then?"

"That's right. Seventeen personal questions. That's all you get. Once you've asked them, that's it."

She appeared to be incredibly pleased, setting the

toothpicks into a perfect line, giving them more attention than she had the ring she'd selected this afternoon. Women. He didn't know if he'd ever figure them out. The way she was acting, you'd think he'd coated the little sticks in gold.

She nudged one of the toothpicks across the table toward him. "Why are you called Hunter?"

"My mother's maiden name."

He picked up the toothpick, broke it in half, and dropped it into his empty bourbon glass. She looked crestfallen.

"What's wrong?" he asked.

"I thought there'd be more to it than that."

"Like what?"

"I don't know. That you were a skilled hunter or when you were a boy you were always out in the woods." She shrugged. "I guess I was expecting a story, something profound, some little hint to your childhood."

"Nope. Mother's maiden name. That's it."

"What's your middle name?"

He held out a hand.

She shook her head. "Nope. It's not worth a toothpick."

"Then you don't get an answer."

"You know, I've asked you questions since that night and you weren't counting them."

"They weren't personal questions."

"So you'll answer questions without a toothpick if you don't think they're personal?"

"Right."

She picked up a toothpick and began tapping it against her chin. He could see the wheels whirring inside that pretty little head of hers. How could she get the most out of him?

"Tell me about your childhood."

"That's not a question."

She glowered at him. "I have a feeling that you're manipulating all the little rules to this game so you only answer what you want to answer."

"The game is twenty *questions,*" he pointed out.

She rolled her eyes, then moved the toothpicks to the side as the waiter set salads in front of them. She picked up a fork and began tossing the lettuce around as though she didn't think the chef had done an adequate job. Hunter speared a generous portion, ate it, went back for more.

A toothpick landed on top of a tomato. He peered up at her, wondering what question she'd come up with that might help her figure him out. Something in her eyes alerted him to the fact that he wasn't going to like the question. He wasn't going to like it one bit.

"Do you love me?" she asked.

Chapter 17

Serena knew the answer to that question. What she was interested in discovering was how he answered it. He couldn't claim it wasn't a question. He couldn't claim that it wasn't personal. It was about as personal as she could get.

It looked as though he was having a difficult time swallowing the food he'd been chewing. But eventually he managed. He set his fork down, pressed his napkin to his mouth, ran his tongue over his teeth, took a sip—which more closely resembled a gulp—of wine, and leaned back.

"You sure you want the answer to that question?"

"I wouldn't have asked if I didn't."

He glanced around as though he was expecting the cavalry to appear and save him. "You sure you want the answer now? Here? This moment?"

"Yes, I'm sure."

He picked up the toothpick, held it between the thumb and finger of one hand while stroking it with the other as though he expected a genie to pop up out of the thing with the answer.

"I like you," he finally said. "I like you a lot. I like your sense of humor. I like the relationship you have with your son and the one you have with your father. I like the protective nature of your character and the way you try to make everyone feel at home, and you hang yellow curtains in your windows.

"Do I love you?" He shook his head. "At this moment, no. But you already knew that answer. What you should have asked was *could* I *come* to love you? And the answer there is yeah, I definitely think I could."

Tears stung her eyes as she watched him place the toothpick back inside his jacket. She didn't know why that small gesture meant almost as much as his answer. And his answer had meant oh, so much. It was what she needed to hear, what she needed to know, what she'd been afraid to ask.

With a trembling hand, she pushed another toothpick across the table. "Could you come to love Riker?"

"Yeah, I could." He pushed the toothpick back toward her. "That one was a freebie. I know if I marry you, Serena, that I'm marrying your family."

"And what about your family? You once told me that you went into foster care when you were eight. You said your parents were long gone, which could mean anything. Do you ever see them, hear from them?"

"No. They're both dead."

He snatched up a toothpick. She stared at him dumbfounded.

"I didn't ask a question."

"Sure you did."

"It wasn't personal."

"Sure it was."

She gathered up her toothpicks and moved them to her lap, beyond his reach. "You don't play fair."

"Maybe not, but I play honest. I know the odds are that our marriage won't work. But I've always been a risk-taker. And I think it's worth the risk to at least try."

"Not when the children might get hurt."

"And how do you think they're going to get hurt?"

"They'll come to love you, and you'll go away. You can't guarantee that you'll always come home—not with this job that you've hinted you have."

"No, I can't guarantee it."

"Would you consider taking some other sort of job?"

"Like what?"

She lifted a shoulder. "I don't know. Law enforcement?"

"You think that's safer than what I do now?"

"I can't judge since I don't really know exactly

what you do now, but at least with law enforcement you wouldn't be leaving for long periods of time. You'd be home."

Home. He wished she hadn't used that word. It appealed to him. But he hadn't really considered giving up what he did for a living. The pay was good, it contained a measure of excitement, and made him feel as though he was making a difference.

"I disliked Steve being in the military. I know some wives adjust. I never could. I didn't like the loneliness or the worry or having to make decisions on my own that affected all of us. I know that makes me selfish—"

"No, I don't imagine any of that was easy. I just hadn't given any thought to resigning. I'll consider it. That's all I can promise."

She nodded as though she could accept that. "Where would we live?"

"I've got no roots. We can live wherever you want."

"I'd want to live in Hopeful."

"Then that's where we'd live."

"How did you know I had yellow curtains hanging in my windows?" she asked, without skipping a beat, as though she thought she could throw him off with a question unrelated to the others.

Grinning, he settled back in the chair. "Figuring people out is what I do. I've gotten to be very good at it."

"So you think you know me?"

Her voice indicated that she was insulted that he'd consider her so easy to figure out.

"I think I have a fairly good idea of what living with you would be like."

"I might surprise you."

He broadened his grin. "I'm not saying what I did simply because I've figured out that you're boring or not full of surprises. Yesterday being a prime example of how you can successfully throw me a curve." He crossed his arms on the table. "But here's what I suspect and you correct me when I'm wrong.

"You cook most of your meals. Not because you can't afford to go out but because you like the feeling that you're providing for your family.

"When Riker plays ball next summer, you'll be the team mom. The one who makes sure the kids have plenty to drink during practice and games. You'll advocate for every kid to be given a trophy even if the team comes in at last place."

"There's nothing wrong with that."

"Of course not. Why make them think that there's a reward in being the best? If you're the worst you get the same reward."

"I see no reason to damage their self-esteem when they're young," she offered, obviously getting a little irritated with him.

Not the goal he was hoping to achieve.

"We can tackle that attitude later. Right now, you're confirming that I'm guessing correctly. You go to every PTA meeting, every school party. You'd never think to purchase your son's birthday cake from the bakery. You wear sexy underwear, but I'm guessing boring nightclothes—"

"Ha! I sleep in the nude."

He laughed as she settled back in the chair with an air of satisfaction—as though she'd just beat him at his own game.

"You don't know me nearly as well you think," she said a little petulantly, as though she'd just realized what she'd revealed, perhaps a little too loudly.

"But I think getting to you know would definitely be fun. If we were to get married, what sort of wedding would you want?"

She fingered the stem of her wineglass like it was a crystal ball that could reveal the answer. "Small," she finally said. "Late afternoon, early evening. At my family's beach house because I have so many fond memories of time spent there. I'd invite only a few friends." She shifted in the chair. "Mostly because I've lost touch with so many people. What sort of wedding would you want?"

"Whatever kind you want."

"This would be a first for you."

"Yep."

"It should be special."

"It would be if you were the one I was marrying."

Blushing, she shook her head. He wasn't sure if she was signaling a negative response to his suggestion or flustered because he thought marrying her would be something special.

He leaned forward. "Look, Serena, I'm not much for fancy words or reciting poetry. But I think there could be something good between us. And I'd work damned hard to make it happen."

The arrival of their steaks had interrupted the discussion of marriage and its possibilities. Taking her to a restaurant had been a tactical error. His house would have served them better. There would have been no interruptions, no distractions.

Of course, there wouldn't have been any food either because he wasn't much of a gourmet. Ham and eggs was about as fancy as he got. So the time at the restaurant would ensure that his stomach didn't growl for the remainder of the evening.

And when he'd asked, she'd consented to go home with him in order to continue the discussion—and, he hoped, get to know him better. He'd stopped on the way home and picked up another bottle of Riesling and a couple of cheap wineglasses. He didn't figure a little more wine would harm her or the baby.

The baby.

Every time that thought went through him, a chill

followed it, but each one was less cold than the one that had come before.

She sat on the couch in front of the floor-to-ceiling window that looked out on the lake. He considered turning down the thermostat enough so he could build a fire, but decided against that desperate action.

He was searching for a romantic mood. He'd actually been surprised that she'd decided to come home with him, but then she was a series of surprises. And she slept in the nude. He still couldn't quite get over that, although the notion had him anticipating all the long nights ahead when she'd be up against his naked body.

He sat beside her and offered her the expensive wine in the cheap glass. She took a sip and set the glass aside. He gulped his, wishing he was drinking something stronger.

He stretched his arm along the back of the couch and began to toy with her curls. They were so soft, as soft as she was. He was encouraged by the fact that she didn't pull away, didn't shrink at his touch.

"It's a nice view," she said quietly. "Won't you miss it . . . if you were to move to Hopeful?"

"Could always come for a visit, a long weekend."

"It's peaceful here."

"Yeah."

She slid her gaze over to him. "Would you want a boy or a girl?"

Alarm bells went off in his head. This was a trick question.

He wrapped her curls around one of his fingers. "Doesn't matter."

She smiled softly. Bull's-eye! Right answer.

"What would you want Riker to call you?"

"Whatever he wants. Whatever you want him to."

"Daddy?"

A hard kick to the gut.

He shifted around so he was sitting at a right angle to her. "Look, Serena, I'm not hard to get along with. I'll handle a threat with overpowering force, but I don't see you threatening me. I'm skilled at adapting to a situation, blending in. My parents didn't offer the best example of what family life should be. So when it comes to what you think is best for you or the kids, I'll follow your lead."

The kids. His kids. Her kids. Their kids. Two months ago, he'd never expected to carry on a conversation that revolved around the possibilities of having children, a family. The thought was still foreign, unbelievable. But he'd hang on like a tenacious rottweiler if that's what it took to make her realize that he only had her best interests in mind. If he died tomorrow, he wanted her provided for.

He leaned close, brushed his lips against her ear, and whispered, "Marry me, Serena."

Serena heard the words, laced with longing. His

warm breath skimmed along her neck as he tucked his mouth beneath her ear, nibbling, stroking with his tongue. Her eyes slid closed and she thought it wasn't fair . . .

It wasn't fair to deny herself the pleasure of his touch.

Yes, they had things to work out, specifics to discuss . . . and yet, she sensed his willingness to work with her. He seemed to like Riker and she was certain that Riker liked him. They got along well, she and Hunter got along well. They hadn't yet come to love each other but she didn't think the moment was far away.

His mouth skimmed along her throat, a leisurely journey to her other ear.

"Marry me."

His voice was like warm honey poured over biscuits. Golden, thick, delicious. They would have this every night . . . at least when he was in town. And when he wasn't . . . she'd have the memories.

"Marry me." His lips brushed against hers as he again voiced the words, wearing down her restraint, eliminating her arguments.

She told herself that she was insane to even be contemplating answering yes. She hadn't known him long, didn't know his past.

But she was fairly confident that she knew *him*, knew the man who was slipping the slim strap of her dress off her shoulder and lightly grazing his teeth over her skin. He wouldn't bite. She was fairly certain that he'd never bark at her. Growl maybe.

But then she was in the habit of doing her own growling.

The attraction was there. She enjoyed being with him. It had all seemed right when she, he, and Riker were together. They would be the family she'd longed to have again.

"Marry me," he repeated.

Her answer came not with a word, but with the slipping off of the other strap. Her heart sang with the echo of his feral growl.

And she knew he wouldn't take her upstairs. That tonight, for them, there would be no bed. That he wanted her here, now.

Which was good, because she wanted him, always wanted him.

Clothes melted away as quickly as the cotton candy she'd eaten at the ballpark. A discarded pile beside the couch, first hers, then his. There wasn't a lot of maneuverability on the couch, but it made no difference.

Their hands and mouths explored. Between the branches of the trees outside, she could catch a glimpse of the stars in the sky, and she thought she was on the verge of traveling there . . . shooting across the heavens in glorious flight.

He was so skilled at carrying her to incredible heights.

"Sweet, sweet, Serena," he whispered near her ear. "I'll make it good for you. I swear I'll make it good for you."

And in a far off corner of her mind, she knew he wasn't talking about this moment. He was talking about the future, about marriage, about their life together.

What was she afraid of?

He'd been committing to her all day—with the purchase of the rings, with marked toothpicks for twenty questions, with words and promises, and now with his body. His strong, virile body nestled between her thighs.

And his kisses. So many kisses from her shoulders to her toes. Hard kisses, enthusiastic kisses. She'd leave here tonight bearing his marks. Which seemed only fair since she was bearing his child.

His tongue was now circling her navel.

"What's the baby feel like?" he asked.

She threaded her fingers through his hair. "I can't feel the baby yet."

He lifted his head, his face limned by moonlight. "I'll do whatever it takes to be a good father. You just tell me what I have to do."

Come to love me.

But what she needed, what they would all need,

couldn't be commanded. It had to arrive of its own volition, in its own time, but she had no doubt that it would. The spark was there, waiting to be ignited into a glorious flame. And it occurred to her that the only reason she could be so certain was because she'd already come to love him.

His strength, his determination . . . the ease with which he read her. His infrequent laughter that she longed to hear more often. There was goodness in him. She'd seen it in the way he treated Riker, had been the recipient of it herself.

He would make a good father without her having to tell him anything. She'd guide him when she could, but she thought he'd be able to follow the path on his own.

He eased up, latching his mouth onto hers, kissing her thoroughly. The kiss spoke volumes. Tender and hungry at once. Asking what he'd already voiced.

Marry me.

I will, I will, I will.

She'd known what her answer would be when she'd stepped out of the house this morning. The hesitancy had only come about because it seemed as though it was expected.

But she didn't want her child to grow up without a father. Wanted Riker to have a man in his life. A good man. And Hunter Fletcher was a good man.

His mouth left hers and he was reaching down,

searching through the clothing—and it suddenly dawned on her what he was searching for.

"You don't need that," she said quietly.

His snapped his gaze to hers. "I've never *not* used one."

She lifted her hips, pleased to know that he would have something with her that he'd never had with another.

He turned away from the clothes, turned back to her. And it was as though the floodgates on his desire had been unleashed. His mouth was hotter as it returned to hers, his hands more demanding as he caressed her.

He emitted a low possessive growl as he joined his body with hers. He stilled. She could feel the tenseness in his muscles, the quivering in his arms as he held himself above her. He released a long, low sigh as though he simply wanted to appreciate the moment, his first of having absolutely nothing separating them.

Then he was rocking against her, pumping into her. Cupping his buttocks, she urged him on. Faster, faster, harder, harder.

Pleasure spiraled through her, higher, higher, higher, until she could climb no higher. They peaked at the same moment, their bodies arching, pulsing. Replete, she sprawled beneath him, his arms shaking as he fought not to place his entire weight on her.

"Was that a yes?" he asked.

Laughing, she responded, "That was a yes."

Chapter 18

Hunter had told her that he understood that marrying her meant marrying her family. So it was time to pay the piper.

As he drove her back to her father's house, he was having a difficult time believing that she'd consented to marry him. Or that he was so incredibly grateful that she had.

He could make this work. He could finally have what he'd been denied his entire life: a normal family.

"Riker will probably already be in bed," she said from her side of the jeep. "But we should probably tell him together. Will you come over tomorrow?"

"Sure."

"And you'll come inside while I tell Dad tonight?"

"Yeah."

He darted a glance over at her. "Did you want me to tell him?"

"If you like."

No, he didn't *like,* but he figured it would earn him points, and he could probably use all the points he could earn. "I'll tell him then."

She reached over and squeezed his hand. "Good. I'll break the news to Kevin."

"Kevin?"

"My brother. He'll be the more difficult of the two."

"I didn't know you had a brother."

"A fancy lawyer up in Dallas." She grinned at him. "Maybe you should have brought some toothpicks for yourself."

He was beginning to think he should have. "Do you have any other surprises waiting in the wings?"

"Not that I know of."

He turned the jeep onto the dirt lane that led to the house. The outside light was on, and he thought that was a habit he'd get into—leaving a light on for his family.

He brought the jeep to a halt, got out, went around, and opened the door for her. Once she stepped out, he kissed her—to shore up his courage and simply because he enjoyed kissing her.

She took hold of his hand and led him to the house, and he thought from this moment on, he'd always have this—her hand to hold, this house to be welcomed into. It was as comforting a thought as it was terrifying. He didn't want to let her down, didn't want to disappoint her.

He'd never had a single person that he'd cared this much for.

She opened the door and walked into the house. A lamp was on in the living room, images were flickering on the TV.

"Dad?"

Her father got out of his recliner. "Well, you're home earlier than I expected." His gaze dropped to their joined hands. "I take it things went well."

She looked over at Hunter, and he realized that was probably his cue to break the news.

"Yes, sir. Your daughter said she'd marry me."

He raised his eyebrows. "She did? Well, I'd say that calls for a little celebrating. Come on in, have a seat. I'll pour us a little comfort."

She patted Hunter's arm. "You go on. I'm going to check on Riker and then I'll call Kevin."

"I'll come with you."

She shook her head slightly and whispered, "You should probably talk with Dad for a minute."

He didn't particularly want to do that, but he figured it was part of the process. He watched her disappear up the stairs, before he walked into the living room and took a seat on the couch.

"Here you go, son," her father said, offering him a glass of Southern Comfort.

Hunter downed it in one long swallow.

Larry chuckled as he returned to his recliner, popped up the footrest, and settled back.

"Not easy asking a girl to marry you."

"No, sir, it's not."

"Harder still to face her father."

"Yes, sir."

"You seem like a decent enough fella."

"I try to be." Leaning forward, he placed his elbows on his thighs. "Mr. Barnett, I care for your daughter. I realize that the circumstances being what they are that it might not be evident that I only want what's best for her."

"If Rena hadn't gotten pregnant—"

"But she did. I'm not a big believer in speculating on the destination of roads not traveled."

Based on the way Larry settled back in his chair, Hunter thought he might have finally said something the old man could approve of.

"What the hell do you mean you're getting married?"

Serena moved farther into the kitchen so no one in the living room would hear her conversation with Kevin. She and Hunter had looked the calendar over and decided a week from Saturday would work.

"You have a college education, Kevin. Surely you can decipher the meaning of 'I'm getting married a week from Saturday—' "

"To whom?"

"His name is Hunter Fletcher—"

"Hunter? What the hell kind of name is that?"

"It's his mother's family name." Thank goodness

for the twenty questions—even though she hadn't used them all.

"Who is he?"

"What do you mean *who* is he? I told you his name."

"I mean who is he? Where does he live? Where did he come from? How did you meet him? What does he do for a living? Why is he marrying you? How long have you known him? Did you run a background check on him? Did you sign a prenup? I don't want you signing a prenup that I haven't prepared. Why the hell are you getting married next Saturday? What's the rush? This is the first I've heard of the guy. What do you know about him? Has Dad met him?"

Finally silence on his end.

"Do you honestly expect me to answer all those questions?" she asked.

"Only the important one."

"Which would be what?"

"Why are you marrying him?"

She picked up a damp cloth and began wiping a counter that didn't need to be wiped. "I don't remember hearing that question in the list you just spouted off."

"Come on, Rena. You call me out of the blue to tell me you're marrying some guy I've never heard of. I want to know why."

"I called you because I thought you'd want to know."

"Damn it, Rena, I'm not asking why you called, and you know it. I'm asking why you're marrying this guy."

She desperately wanted to say because she loved him. Wasn't that really the only reason to get married? Because you loved the person, wanted to build a life with him, wanted to hold his hand when you were both old?

She turned and there was Hunter standing in the doorway. Tall, proud. So damned sexy, so incredibly serious.

"Need me to talk to him?" he asked quietly.

And that was all it took. Those few words, earnestly offered, and although she couldn't say that she was marrying him because she loved him, didn't want to say she was marrying him because she was pregnant, she did suddenly know why she was marrying him. Probably not the best of reasons, but it was an honest reason.

"I'm marrying Hunter because I want to," she said succinctly, her gaze holding his, feeling a thrill skid through her when satisfaction hit his eyes. "Are you coming to the wedding?"

"I'll check my calendar. Hell, yes, I'm coming," he barked, not sounding at all pleased that he was. "I want some time alone with this guy before the ceremony."

She considered Hunter's broad shoulders, his muscular arms, his wide chest, his determined stance. She almost laughed. Kevin would be a toothpick standing next to a mighty oak. "No, Kevin, I really don't think you do."

And then she let her irritation with Kevin's third degree float away, and she recognized what was behind the interrogation. "I love you, Kev."

He sighed. "I love you, too, Sis. I just hope you're not making a mistake."

He hung up, denying her the satisfaction of hanging up on him. She returned the phone to the cradle and gave Hunter an impish smile. "He wants some time alone with you."

"Based on what I overheard of your end of the conversation, I'd say I need some time alone with him."

She patted his arm. "Go gentle with him."

"Only if he deserves it."

"He does. He's simply being an overprotective brother."

"Overprotectiveness seems to run in your family."

"Yeah, it does." She knew it was late, knew she should let him go home, but it had been such an overwhelming day. "Will you sit on the porch for a while before you leave?"

"Sure."

The night was warm, only slightly humid, as they sat on the bench swing. His arm seemed to automatically come around her, and she thought there was a tenderness to him that he didn't even know existed. The silence between them contained a comfortableness . . . nothing forced. No pressure to converse.

With a sigh of contentment, she settled her head within the nook of Hunter's shoulder. And decided this marriage had a chance of working.

Chapter 19

⁓

The silver Jaguar screeched to a halt inches from the front porch where Hunter stood waiting. He hadn't flinched, blinked, or tensed. He'd trusted Dan Becker with his life too many times to think that the guy couldn't judge the braking distance he needed not to hit the porch.

Dan smoothly unfolded his body as he got out of the car. Like everyone assigned to Hunter's group, he was deeply tanned with black hair, dark eyes. Diversity enthusiasts would probably have a fit if they ever caught sight of the men Hunter worked with. They all looked like clones—but then fair haired, blue eyed people tended to get too much attention in the places they frequented.

Dan grinned. "Damn, I kept telling myself the whole way down here that this was a practical joke. It is, right? You've suddenly sprouted a sense of humor, and thought you'd yank my chain? Because there's no way, man, that you're getting married."

"I'm getting married."

"Man, I can't wait to meet this lady who sunk her claws into you."

"No claws. She's definitely not your type."

Dan shook his head, his grin growing even wider, as he walked up the steps and clapped Hunter on the shoulder. "Wait until you see what I have in mind for the bachelor party."

"Since the wedding is this evening, I'm afraid you're going to be doing that solo."

Dan shrugged. "Works for me. I have a list of local gentlemen's clubs. I plan to start with the Yellow Rose. I like the dancers."

"Why don't you come in, get settled?"

He led Dan inside, went straight to the refrigerator, and pulled out two beers.

"Your timing's lousy," Dan said, all humor gone. "They'll pull you off—"

"Not this one. I've put too much into it, and I've already gotten permission to finish the job."

It was a requirement that the men in his group be single, no family affiliations. The risks were too great, and they needed men who could stay focused, and if necessary, stay out of the country for a long time.

"That surprises me, and I'm not very often surprised."

"At this point, it's not a traditional marriage. We're getting married because she's pregnant."

"Shit. You gonna be thinking about that—"

"No. But if something happens to me, I want her and the kid taken care of."

"And if nothing happens to you, then you're latched to a ball and chain. I've been there, man—"

"Three days. You were married for three whole days."

"And it's hell. I'm telling you. Marriage isn't for guys like us."

"Maybe not." But being an unwed mother wasn't for women like Serena either.

"What time does this shindig get started?" Dan asked.

"Seven. And we need to get down to the coast before then."

When Serena's grandfather had passed away, his will had stipulated that his retirement home would be left to his descendents, along with a trust fund with enough capital in it to ensure the interest would handle the upkeep and maintenance costs required to keep the waterfront property manageable. He'd written that he wanted a place where his family could always gather.

Kevin managed the property and the trust, but he rarely took time to enjoy their grandfather's legacy. Serena on the other hand, loved to spend time here. She'd spent long weekends here with her parents. She often invited Jack and his family to join her. It was simply a place that cried out for company.

The three-story house with a crow's nest sat on an inlet that jutted into the bay. Following a sand and shell trail, she would reach the beach, where the Gulf of Mexico washed over the shore. She was tempted to go there now but people would soon be arriving, and in a couple of more hours she'd be married. She couldn't believe it, as she gazed in the mirror in the main bedroom on the second level, trying to determine what was missing.

The dress was pale, pale lavender with a scooped neck and a scooped back that gathered into folds. The dress flowed without a waist into a hem of tiered ruffled layers, cut at an angle that swooped down from her knee on one side to her calf on the other. Elegant, a little sexy. Nothing traditional.

But then this evening was probably more for her than it was for Hunter. She imagined he would have been content to slip down to the Justice of the Peace's office with no one else in attendance.

But she needed the ceremony, the gathering of family. Kevin had flown into Houston Hobby from Dallas, rented a car, and arrived at the beach house with a card in hand that she was certain contained a generous check. He'd hugged her, glanced at his watch, and announced he was catching the last flight out that night—the ceremony would take place on time, right?

She'd wanted to smack him. Instead she'd come

into the room to get dressed. Jack and his family would be arriving at any time, as would a few other family members and a few very close friends. She'd hoped the groom would have arrived by now, but he'd needed to wait for the arrival of the best man. Everything seemed so unorganized, so last minute. Until the groom showed, she was going to worry.

She turned at the knock on her door.

"Come in?"

Kevin stuck his head inside. "You sure?"

She smiled. "Yeah."

He had her fair coloring, brown eyes. He slid his hands into the trouser pockets of a suit that probably cost more than her entire wardrobe.

"You were peeved at me earlier because I'm not staying," he said.

"It's your life, Kevin. I'm glad you were able to make it for the ceremony."

"Me, too. He's here. We talked."

"Hunter?" she asked, surprised. "He's here?"

"Yep. Him and the best man. Dan Becker. Pair of bookends I wouldn't want to get between."

"I know Hunter can be intimidating." And she assumed his friend was chiseled from the same block of granite.

"Tell me about it."

She stepped nearer, not accustomed to seeing her usually confident brother exhibiting any self-doubts.

"Other than that, what was your impression of Hunter?"

"That he cares a great deal for you."

His words surprised her almost as much as his guarded expression. "Why do you look like that's a bad thing?"

"It's not. A guy would be insane not to be crazy about you. He's just a little different than I expected, that's all. I think you'll be all right with him."

Well, that wasn't exactly a glowing endorsement but she didn't really need it. She trusted her own judgment on the matter, and she was certain things would be fine.

"Oh"—he reached into his jacket and brought out a small white-wrapped box with a white bow—"he wanted me to give you this."

She took the gift, pleased beyond measure that Hunter had given her a wedding present.

She removed the ribbon and the paper. Nestled inside the box was a heart-shaped pendant encrusted with diamonds. She wondered if he'd given her the necklace because he couldn't give her his real heart. Or was he offering his heart without words?

She took it out of the box and started to put it around her neck.

"Here, I'll clasp it for you," Kevin said as he came around behind her. "I want you to be happy, Rena," he said quietly.

"I want that, too, Kev."

She looked in the mirror, touched the heart-shaped pendant that looked perfect just below her throat, and she realized with astonishing clarity what was missing from the day.

A man who loved her.

"Oh, man, I should have brought a date," Dan lamented as he and Hunter stood off to the side, near the storage shed that provided part of the support for the stilted house. "Doesn't your bride know anyone under the age of fifty?"

Hunter grinned. "I think most of these people are her family. I wouldn't want you getting involved with any of them anyway."

"What was up with the brother?"

"Protective."

"He know what you do for a living?"

Hunter shook his head. "Only Serena knows. Anyone else asks—I'm in security."

"Computers," Dan said. "I'm in computers."

Which he was. The magic he could work with computers was truly amazing.

"Hunter?"

Turning, he smiled at Serena. Sweet Lord, but she looked lovely, and the necklace he'd given her was perfect. "Hey."

Reaching out, he took her hand and drew her near. "This is Dan, a good buddy of mine."

Dan winked and gave her his million-dollar smile. "You wouldn't happen to have a sister would you?"

"Afraid not," Serena said. "We're glad you could come."

"I wouldn't miss it. I had to meet the lady who reeled this guy in. He's been slipping off the hook for years."

She turned to Hunter. "You don't have to wait over here, away from everyone else."

"It's a good place to people-watch."

"Has Dad introduced you around?"

"Yep."

"If you forget who someone is, just ask," Serena said. "No one expects you to remember all the names."

"Are you kidding?" Dan asked. "He's not going to forget names. He has a memory like a steel trap. You could line everyone up and he could tick off their names without missing a beat."

"Thanks, Dan, for that commentary," Hunter said, a little irritated that Dan was jabbering. As a rule, he tended to be as quiet as Hunter was.

"Hey, I just call it like I see it," Dan said.

Serena angled her head to the side. "You're not the buddy who married the stripper are you?"

Dan continued to smile. "I can't believe he told you about that. I was drunk and she was hot. Drive-thru wedding. Best six days of my life. Knew her for three, was married to her for three."

Serena laughed lightly. "I'm hoping ours will last a little longer."

"It will. I have a good feeling about all this," Dan said.

Another minivan pulled into the yard. Riker and his dog were running toward it. Serena smiled as though she'd never been happier.

"There's Jack and his family. Come on, I want to introduce you."

Hunter watched as people clambered out of the van. A tall man with dark hair caught his attention and held it. She'd mentioned Jack, her neighbor, her best friend, several times. He'd never asked how they'd come to know each other. He'd never put two and two together.

"I'll catch up with you," Hunter told her. "I need to talk with Dan for just a minute."

"Okay." She leaned up and kissed him on the cheek. "Don't take too long. I'm anxious for Jack to meet you."

He watched as she hurried to greet the newest arrivals.

"What's wrong?" Dan asked.

"I just needed to give you the ring." He removed it from his pocket and handed it off to Dan.

"That could have waited, man. What's going on?"

"Remember that trouble I got into about six years back?"

"In Afghanistan?"

"Yeah. I think that guy might have been one of the guys sent to get me out."

"It was a classified mission. He's not going to say anything."

"Serena's husband was killed on that mission. I have a feeling he and Jack were friends."

"Shit. Serena doesn't know—"

"My connection to that mission? Like you said, it's classified. By the time I realized who her husband was, I'd convinced myself that it wouldn't hurt to keep seeing her, and there was no reason for her to know. I think that decision is about to come back and bite me."

"Not necessarily. They were told only your code name. And after ten days with your torturers, you were so badly beaten that I barely recognized you when I saw you in the hospital. He's not going to recognize you."

"I hope you're right."

Because if he wasn't, then all hell was going to break loose.

"I can't believe that you're marrying someone I haven't met," Jack said, holding Serena close against his side, his arm around her shoulders.

"Everything happened quickly, but you'll like him. He's your kind of guy."

"My kind of guy? What the hell does that mean?"

"Tough, strong. He was in the army for a while. You can probably swap war stories."

"No, I'll keep my war stories to myself, thanks all the same."

She spotted Hunter standing in the shadows of the outer stairs, isolated, suddenly alone, and she wondered where Dan had gone off to. Hunter struck her as he had so many times when she looked at him without expectation: filled with loneliness. It was as though it rolled off, only to return, like the undulating tides.

But he was a good man, she knew that, and she knew in her heart that they could make this work. She motioned him over, surprised that he seemed reluctant to join them. But eventually, his long strides began to eat up the distance separating them.

Hunter stopped a short distance in front of them. His eyes were emotionless. His face revealed nothing of what he was thinking, and she wondered briefly if he was jealous of her relationship with Jack, with the way that Jack so easily hugged her, kept her close. She stepped out of Jack's embrace and went to Hunter, welcoming his arm around her waist.

"Hunter, this is Jack Morgan."

Hunter extended his hand. "It's good to meet you. Serena has told me a lot about you."

Jack shook his hand. "She has good things to say

about you, too. She said you were in the army. We've never met, though, have we?"

"I don't think so."

"You seem familiar."

Hunter shook his head. "Can't imagine why."

"It'll come to me."

Hunter hoped not.

"Jack, put the badge away," an attractive blond woman said as she nestled up against his side.

Jack slipped his arm around her. "This is my wife, Kelley."

"You have to forgive him," Kelley said. "He has a difficult time turning off his police chief mode, and he's always been protective where Serena is concerned."

Police chief. Serena had failed to mention that.

"That's Madison, their daughter," Serena said, pointing to a young girl that Hunter put at sixteen or seventeen. "And the boy talking to Riker is Jason."

"Nice family," Hunter said.

"We think so," Kelley said. She patted her husband's arm. "Come on. We need to go say hello to Larry. It was nice to meet you."

Thinking Jack left rather reluctantly, Hunter had a feeling that the reason he looked familiar to Jack was going to gnaw at the man. Hunter knew it would gnaw at him if their situations were reversed.

"Is everything all right?" Serena asked.

"Everything is great."

"I figured you and Jack would get along."

"We'll get along just fine." As long as he never realizes where he knows me from.

Chapter 20

～

The sky was awash in orange, purple, and pink as Serena stood before the minister with Hunter beside her. It was an extremely informal gathering. Family and friends formed a half circle around the couple.

When the minister had asked who gave the bride, her father had responded, "Her son and I, her father, do."

She'd thought she was going to burst into tears at that very moment. And if Hunter hadn't taken her hand, squeezed it, and held her gaze, given her his strength, she would have wept.

But he was so strong, so sure, so confident. He wasn't trembling as she was. He had no doubts, and because he didn't, she found herself casting her doubts aside.

She didn't think he'd ever looked more handsome than he did at this moment in his tuxedo. Traditional black and white. The only bit of color he wore was the yellow boutonniere that matched her bouquet of yellow roses.

The minister spoke all the right words, and she discovered that she didn't feel that they were making a mockery of the marriage. She supposed people got married knowing much less about each other.

How did you learn everything about a person when you hadn't grown up with them?

She would probably never know all there was to know about Hunter Fletcher, but standing here beside him, she was convinced that she knew enough to be certain she'd made the right decision. Riker would have a truer father-figure than Jack. This baby would have both parents.

And she thought love for this man hovered just over the horizon, that it would arrive when she was least expecting it.

And the manner in which he continued to hold her gaze, hold her hand, led her to believe that in time he would come to love her as well. He'd promised to do whatever it took to make the marriage work. She would as well.

Those were the silent vows she was taking today. But she would remain as true to them as she would to those she spoke aloud.

Hunter's voice boomed loudly and clearly when he repeated his vows, and she heard not an ounce of doubt. She'd repeated her vows with equal conviction. They exchanged rings.

And when the minister gave Hunter permission to

kiss the bride, the kiss was more tender than any she'd ever received. It spoke of promises made, of his commitment to her, of his determination to make this marriage work.

And she knew in that single moment that everything would be all right.

Hunter had shaken more hands, received more kisses on the cheek and more slaps on the back than he thought it was humanly possible to receive in the hour since he and Serena had exchanges vows.

They'd just had their photos taken cutting into the cake. Now someone wanted to take a photo of them holding champagne glasses with their arms all twisted around each other's. He felt like an awkward fool, but based on the warm smile Serena was bestowing on him, he had a feeling that it didn't show.

He took a sip of the champagne, wishing he was free to down it and a few more. He wondered if Dan had brought anything stronger to drink.

People clapped, and he tried not to feel stupid doing all these little rituals which meant nothing to him, but obviously meant something to Serena. For her sake, he could pretend that they all mattered.

He heard a tapping on glass, turned to see Dan grinning broadly, and had a feeling that he wasn't going to like whatever was about to happen.

"Well, now," Dan said, lifting his glass slightly

once he had everyone's attention. "I think as best man that I'm supposed to make a toast."

Damn. Hunter knew what was coming, something lascivious, crude, and rude that would refer to the wedding night—and he didn't know how to stop it.

"Well, this is a day that I never thought I'd see, so Serena, darlin', although we just met, I know you're special. And in case you haven't figured it out yet, so is the guy you married. I'd trust him with my life. More than that, I'd lay down my life for him, without hesitation, and there aren't many I'd do that for. I wish you both a long life and happiness and lots of kids. Cheers!"

There was a round of cheers. Hunter hadn't expected such a heartfelt acknowledgment. He was deeply touched, because if there was any man he'd lay down his life for, it was Dan. When he looked at Serena, she had tears in her eyes.

"He works with you, doesn't he?" she asked.

"Yeah."

"He just told me a whole lot about you, Hunter, things I'd suspected, and now have confirmed." She gave him a sweet, gentle kiss. "I think we're going to be okay."

"I know we are."

Smiling at Serena, Hunter took another sip of the champagne and hoped the traditions were about over.

"Well, son, I want to officially welcome you to the family," Larry said as he extended his hand.

"Thank you, sir."

Larry winked. "Riker and I are going to go to Hopeful for the night."

"Thanks, Dad," Serena said.

Larry leaned over and kissed her cheek. "You're welcome, sweetie. I can't help but believe that your mom and Steve were looking down this evening with approval."

Hunter's gut clenched. He would have preferred to have no reminders of Steve Hamilton today, but they kept popping up.

Her father walked off. Dan came over, grinning like a Cheshire cat. "Nice toast, huh?"

"I never took you to be such a sentimentalist."

Dan patted his chest, just above his heart. "Deep in here, buddy, and I meant every word I said."

Hunter felt his throat knot up with unexpected emotions. "I'd do the same for you, you know."

"Yeah, I know, but we keep walking this trail and I'm going to start crying."

Hunter had a feeling that he meant those words as well.

Dan's grinned broadened. "I don't think I've kissed the bride yet."

Hunter put his hand on Dan's chest. "You kissed her."

Dan wiggled his brows and winked at Serena. "You ever get tired of this guy, you come see me."

Serena laughed. "I think I'll stick with what I have."

Her words surprised him, but Hunter felt they were more freely given and possibly truer than any of the vows they'd exchanged.

"It really was a nice toast," Serena said. "I appreciated the sentiment."

"Like I said, I meant every word. Don't let him fool you. He's a special guy. He'll spend the rest of his life trying to convince you otherwise. But the bottom line is that they don't get no better than him."

"So I'm coming to realize."

He leaned toward Hunter. "If you'll excuse me, I'm going to go check out that babe over there."

Looking where Dan was, Hunter shook his head. "I wouldn't. Her father is the police chief." He pointed toward Jack. "Right there."

"Well, that's not fair." He patted Hunter's shoulder. "When the time is right, I'm just going to slip away. Might not see you before I go."

"All right. I'll see you in a couple of weeks."

Dan leaned over and kissed Serena's cheek. "Honestly, darlin', I wish you the best. Keep this guy out of trouble and happy."

"It was nice to meet you, Dan."

"You bet it was. It always is."

Laughing, he walked away.

"The last thing I expected was for you to have such a talkative friend," Serena said.

"Opposites attract."

"I suppose. Why are you going to see him in a couple of weeks?"

"Let's not worry about it tonight, okay? Tonight, I just want you to be happy."

Chapter 21

Serena loved the beach at night. She could hear the rush of distant water, an occasional foghorn, and the breeze whispering over the water, sand, and grass.

Standing outside with Hunter's arms around her, his chest to her back, she watched as the taillights on the last car disappeared down the sandy road. Her father was taking Riker to Hopeful so the newlyweds could have some time alone.

She wanted to be what Hunter wanted her to be: happy. But it was difficult when the future held such uncertainty. He would be leaving soon. He couldn't tell her where he'd be going or what he'd be doing. She despised the secrecy, because she knew it was a harbinger for danger.

She didn't want to think about his friend, or how he'd done exactly as he'd promised—snuck away without being noticed. And she didn't want to admit that Hunter was probably in the habit of doing the same thing: arriving places without drawing attention and then stealthily slipping away. No more than a shadow.

But tonight he was flesh and blood, warm and firm, distracting her from her worries with a slow trailing of his mouth along the curve of her neck.

"Do you know the problem with an outdoor wedding on the Texas coast in July?" she asked, angling her head, exposing more skin to his questing lips.

"No."

"You get all sticky." She turned and wound her arms around his neck. "I want to take a bath."

"All right."

His lips met hers before his words were fully out of his mouth. She didn't hesitate to return the kiss. He was her husband. She still had a difficult time believing it.

The rapidity with which everything had happened astonished her, and yet she was convinced she'd made the correct decision to marry him. He had a loyal friend, and meeting Dan had told her more about Hunter than any silly game of twenty questions she could ever play.

Breaking off the kiss, she took his hand and led him into the house and up the stairs to the main bedroom. She was surprised to see a bottle of champagne chilling in a bucket of ice.

"What is this?" she asked, as she walked over to it. A small envelope was taped to the bottle. She removed it and read the note.

"Who's it from?" Hunter asked.

"Kevin." She waved the note in the air. "He wishes us the best, and knowing him, this champagne is probably the *best*. Will you open it, while I get the bath ready?"

"Sure."

She went into the bathroom. She'd always loved the claw-footed tub. She turned on the water, dropped in a capful of bubble bath, and lit the candles. She removed her clothes. When the tub was almost filled, she climbed into it and sank into the heavenly warm water.

She was tired, but it was a good kind of tired. Brought on by a day of joy. Hearing footsteps, she looked toward the door. Hunter came in carrying two flutes of champagne.

"Just as I suspected," she said. "Expensive stuff."

She reached a hand through the bubbles and took one of the offered glasses.

"How can you tell?" he asked.

"The teeny tiny bubbles. The more expensive the champagne, the tinier the bubbles."

He tapped his glass against hers. "To us."

"To us," she repeated.

They each took a sip of the bubbly brew, and then he leaned down and kissed her.

"There's room in here for you," she assured him.

"Glad to hear it."

He placed his glass on the small table beside the

tub. She watched in fascination as he began to re-move his clothes.

"You know, we really need to find more excuses for you to wear a tuxedo." She released a tiny growl. "You looked really good tonight."

And he looked even better as he dropped his clothes to the floor, piece by piece. The only light in the room was the flickering candles. She watched the shadows and light play over his skin as it was revealed to her.

"Have I ever mentioned that I love the way you look?" she asked.

"I don't think so."

"Well, I do."

She brought up her knees as he stepped into the tub, slid down, and placed his feet on either side of her hips. She took his flute off the table and passed it to him. "Another toast." She clinked her glass against his. "To hot nights that have nothing to do with the weather."

"I'll drink to that."

Wiggling her toes, she ran her foot along his thigh, his hip, and up his chest. He wrapped his hand around her foot and began to knead her sole with his thumb.

She closed her eyes and took another sip of cham-pagne. "That feels good."

"You were beautiful today, Serena."

His words pleased her beyond measure. "It was a perfect day, Hunter."

He closed his mouth around her toe. The heat traveled from her toes all the way up her leg. She'd never realized how sensitive her foot was.

He downed his remaining champagne, set his glass aside, and went to work in earnest on her foot, rubbing, massaging, kissing, nibbling.

"Maybe you need to come nibble at this end," she suggested.

"It would be easier if you came this way so you were on top."

She finished off her champagne and placed the glass on the table. Easing up, she straddled his thighs and shifted her weight until she was lying against his chest. He dipped his head and took possession of her mouth.

The heat was instantaneous and she wondered if it would always be this way with them. A fire that started so easily and burned so brightly.

With one hand, she cradled his face, changed the angle of the kiss and slid farther into the water where his hands were skimming over her body, stroking, and pressing her to him. They had all night. With no one waiting on them, no one expecting them.

They had the rest of their lives.

"Promise me you'll come back," she whispered, her mouth only a breath away from his.

He opened his eyes and held her gaze. "I'll do everything in my power to come back. That's all I can promise." Water rained down his arms as he lifted his hands out of the water and bracketed her face. "But know this, Serena. Never in my entire life have I ever cared about coming back as much as I care now. I'll admit that I was reluctant to get married. But you're mine now. You, Riker, and this baby. I've never cared about anything as much as I care about you. It scares the hell out of me to feel this much. I never knew a chest could ache with gladness. I can't even describe what I feel, because I've never felt it before."

She felt the tears sting her eyes as his arms came around her and he hugged her tightly. "Hunter—"

And then as though what he felt was beyond words, he tangled his fingers through her hair, gently pulled her head down, and latched his mouth onto hers, pouring whatever he was experiencing into the kiss.

She couldn't help but wonder if it might be love. If a man of his past would even know what love felt like, would recognize it if it grew within him to embrace those around him.

What she was coming to feel for him was beyond words, beyond anything she'd ever known. It frightened her as well, because she didn't want to contemplate not having him with her first thing in the morning, last thing at night, and all the minutes in between.

Rising up out of the water on her knees, she slid her body along his, breasts to chest, as he rained kisses over her flesh, a thousand heated sparks. And when she glided down, he was waiting, hot and hard as she welcomed him home. The bubbles surrounding them made tiny popping sounds as each ceased to exist. His kiss turned feral, his low growls guttural. Their skin was slick as they found their rhythm, the water undulating with their movements as the pleasure increased. She hadn't thought it possible for their lovemaking to become any more intense. But it did.

Every nerve ending cried out for release. She clutched him, felt him holding her tightly. Her fulfillment arrived in tandem with his, their bodies tensing in glorious rapture. Together, complete, with the possibility of love flickering in the candlelight.

Tonight they were husband and wife. Tomorrow they would become a family.

Chapter 22

From what Hunter had seen so far after coming through the front door, Serena's house was exactly as he'd envisioned it. Bright colors. Clean. Cheery.

Having arrived only a few moments before, they now stood in the living room while Serena quizzed Larry on Riker's night: what he'd eaten, how he'd slept, what he'd done. Listening, Hunter felt like an intruder, although he supposed that he'd be part of all future moments like this, and her inquisitiveness would extend to their child. While he appreciated her involvement with her son, he also was concerned that she was too overprotective. The kid was nine. By the time Hunter was that age, he was pretty much on his own.

Based on Larry's ready responses, he was accustomed to the interrogation. So far, Hunter had gleaned that all had gone well and that Riker was presently next door playing with Jason.

"And I think I'll just mosey on home now," Larry said, with a clap of his hands as though to signal the end to the questions.

"Dad, you don't have to rush off," Serena said. "Stay for a couple of days."

Larry shook his head. "Honey, your new family needs time to become a family. And you don't need me around for that."

"At least stay for supper."

Larry smiled gently and touched her cheek. "My bags are packed, in my car, and I'm ready to go. I want to be home before dark. I'm going to go next door and say good-bye to my grandson. But I'll say good-bye to you now."

"Oh, Dad."

Hunter looked away as Serena hugged her father. He felt an unaccustomed knot in his throat because his child would be raised in a family where parents displayed affection. He was as grateful for that as he was uncomfortable with it, because it was alien to him. But for his children, his new family, he'd learn how to embrace and show affection. It might take a while, but he'd learn.

"Well, son."

Hunter turned to his father-in-law. That was certainly a term he'd never expected to apply to anyone in his life. "Larry."

"You take good care of my daughter and grandson."

Hunter shook the offered hand. "I will, sir."

"I don't doubt that for a minute. Take good care

of yourself, too." He patted Hunter's shoulder. "Come back home safe from this business trip you're going on."

Hunter suddenly realized with startling clarity why they selected only men who had no family for the missions he went on. It was difficult to think about leaving knowing there was a good chance he might not come back home—and to know people would be waiting. Never before had there been any-one waiting.

He shifted his gaze to Serena. She looked as though she was anxiously awaiting his promise to her father that he would return. "I'll try, sir," was the best he could offer.

"According to Yoda there is no try."

"Yoda?"

Larry chuckled. "Ask Riker."

Hunter waited while Serena walked her father to the door. He figured they'd need one more good-bye before Larry truly left. He was learning that this family wasn't the most efficient. They hugged, re-hugged, and then for good measure, usually hugged again. A kiss on the cheek. Another hug.

Not that he minded. He much preferred their way to the one he'd grown up with. A slap. A re-slap. Then another for good measure.

He wandered over to the far wall. A television was in the center. Shelves holding various entertainment systems were on one side of the TV. On the other side were shelves holding books. The two lower shelves held a set of encyclopedias, various *National Geographic* books, and other books that were obviously Riker's. The remaining shelves held books that he was fairly certain belonged to Serena.

He heard her quiet footsteps and slowly turned.

She smiled softly. "Well, Dad's gone to say goodbye to Riker, and then he'll drive away." She crossed her arms over her chest and released a deep sigh, as though she suddenly didn't know what to do with this man in her house.

Hunter jerked his thumb over his shoulder. "Have you read all those?"

She nodded, her smile growing. "Those are my keeper shelves."

"Keeper shelves?"

"The books that I really enjoy reading, I place on those shelves in case I want to read them again. I donate the rest to the library."

"You read a lot."

"Not as much since I met you." She took a step back. "Let me show you the rest of the house."

"I like what I've seen so far."

She beamed at that.

"I assume all your windows have Window Dressing originals," he said.

"Of course."

"Maybe I should let you do the windows out at the lake."

"I could work up some designs."

"I need to get you a key." Hunter needed to get her a lot of things, before he left. Needed to have all his affairs in order before he left on his mission.

As though she realized the direction his thoughts had just gone in, her smile left her eyes. "Come on. Let me show you upstairs."

Hunter followed her up the staircase. One side opened onto the living room, the other side was a wall lined with photos of her son. He'd never seen so much organized clutter in a house. She had flowers, statuettes, knickknacks—items he'd never think to purchase much less to display. And yet everything seemed as though it belonged exactly where she'd placed it.

The top of the stairs opened onto a large room that had another TV in it, a couple of recliners, a toy box, and a wall of shelves with more books.

"This is the game room," Serena said. "Riker plays his video games on that TV."

"More keeper shelves."

She blushed at that. "Yes. Well, sorta. Some are keepers, some I haven't read yet."

"I've never known anyone who reads that much."

"I love reading. It's an escape. I probably rely on it too much sometimes, but books keep me company. Do you read?"

"Yeah, but not like that."

She walked past him toward the hallway. "You're welcome to read any of my books."

Based on the titles he'd read he figured they weren't his type of reading. "I'll pass, thanks."

"Jack reads them."

"You're kidding."

She glanced over her shoulder. "Nope. Don't be a snob. I bet a romance novel isn't anything like you think it is."

He grimaced. No way was he reading a romance. All that lovey-dovey stuff. "I'll stick with nonfiction, thanks all the same."

"Suit yourself. This is Riker's room."

He peered inside. Spiderman was on the walls, bed, and window. It was the kind of room that a boy would feel at home in.

"The Spiderman on the walls is glow in the dark," she said. "I thought I should warn you because it nearly gave my dad a heart attack the first time he walked down the hallway in the dark, looked in on Riker, and saw Spiderman leaping toward him."

"Appreciate the warning."

"This room down here is another bedroom, but I use it mostly for storage. I've been meaning to get Jack to put planks down in the attic so I can move the boxes up there and make this a real guest room."

"I can do that for you," he said. She didn't need

Jack doing for her now that she was married to Hunter. He could take care of his own.

She looked over at him. "I thought we might use it for the nursery now, rather than a guest room."

"Right. A nursery." A room where his kid would sleep. It was like a punch in the gut. The reality that he was going to have a child who would need a room to sleep in.

"I know it seems kind of soon, but since you don't know how long you'll be gone, I thought maybe we could decorate the room before you left, so you'd at least know what it looks like."

"I'd like that."

Worry lines eased between her brows. "Will I be able to write you?"

He shook his head. "You could, but I won't get the letters until the mission is completed. And then I'll be on my way back, and you can tell me whatever you wrote me."

She nodded jerkily. "I'll keep a journal, so you can read about what happened when you were gone. Because I know I'll forget something that I wanted to tell you."

He saw a tear escape out of the corner of her eye. He didn't know if in his entire life anyone had cried for him. He certainly didn't want this brave woman to cry over him. Reaching out, he wiped the tear away with his thumb. "Babe, don't think about it yet. We've got a couple of more weeks."

"I know. I can't change it. I need to focus on the present." She gave him a shaky smile. "Come on. I'll show you our room."

Our room. He followed her back down the hallway to a door across from Riker's. She opened the door and stepped inside.

Their bedroom was lace, frills, and femininity. Yellow, pink, flowers, and gewgaws.

And a king-size sleigh bed.

"I can redecorate it if you don't like it," she said.

He slid his gaze over to her, wondering why she was so worried about what he liked and what he didn't. She could have bare walls and he wouldn't care. Reaching out, he pulled her up against him, looped his arms loosely around her. "I'd like to have a few things changed."

"Like what?"

He grinned. "I'd like to have you naked."

Laughing, she broke free and stepped back. "You're crazy."

"Crazy about you." He took a step toward her. "Take your clothes off."

"No, it's the middle of the afternoon."

"So I'll have the opportunity to see you better. Take your clothes off."

"Riker could be home at any minute."

"I'll hear him the second his feet hit the yard." He

stepped toward her. "Come on. Let me see how the room looks with you naked in it."

She shook her head, but her smile and sparkling eyes belied her actions.

"I won't know if I like the decorating until I've seen you naked," he assured her.

"The honeymoon is over."

"For us, it's never going to be over."

He rushed her as gently as he could, tumbling her onto the bed, pinning her arms over her head, straddling her hips while her shrieks and laughter echoed around him.

"You can't do this," she said.

"Watch me."

He lowered his head and silenced her protests with a searing kiss. The fact that she returned it as eagerly as he delivered it told him that her objections were insincere. Her tongue parried with his. She didn't try to free her hands from his light grip, didn't try to buck him off.

He trailed his mouth along her throat. "So far I like the bed," he rasped.

Still holding her wrists with one hand, he reached down with the other and began to tug up her top, over her breasts, up over her head, along her arms, releasing her hands for only a second so he could move it over them. He tossed her shirt onto the floor, then closed his hand back around her wrists.

He skimmed his hand over the curve of her breast.

"We really shouldn't do this." Her words came out breathy, sexy.

"Yeah, we really should." He eased the cup of her bra down. "We definitely should be doing this." With his tongue he circled her nipple.

Moaning, she twisted her body up toward him, giving him easier access. He closed his mouth around her hardened nipple and suckled.

"Let go of my hands," she ordered.

He complied. She tugged on his shirt, eased it out of his jeans, and began undoing the buttons. To hell with that. He pulled his shirt over his head and tossed it aside. He shifted his weight until he was nestled between her thighs.

While she combed her fingers through his hair, he dipped his tongue into her navel. She wrapped her long legs around him and squeezed. Oh, God, he thought he might explode before he ever got their jeans off and buried himself inside—

"Mom!"

Her knee came up, hitting him in the nose. Fire burst through his face. Tears stung his eyes.

"Get off!" she whispered frantically, "Get off!"

He didn't think his nose was broken, but it still hurt.

"Move!" she whispered.

"Just a minute."

"We don't have a minute."

"Mom!"

He heard the footsteps now. On the stairs. He rolled off the bed, grabbed a shirt off the floor, and tossed it to her. Snatched the other up and put it over his head, slid his arm into a sleeve—damn thing had shrunk.

Riker bounded into the room. "Mom?"

"Riker, honey, you're home," Serena said, her voice a little too high, a little too cheerful.

"What are you doing?" Riker asked.

"Nothing," she said.

Riker's brows puckered as he pointed at Hunter. "Why is he wearing your shirt?"

Serena spun around, horror in her eyes as her gaze fell on Hunter, her shirt wrapped around his neck with only one of his arms stuck in a sleeve. In her panic, she'd obviously not realized that she was wearing his. Hunter couldn't wait to hear her explanation for this mess.

"Uh," she began. "Uh."

Hunter pulled off the shirt. "I was looking for a shirt that I could use when I lift weights. I like to wear them tight. I thought your mom's might work, but it's a little *too* small."

"Cool! You lift weights?" Riker asked.

He'd figured Riker would latch onto the manly part of the story instead of the stupid part. "Yeah. I like to work out in a gym three times a week."

"We don't have a gym," Serena said.

Hunter shook his head. She wasn't helping to divert her son's attention from the true state of their affairs.

"Wish you'd told me that before I tried to put on your shirt."

He saw comprehension dawn and she turned to her son. "Riker, why don't you go downstairs and give us a minute up here?"

"Why?"

"Because we just got home and we're trying to get settled," Serena said. She waved her hand toward him. "Go on. Do as I say."

With a shrug, Riker disappeared from view. Serena pressed a hand to her mouth and started laughing softly. "A shirt to exercise in?"

"It was better than uh, uh, uh," Hunter pointed out in his own defense.

She fell against him, her shoulders quaking with her laughter. "I tried to warn you."

"That kid is too quiet. We need to lace bells to his shoes."

Her shoulders shook harder as she lifted her face, tears of mirth in her eyes. "Maybe I'm just good at distracting you."

"Oh, you are definitely good at that."

"Riker probably didn't know what to think. I've never had a man in my bedroom."

Although he'd known that, he still didn't mind hearing it. "From now on we close and lock the door."

"Definitely."

He kissed her. "I'll take my shirt back now."

"This is the deck," Riker said as he and Hunter stepped out through the back door that led from the kitchen. "Uncle Jack built it."

Of course. Uncle Jack had hung pictures and put in shelves and been a regular handyman for Serena.

"It's nice."

"Be better if we had a pool."

"Why don't you have a pool?"

"Too expensive."

"How much are they?"

Riker blinked, furrowed his brow, and shrugged. "About a million dollars."

"That seems a little unreasonable."

Riker shrugged again. "Mom says they're too expensive, so I figured that's about what it costs. Come on. I'll show you my fort."

Hunter followed him across the well-maintained yard. Flowers surrounded the house, lined the fence. If he were a betting man, he'd bet that Serena was responsible for the colorful flowers and her neighbor for the manicured lawn.

"This is it," Riker said.

"It's great," Hunter said. More than great. It was

a kid's paradise. The wooden structure stood on stilts and straddled the neighbor's fence, so the boy next door could easily play in it. Hunter didn't have to ask who had built it. He knew it was the same guy who had built the backyard deck. Jack Morgan.

Neighbor. Friend. Idiot if he'd never put a move on Serena. How could he have not been attracted to her? Made no sense. No sense at all.

"Want to come inside?" Riker asked.

Hunter nodded. "Sure."

He followed Riker up the ladder and ducked in through the narrow doorway. He was impressed. There was a small table and two chairs. Drawings on the walls. Maps. Diagrams. Obviously these boys played some sort of war games.

"Very nice," he said, figuring that's what Riker needed to hear.

"I'm almost too old to be playing in forts," Riker said.

Hunter shrugged. "Sometimes a guy needs his own space."

"Yeah, especially during that time of the month."

Hunter narrowed his eyes in speculation, wondering if Riker meant what Hunter thought he meant. "What time of the month?"

"When Mom is grumpy. Uncle Jack says, 'it's just that time of the month.' It's kinda like werewolves and a full moon, I guess. Doesn't happen often, but when it does, you'd better watch out."

Hunter fought not to laugh. He had a few months before he'd have to deal with PMS. "Seems like Uncle Jack tells you a lot of things."

Riker nodded quickly. "He's the greatest. But he's not really my uncle. Uncle Kevin is my uncle. He's not as much fun, though." His eyes widened. "But he's rich. He always sends me a hundred dollars for Christmas and my birthday."

"Sounds like a good guy." But Riker was right. Not nearly as good as a guy who builds you a fort.

A loud knock caught his attention. "Hey, are y'all going to spend the night in there?" Serena called out.

Hunter stuck his head through the door. "No, I was just getting the grand tour."

"I don't have anything to fix for supper. I need to go to the grocery store. If you want to give me a list of some things you like to eat—"

"Why don't we all go?" Hunter suggested.

"Grocery shopping?"

"Sure. Give me a better feel for the town. Then I can just pick up what I want."

He didn't know why she looked uncomfortable with that idea. And talking to her through the opening of the fort had him at a disadvantage. He climbed out and down the ladder and faced her. "You don't want me going to the grocery store. Am I going to discover you were more than friends with the butcher?"

Laughing lightly, she rubbed her hand up and down his arm. "No, it's just that I've discovered if I don't take a list to the store then I tend to go over my budget. My business brings in some money, but not a lot. I've always felt that spending time with Riker was more important than spending money on him, so I have to carefully watch my budget."

"Not anymore."

She shook her head, nodded, shook her head. "We need to talk about finances and how we're going to divide expenditures."

"It's pretty simple. You buy it. I pay for it. Whatever money you make from your business is yours to spend however you want."

"Mom, we could get a pool then." Riker was sitting in the doorway of his fort, obviously listening.

Serena shook her head. "Riker, this is between Hunter and me."

"But we're a family. We're supposed to make decisions together."

"Some decisions. Not all decisions."

Hunter slipped his arm around Serena, drew her up against his side. "Look, we obviously have some adjusting to do all the way around. For tonight, why don't we just get the groceries, and we'll address the other issues later."

"All right. But we will address them."

"Sure." Hunter looked over his shoulder and winked at Riker. If the kid wanted a pool, he was going to get a pool.

Serena's house suddenly seemed much smaller with Hunter prowling through it. And prowling was the best word to describe the way he moved. Serena had always thought that Hunter possessed a predator-like stillness but tonight he seemed antsy.

They'd gone out to get pizza for supper, and then at Riker's request, they'd stopped by the video store and picked up *Lord of the Rings: The Two Towers.* Riker was lost in the story—even though he'd seen it twice before. Every time she got absorbed in the movie, Hunter would shift his body, distracting her.

He moved from the couch to the chair, to the kitchen for a drink, back to the chair, to the couch, petted Lucky, sighed, then leaned toward her and whispered, "I'm stepping out back for a minute."

She watched him head back to the kitchen where he'd have access to the back deck, the beagle trailing along after him. Riker paused the DVD and looked at her.

"What's wrong?"

"Nothing's wrong."

"Why'd he leave?"

"I think he's already seen this movie."

Riker shook his head. "He didn't even know who Frodo was, Mom. And he asked me about my friend, Yoda. There's a lot of stuff he doesn't know."

She hugged him. "He'll learn. You keep watching your show. I'm going to go talk to him."

She found Hunter on the top step of the deck, Lucky on one side of him, his head on Hunter's lap, Hunter scratching behind his ear. She sat on the other side, slipped her arm around Hunter's and leaned her head against his shoulder. She'd been afraid that the only thing they'd really have together was sex.

"Married life not to your liking?" she asked softly.

He kissed the top of her head. "I'm liking it just fine. I'm just not much into watching TV. And that guy on that show that's supposed to be an elf?" He shook his head. "I always thought elves were little, flying around flowers and stuff."

Smiling, she squeezed his arm. "It's all fantasy. Elves can be whatever you want them to be."

"You don't have to sit out here with me," he said quietly.

"I know, but I want to."

He looked up at the sky. "With the lights from the town you can't see the stars very well."

"You like looking at the stars."

"I like being outside. I get claustrophobic when I'm inside and don't have to be. Which is odd because a lot of my job involves being in tight places, being absolutely still, not scratching an itch, just listening and waiting. I can be cold, wet . . . scared. But I wait until I can do what I've been sent to do."

"What are you sent to do?"

He shifted his attention to her, and in the pale light spilling out through the kitchen window, she could see his somber smile. "Is this one of your twenty questions?"

She wondered if she really wanted an answer. "We're married, Hunter. I should be able to ask all the questions I want. Personal or otherwise."

"For better or worse?"

Swallowing hard, she nodded. "For better or worse. I want to know who my husband is."

"I neutralize threats."

Her heart thudded against her chest. Her imagination shifted into overdrive. She could interpret his words several different ways, and she suspected that he was trying to soften the truth, to protect her from gaining the knowledge of what he truly did. "Do you do that by killing them?"

He released a deep sigh, but held her gaze. "Sometimes. You're trying to make it personal, and it's not. Sometimes I'm simply sent to gather information. That's not always a pretty process. I don't deal with the good guys, Serena. Sometimes I'm not even sure that I'm a good guy."

"You are."

"I want to be. For you, your son, the baby. I'm usually able to blend in—wherever I'm sent. But I don't know how to blend in with yellow curtains."

"I can always change the curtains."

Reaching out, he cradled her cheek with the most tender touch she thought she'd ever received. "I don't want you to change anything. There have never been yellow curtains in my life, Serena."

He kissed her, and she wanted to hold him close and never let go. Keep him with her, not let him go away on a mission that might turn ugly. She wanted more windows in the house, more yellow curtains, wanted to fill his life with bright colors and sunshine.

He ended the kiss and said in a low voice, "I think we should get a pool."

She drew back. "What?"

"Riker wants a pool. I think we should get one."

"They're expensive."

"Yeah, he told me. About a million dollars."

She laughed lightly. "Not quite that much, but you don't have to buy him a pool."

"I want to. I want to be the best dad that I can be."

Her heart aching, she ran her hand along the side of his face. "Then give him your time."

Hunter felt like a visitor in a strange world. He'd lived in foster homes where meals were eaten together, chores dished out, kindness offered. But he'd never thought of himself as being part of a family—and that's what he had now, what he wanted to hold onto.

He really thought Riker would prefer to have a pool, but he figured Serena knew her son better than he did, so he'd work on figuring out how to give the boy his time. He and Serena returned to the living room about the time some major battle was going on. Riker's gaze was glued to the TV, and every now and then, he'd give a little bounce as though he was imagining himself in the thick of things. Watching the kid was more interesting than watching the movie.

He couldn't remember a time in his life when he'd ever had that much enthusiasm about anything. This boy lived in a safe environment where he didn't have to worry about being hit or hurt or screamed at for having his feet in the chair and not being still. And that was good, because that's what he wanted for his own child.

He wanted his kid to grow up in this home with this woman and this boy.

Serena sat on the couch and rubbed her hand over the empty spot beside her. He joined her, rested his arm along the back, and began toying with her hair. She snuggled up against his side. He loved that aspect of her—that she was quick to offer comfort, even if it wasn't asked for.

When the movie was finally over, Serena picked up the remote and turned off the TV. Riker twisted around in his chair to face them, his brow furrowed.

"Do I have to go to bed already?"

"In a little bit. Right now we want to share some good news with you."

"We're getting a pool?"

Hunter tugged on her hair. She rolled her eyes at him, before looking back at Riker. "We're still discussing that. What we wanted to tell you was that . . . we're going to have a baby. You're going to be a big brother."

"Okay."

She looked at Hunter and he wondered if she was expecting him to say something profound. What the hell could he add? He shifted his gaze to Riker, who also looked as though he was waiting to hear more.

"We'll be a family."

Riker nodded. "Can I call you Dad?"

Hunter's stomach clenched and his heart kicked an extra beat. "Sure, I'd like that."

The words sounded strangled, but Riker didn't seem to notice. "Great."

"Do you have any other questions?" Serena asked.

Riker shook his head.

Serena smiled. "All right then. Go get ready for bed, and we'll be up in a minute."

"Can't I stay up longer?"

"Not tonight," Serena said.

"But I don't have school tomorrow."

"I'm tired, Riker. We're going to bed."

"I could stay up with him." He pointed at Hunter.

"Not tonight."

Hunter thought about saying he'd stay up with the kid, but he didn't want to spoil any routines, wasn't exactly sure what his role should be. So he kept quiet and watched as the kid slowly made his way up the stairs, holding onto the banister as though he was scaling the summit of Mount Everest.

Serena got up, went to the TV, and popped out the DVD. She turned to him and smiled. "That went easier than I expected. He usually has more excuses for staying up."

"I don't mind staying up with him," Hunter offered. Okay, he minded a little. He and Serena still had unfinished business from this afternoon.

"He needs to keep his routine."

Hunter nodded. He figured that. "How did you learn all this parenting stuff?"

"Mostly I called and asked my mother. I'm really going to miss her when this baby is born. She stayed with me after Riker was born. I was so afraid I'd do something wrong."

He was worried he'd do something wrong now. "Look, if I do something that's not what I need to do for these kids, you let me know."

"I don't think that's going to be a problem. I think you'll be a good father."

"Mom, I'm ready!"

She narrowed her eyes. "Definitely too cooperative. He might be trying to impress you."

Hunter stood. "He impressed me the first time I met him. Just like his mom."

Smiling softly, she lifted up on her toes and kissed him. Briefly, but with a hint that there was more to come.

"I'm going to tuck him in," she said.

"I'll go with you."

It seemed the right thing to say, the right thing to do. And it was certainly something that he wanted to be part of. He wanted them to be a family. The fact that he only had a vague idea of what that entailed wasn't going to deter him. He figured Serena was a model to follow—and he intended to do just that. Follow her up the stairs and see where things led.

In Riker's room, he was surprised to see the boy already beneath the sheet, reading a book, the dog nestled at the foot of the bed. Serena took the book from him and placed it on the nightstand beside the bed. Riker scooted down onto his back. Standing beside the bed, Serena combed her fingers gently through his hair.

"Sweet dreams."

She leaned down and kissed his forehead.

Hunter wondered how many times they might

have exchanged those words, those actions. She returned to his side and turned off the light.

"Good night, sweetie."

" 'Night, Mom . . . 'night . . . Dad."

Hunter felt as though he'd been ambushed and taken a devastating blow to his heart. A fierce protectiveness he'd never before experienced welled up inside him. He'd been completely unprepared for the impact of that one word, delivered to him with a young boy's voice and doubts.

He was crossing the room before he even realized he'd made the decision to do so. He reached Riker's side, folded his hand around the boy's skinny shoulder, and squeezed. "Good night, Son."

He took another blow to the heart as the boy's face—limned by the light from the hallway—split into a wide grin. He thought he could stand here all night saying those three little words and watching the boy's reaction to them.

" 'Night, Dad," Riker said again, with more confidence and sureness echoing in his voice.

Hunter grinned. " 'Night."

He walked back to the doorway where Serena was waiting, smiling, her eyes glistening. And he suddenly felt as though he'd found what he'd been searching for his entire life. He couldn't name it, describe it, or pinpoint it. He only knew that he'd found it.

Chapter 23

Having a husband in the house wasn't like having a guest in the house. Her completely feminine pale pink bathroom now had male accoutrements in it: an additional toothbrush, shaving gel, razor. And she'd hung out another towel, so Hunter wouldn't have to go scrounging through the linen closet for it.

She'd thought of this house as hers and Riker's. She'd never had another man other than her father sleep in the house. Yet even now she was aware of Hunter prowling through the rooms, checking the doors, windows, and locks. The house simply had a different feel to it, and part of her wondered if they should start over. Buy a new house. Turn it into theirs, rather than slowly converting this one.

As she removed her clothes and slipped on her silken robe, she realized that her life was filled with rituals that were slowly changing, evolving. Riker now had two parents to tuck him in. Her heart had expanded as she'd watched the initial shock on Hunter's face give way to wonder after Riker had called him Dad. She didn't think it was so much that he was surprised that her son had called him Dad. After all, Riker had asked right off the bat if he could have that privilege.

No. She suspected that Hunter had been unprepared for all he would experience when that powerful word was applied to him.

Unlike her, he wasn't easy to read, but she was beginning to recognize the moments when he was disarmed. The evidence was subtle, a vulnerability expressed only with his eyes.

She imagined that his occupation required that he keep all signs of weakness hidden. He had to always appear strong, in control, powerful. The elements that had first attracted her to him.

But it was the small kindnesses, the strangled rasp of his voice as he'd said good night to Riker, his desire to do right by them, to be a good father and husband, that would keep him with her.

She tightened the sash of her silky robe, walked into the bedroom, and turned down the covers to her bed.

Her bed?

Their bed.

It didn't quite seem like theirs yet. He hadn't brought a lot of items with him. Only a couple of bags. She'd cleaned out a drawer for him and made room in the closet. She supposed once he returned from this mission, he might move other things to her—their—house.

She would redecorate while he was gone. The nursery, but also this room. Add a masculine touch.

She'd expected him to return by now. Where was he?

She stepped into the shadowy hallway.

He was standing in the doorway to Riker's room. Still. Unmoving.

She crossed over to him, wrapped her hand around his arm. "What's wrong?"

"Nothing's wrong. Nothing at all. He's just so"— he shook his head—"innocent, trusting, happy."

"He's had no reason not to be."

"We're getting a pool."

She sighed. If he had the money for it, she supposed there was no reason to argue against it. "All right."

She thought she detected satisfaction in the slight nod he gave her.

"You like the glow in the dark Spiderman?" she asked.

"He's a little frightening."

"I thought we could have glow in the dark stars in the nursery, since you like stars."

"I like that idea."

Reaching down, she took his hand and led him back into the bedroom.

"Close the door," she instructed.

He did, and she moved over to the bed, slid her finger into the sash, loosened it, and slipped off her robe.

"Lock it."

She laughed softly with triumph as he tumbled her onto their bed.

Hunter awoke thinking that there were definite advantages to being married. A woman's sweet perfume filling his nostrils through the night, her warm body nestled up against his, her soft breathing a calming cadence, her hair tickling his chin, her arms around him.

With Serena he had more than all that. He was acquiring a familiarity—something he'd never had with any other woman. He knew that she preferred to sleep on her side. That she rubbed one foot against the other until she drifted off to sleep. And he knew that he slept more deeply with her beside him. That she held his loneliness at bay.

And that she made him grateful to wake up.

He skimmed his hand along her hip, down and up. He kissed the curve of her neck, the back of her shoulder. He rose up on his elbow—

"Don't move," she whispered.

He stilled, listening, his senses on alert. "What's wrong?" he asked, quietly, barely breathing.

"Morning sickness." She released a tiny moan. "It comes and goes."

Morning sickness wasn't a totally foreign concept to him, but since almost every man he worked with was also single, it wasn't something that he knew a great deal about.

"How long does it last?" he asked.

"Depends."

"What exactly are you feeling?"

"Nauseous."

"What do you need me to do?"

"Could you make me some hot tea? Bring me some crackers."

"Okay. Sure. Be right back."

Concentrating on his muscles, his movements, he eased himself off the bed. He snatched his jeans off the floor—

"My God!"

He spun around at her exclamation. Looking over her shoulder at him, she was raised on her elbow.

"What?" he asked.

"I didn't even feel you get up."

"I thought if you felt the bed moving, you'd get sick."

She rolled over, stretched out on her side, and studied him. "You're amazing."

He grinned at her. "I'll take that as a compliment."

"It was meant as one."

He could tell from looking into her eyes that she didn't feel well. The sparkle was missing. He wanted to get back into bed with her and just hold her, comfort her.

Instead he pulled on his jeans. "I won't be long."

He headed into the hallway and stopped briefly to look in on Riker. This experience was foreign to him—waking up in a house full of people. But he liked it. He liked it a lot.

The dog lifted his head before leaping off the bed. Riker groaned and rolled over.

Hunter reached down and petted the dog. "Come on, fella. Let's see if we can figure out where things are in the kitchen."

Serena's kitchen held a lot more items than his did. He managed to find the tea bags and pots so he started boiling water. Then decided he'd surprise her with a little more than crackers. He put on a second pot of water and placed a couple of eggs in it. Then he rummaged through the pantry until he located the saltines. Toast was fairly bland so he grabbed the loaf of bread.

He wanted to give her more than she was expecting.

He located a shallow wicker tray that he thought might be an actual breakfast tray so he decided to use it to carry everything upstairs. He popped outside, swiped a few flowers from her garden, and placed them in a glass of water. The water was boiling in both pots. He started timing the eggs and poured water over a tea bag in a cup.

Then he turned to go in search of the sugar and came up short. Riker stood in the doorway, scratching his head, yawning, wearing nothing more than his underwear. How did this kid constantly sneak up on him?

"What are you doing?" Riker asked.

"Making your mom some breakfast. She's not feeling well—"

"What's wrong with her?" He appeared terrified. "She's not going to die is she? Grandma didn't feel good and she died."

"Oh, no, she's not going to die. The baby . . . makes her feel kinda sick." He wondered how much the boy knew about the birds and the bees. If he even knew where babies came from. How much he should explain?

"Jason's mom is going to have a baby."

"Yeah, I heard."

"Jason said she cries all the time."

Great. "I don't think your mom will cry."

Riker walked farther into the kitchen and peered over the stove. "Are you making egg boats?"

"Nah, just boiling eggs."

"When I'm not feeling good, Mom makes me an egg boat. Can we make her one?"

"I don't know how."

Riker's eyes widened with enthusiasm. "It's easy. I'll show you."

Hunter wanted to tell the boy that he needed to get upstairs quickly and didn't have time to be building any boats, but he didn't want to hurt his feelings.

"How long does it take?" Hunter asked. "The tea is almost ready."

"Not long." Riker was digging into a drawer, removing paper, scissors, and pencils. "When the eggs are done, peel them and cut them in half."

"Where's the sugar?"

"Mom has a special sugar shaker." Riker retrieved it and put it on the tray. "Better let her do it. She likes lots." He returned to the drawer where he'd taken out his supplies.

Hunter finished preparing the tea and followed Riker's orders for the eggs. Riker returned to his side and handed him what looked like a toothpick sticking through a white flag—the flag being a scrap of paper cut into a triangle.

"We stick these in the eggs," Riker explained. "Then we have a sailboat."

Hunter nodded. "Clever." He moved to stick it in one of the eggs—

"But first you have to write your message."

He stopped and looked back at Riker, who was extending a pencil toward him. "What?"

"You have to write her a message. So she can feel better." He wiggled the pencil at him. "You write one and I'll write one."

"A message."

Riker nodded. "Yeah."

Hunter took the pencil. Riker climbed onto a stool at the counter and started writing. Hunter glanced around the kitchen, searching for inspiration.

Riker returned to his side. "What did you write?"

"I haven't yet."

"How come?"

"I don't know what to say to make her feel better. Let me see yours."

Instead of handing it over, Riker poked it into one of the eggs.

I love you.

With hearts surrounding the words.

How was Hunter going to top that? He couldn't. No way. He tapped his pencil against the edge of the counter. What could he write? What could he write? The tea and eggs were getting cold. Damn it.

Get well.

He drew a couple of sorry looking stars next to the hastily scribbled and inadequate words and jabbed the toothpick into the egg in such a way that sent it skidding off the plate and onto the floor. The dog pounced onto it. Hunter went to grab him, his elbow hit an empty pan and sent it crashing to the floor.

"No, Lucky!" Riker yelled. "You can't eat a toothpick."

The dog took off around the island. Riker hurried to the other side. The dog circled back around and Hunter planted his feet squarely to block the way. The dog spun around and went back the other way, as though he couldn't figure out he was trapped.

"Lucky!" Riker screamed.

The dog came back around, barreled toward Hunter. He reached down to catch him, the dog skidded, yelped, scrambled around—

"Come here, dog!"

"Lucky!"

"What is going on!"

Hunter spun around. Serena stood in the doorway in her robe, her arms crossed over her chest.

"Lucky has an egg boat, Mom. He's going to choke on the toothpick!"

Serena knelt down. "Come here, Lucky, come here, baby."

The dog lowered his belly to the tile and crept toward her. Somehow Serena managed to get the toothpick sail out of the dog's mouth before the animal started downing the egg.

"We were making you egg boats so you'd feel better," Riker told her.

"Were you?" she asked, smiling, looking up at him.

"Yeah, but then he dropped *his,*" Riker said, pointing a finger at Hunter.

"I didn't drop it. It just slid off the plate."

Only she didn't appear to be listening. She was reading the stupid message he'd written on the sail. She looked at him and did the very last thing he'd expected. She started crying.

Riker cast a knowing glance at Hunter. "Told you so."

Sitting in a chair with her feet curled beneath her, sipping her tea, she stared out the window and waited for her husband and son to return. Once everything had calmed down in the kitchen, Hunter declared that he'd needed to go for a run.

Riker promptly asked if he could go with him. Hunter had grumbled that he could go. She didn't think he was upset with Riker. He was upset that she'd started crying. She'd upset herself as well.

She didn't know why she hadn't been able to hold back the tears. Riker had patted her shoulder and told her it was okay. It was because she was going to have a baby. But she thought it was more than that. It was because Hunter was trying so hard to please her—and because he had no frame of reference.

Yet, everything he did touched her deeply.

Even taking a pair of scissors and cutting the sleeves out of Riker's T-shirt because her son wanted to be dressed like his new dad. Although Riker's slender arms didn't look anything like Hunter's muscular arms. Or his legs.

Although she'd slept with those arms and legs wrapped around her, she still enjoyed viewing them. His T-shirt had molded to his torso.

She picked up the sail he'd made her and twirled it between her fingers. Riker gave his love freely, innocently, wholeheartedly. He'd been too young to really understand when his father had died.

And now he had a man in his life whom he fairly worshipped. Serena had to admit that she thought his feelings were well-placed.

She was feeling better, the morning sickness had subsided, and she had a lot to get done now that they were home. She went upstairs to her bedroom and got dressed. She needed to do laundry.

She gathered up her clothes and then decided that she'd wash Hunter's as well. The clothes he'd worn yesterday were folded neatly on a chair. She picked up his jeans and began setting the contents of his pockets on the dresser.

She stilled when she recognized a matchbook for the Paradise Lounge. Steve had worked at the Paradise Lounge before he went into the Army.

It was an old matchbook. Faded, worn. It didn't carry their new logo, but the one they'd had when Steve worked there. How funny.

She wondered if Hunter collected matchbooks and boxes like Steve had. Every place they'd ever gone—even though neither one of them smoked—he'd pick up a matchbook and write the date inside.

"Years from now we'll have a record of all the places we've been and when we were there."

She opened the matchbook—just out of curiosity—to see if Hunter wrote anything in his like Steve did. And there was a date—6-15-1994—written inside a heart. In handwriting she'd recognize if she lived to be a thousand.

Her nausea returned in full force.

Hunter ran the last mile with Riker on his back. The kid was as light as a feather, and a pretty good runner in his own right. Hunter envisioned him running around the bases next season when he hit home runs during baseball games.

They got to the house and Riker slid down to the ground. "That was cool. Are we going to run tomorrow?"

"Maybe the day after. If we had a gym, tomorrow would be free weights."

"We need a gym."

"I can bring some weights from my house."

"I like having you living with us," Riker said.

Hunter patted the boy's shoulder. "I like living

here. Let's go in and take showers. I'm going to check on your mom and then we'll see about lunch."

"I'm going to go see Jason first. Tell him that we're running."

"Okay." He watched as the boy bounded across the yard, then he went inside. He didn't see any sign of Serena downstairs.

He found her in their bedroom, sitting on the edge of the bed. She looked awful. Absolutely awful.

He wondered where the nearest hospital was. If he should take her there now. If he should dial 9-1-1.

He wouldn't have left her to go for a run, but she'd seemed fine. He moved farther into the room. She didn't acknowledge his presence. She seemed to have gone into some sort of shock.

He knelt before her. "Serena? Babe? What's wrong? What do I need to do?"

She blinked and looked at him as though she didn't know him. "Where did you get this?"

He looked down at what she was holding in her hand. The matchbook. Damn it.

"I was going to wash your clothes. It was in your pocket," she said flatly. "Steve had one just like it. And you know what?"

She opened the flap, folded it back. "He used to work at the Paradise Lounge. I went there the afternoon I discovered I was pregnant, and he wrote the date down on a matchbook. He always did that.

Used matchbooks to mark important occasions so he'd remember where he was when something happened."

Tears welled in her eyes, spilled over onto her cheeks, and he felt his heart being ripped through his chest.

"June 15, 1994. He put a heart around the date, because he asked me to marry him that day, and I said yes. And he promised he would always carry it with him. It was his good luck charm. So why do you have it?"

"Because I'm the reason he died."

Chapter 24

It had never taken Hunter more courage to do anything than it had to utter those few words and then to look at the woman sitting before him. Always before, the only thing he risked losing was his life.

Now he risked losing her. And he realized with startling clarity that he didn't want to lose her. She might never have with him what she'd had before, but they could have something good, something worth coming home to.

He gave her credit for holding his gaze when he was having a hard time holding hers.

"I don't understand," she said.

Of course she didn't, because he hadn't explained anything—and couldn't reveal most of it.

"The mission in which he was killed is classified, so there's a lot I can't tell you."

She circled her finger in the air as though trying to draw a boundary around everything. "But this whole time that we've been seeing each other, you knew who Steve was, knew I was his wife—"

"No, not until late the second night. And then I wasn't a hundred percent sure that it was the same guy. Steve Hamilton—nothing uncommon in that name. I convinced myself that it was simply coincidence."

"And the coincidence was that you just happened to pick me—"

"I don't know how much coincidence it was. I settled in the area because he told me it was paradise. I was looking for whatever it was that he thought was so damned special about the place. I have a feeling it was you."

"When would you have told me?"

"I wouldn't have. Keeping secrets is what I do."

She held up the matchbook. "And this? How did you come to have it?"

"I was with him shortly after he got wounded. He wanted it, so I dug it out of his pocket. He died holding it, but in the insanity that followed, I somehow ended up with it. It became my talisman."

"Why are you the reason he's dead?" She shook her head. "You're not the one who shot him."

"No, but I'm the reason he was there. It cost him his life. It cost you."

Six years of loneliness, dreams unfulfilled. A son without a father. She felt angry, but more she felt betrayed. Not because she thought he was totally responsible for whatever had happened that night, but because he hadn't trusted her enough to tell her.

Because he had known and he'd kept the information from her. They'd exchanged vows: for better or worse. And he'd kept the worst to himself. How could she come to love a man she couldn't completely trust? A man who didn't completely trust her?

She'd had hopes for this marriage, for this relationship, for her life with this man.

How could she love him when he held secrets? How could she trust him when he didn't trust her? They were building a house without a strong foundation beneath it. It was destined to crumble and fall.

She felt as though she'd betrayed Steve by sleeping with the enemy. Only Hunter wasn't the enemy. He was a man she'd come to care for.

"Why didn't you tell me when you figured it out?"

"Because you loved him so much. Because I was responsible for his dying. Because I knew I couldn't do anything to make it up to you. Because I enjoyed being with you. I kept thinking, 'I'll just see her one more time, and then I'll get out of her life.'

"And when I'd finally found the strength to do that, to walk out of your life, you show up on my doorstep and announce that you're pregnant. With my kid. My kid is growing inside you.

"So am I supposed to tell you then that the reason it's not *his* kid is because he died getting me out of a jam? I wanted to marry you, Serena. I wanted to provide for this child, and omitting this information didn't seem likely to cause as much hurt as the admission of my role in his death. I was trying to protect you and what we had."

She released a self-deprecating laugh. "What we had? We don't have anything."

"We do have something—"

"No. It's not real, Hunter. With you, I needed more than a game of twenty questions. I needed a thousand, because you'll never simply reveal information about yourself. Everything has to be pried out of you. And now I have to wonder what else you haven't told me. What other secrets are lurking, waiting to jump out at the most inopportune moments."

"There isn't any other secret that will hurt you."

"And how do you know if you haven't told me? How can you judge what will hurt me and what won't? We have children to consider."

"I'm aware of that."

"What do I tell them? What do I tell Riker?"

"It's not something that they really *need* to know."

"Need to know? That's your mantra, isn't it? What do people *need* to know?"

"It's what I've been trained to consider. I've been taught to analyze risks—"

"And you knew telling me was a risk. That if you told me, you might lose me?"

"Yes."

"And you're losing me now because you didn't tell me. Can you at least tell me why you are responsible for Steve's death?"

"Because I'm the one they were sent in to rescue."

Serena stared at him as though he'd spoken in a foreign language. "Rescue? From what?"

"I'd been captured."

"Where?"

"I can't say."

"Because you didn't know?"

"Because it's classified. Where I was, what I was doing, what I was to accomplish . . . it can't be discussed. Leaks could jeopardize other operations. You have no idea the things that go on, that can't be talked about."

Serena kept feeling as though she'd been dropped into a bad movie. "Were you tortured?"

"What difference does that make?"

None, she supposed. Why couldn't she have fallen for an insurance salesman?

Because an insurance salesman didn't appeal to her. Hunter did. He made her heart pound with longing, her skin tingle with desire. He made her smile and laugh. He made her grateful that she was in his life and he was in hers.

He was taking on too much responsibility for Steve's death. He'd been a prisoner, they'd gone in to rescue him. How did that make him responsible? She didn't see that it did.

But she didn't trust him. She was beginning to think she didn't trust herself, her ability to make a good decision.

"I don't blame you for what happened to Steve, but I don't trust you either. I don't understand this world you inhabit. You and Dan speak in code. If I make a wrong assumption, you let me live with it."

"You're talking about the unemployment—"

"I'm talking about everything. I can't live like this. With secrets. You won't talk about your job, your family, your childhood." She held up the match-book. "This man was an important part of my life— and you knew him. But you didn't trust me enough to reveal what you knew about him. If you don't trust me, then you can never love me, because you can't love someone you can't trust."

She felt the tears stinging her eyes. "And I can't trust you." So I can't love you. Those were the words she needed to say, but couldn't. "I need you to leave. You can't live here with me and Riker."

"Okay. I'll gather up my things. Check into a motel."

"There's really no need for you to stay in town."

"I want to be in town in case you need me. At least until I have to report to Langley."

"Do what you have to do."

"What about Riker?"

"I'll explain things to him."

"Did you want me to be there with you when you talk to him?" he asked.

"No."

"Serena, it was never my plan to hurt you."

"You might not have planned it," she said, "but you accomplished it just the same." She paused. "I may want a divorce right after this baby is born," she told him, wanting to hurt him as much as she was hurting right now.

He nodded. "If you think that's best. I told you that I wouldn't fight you on anything you wanted. I meant it."

"But you said he'd be my dad."

Serena had never felt so desolate. It had hurt watching Hunter pack up his things and leave. It had hurt when he'd called to give her his room number at the motel. And it had hurt more than she thought possible when Riker had come home from Jason's looking for his dad.

"I know I told you that he would be your dad—"

"So he should live with us."

They were in the kitchen, Riker standing mulishly before her, refusing to give any ground in the argument. He needed a father and she'd thought she'd found him one.

"Riker, Hunter and I got married before we knew each other very well, and we've discovered that we need a little more time before he lives here with us."

"Why?"

Because he didn't trust me enough to tell me that he knew your dad. Because I don't know what other secrets he has. And because you're too young to understand and I don't want to hurt you, I can't tell you any of this.

"For a man and woman to live together, they should love each other."

"Don't you love him?"

She did. In spite of everything, she did. And that was the reason that it hurt so badly that he didn't trust her. "Riker—"

"When will I see him?"

"I don't know."

"But he was going to teach me more karate. And take me to ball games. We had it all planned."

"I'll talk to him, but you shouldn't make too many plans or get too attached to him, because he'll be leaving in a couple of weeks."

"Why?"

"He has to go to work."

"But he can work here."

"No, he works for a big company, and he can't do his work here."

She hated the vagueness, hated trying to juggle her comments so she protected her son.

"Can I go back over to Jason's?"

"Yes. I'll call you home for supper."

As he headed out the door, she heard him murmur, "This sucks."

Unfortunately, she had to agree.

It was close to midnight when she heard Jack drive up. As police chief, he kept the most atrocious hours.

She hurried out the front door and across the lawn. "Jack!" she called out softly.

He stopped walking toward his house, glanced over at her, and grinned. "Hey, Serena."

Then she was in his arms, and she thought a hug had never felt so good. She didn't know where she'd find the strength to let him go, but she knew she had to. She leaned away from him. "I need to talk to you. Can you come over for a little while?"

"Sure, let me check on Kelley and I'll be right over. What's up?"

"I don't want to give it to you in bits and pieces. I'll wait until you come over." She didn't know where to begin, and she was afraid once she got started, she wouldn't be able to stop.

She scampered back across the damp lawn, went into the house, and waited what seemed an eternity. She scrubbed down the kitchen counter and had just started working on the sink when she heard the rap on the back door. She'd known Jack would come to the back. He always did.

She opened the door. "Come on in. Can I get you something to eat or drink?"

"No, I'm fine." He yawned. "Just tired. What's up?"

Guilt assailed her. He'd been working all night, and here she was infringing on his time, keeping him from his family. It was so unfair. She had to let him go, had to learn to handle her own problems.

"I'm sorry, Jack. Go home. It's not important. We can talk about it tomorrow."

He crossed his arms over his chest and leaned against the counter she'd just scrubbed. "Serena, you don't dash across the lawn at midnight for something that's not important. What's wrong?"

She couldn't stop the stupid tears from filling her eyes. She knew it was because she was pregnant and her emotions were on high alert, but it was still irritating. "It's Hunter."

"Did he hurt you?"

She nodded.

"Where is he?" His voice had gone from friend to police chief in a heartbeat.

"The motel."

"I'll take care of it."

He was reaching for the door when she cried, "No!"

He held up his hands. "Serena, you know how I feel about men hitting women, and I don't care if he is your husband—"

"He didn't hit me."

"But he hurt you."

"Jack, do you know who he is?"

Jack leaned back against the counter. "Is this a trick question?"

"I don't understand why you didn't recognize him. He told me he was responsible for Steve's death."

Jack slowly shook his head, then stilled as knowledge obviously dawned. "*That's* where I recognized him from." He dropped his head back. "Damn."

"So you do know him?"

"Yeah. What did he tell you?"

"Only that he was being rescued."

He nodded.

"Why didn't you recognize him?" she asked.

"They'd beaten him so badly, Serena, that his own mother wouldn't have recognized him. He was a lot skinnier, too. I doubt they were feeding him much. And I only knew his code name."

She crossed her arms over her chest. "I don't like this cloak and dagger stuff."

"That particular night neither did we. I don't understand the reason he thinks he's responsible for Steve's death. We went in to retrieve him. I don't know if I've ever seen anyone more courageous than he was that night. When Steve got shot, he stayed with him while the rest of us went to figure out a new exit strategy."

"Then why did he say he was to blame?"

"Survivor's guilt, maybe? Steve was standing right beside me when he went down. Could have been me. For the longest time, I felt guilty because it wasn't."

"And you think he feels the same?"

"You'd have to ask him."

She sighed. "He doesn't allow personal questions to be asked without a toothpick."

"I beg your pardon?"

She shook her head. "It's a private joke."

"Kelley swears the marriages that last do so because the couples know how to make each other laugh."

He'd obviously not picked up on the sarcasm in her voice. As far as making each other laugh, so far she thought she and Hunter were batting almost zero on that.

"I'm not laughing, Jack. He doesn't trust me. He has this little world of secrets and games—"

"What exactly is it that you want to know?"

"I want to know that he trusts me. I want to know that he could love me. He promised that he'd always give me honest words. I want that honesty when there's silence."

"Serena, you're confusing the man with his job.

His profession is to keep secrets. The president of the United States trusts him to keep secrets. The director of the CIA trusts him to keep secrets. So I'm going to make a guess that Hunter has a greater respect for trust than you or I will ever have.

"The night Steve died, our orders were to go in and extract a hostage. If anyone asked, we were never there. If anyone asked about the man we were sent after, he didn't exist.

"Your husband's job requires that he carry the burden of secrets. That he carry them alone. Imagine the weight of never telling a soul what you know—not because you don't trust someone, but because someone else has trusted you not to betray their trust."

She shook her head. "I understand that, Jack. I'm not asking him to reveal his secrets. I'm asking him to trust me with the things that aren't secrets."

"He might not be able to tell the difference, Serena. He works in a world of espionage. I would think a town like Hopeful is surreal to him."

"I always thought you left the Army because Steve died and no one would talk about what happened."

"I left the Army because I didn't want to carry the weight of the secrets. I know they're out there, but I don't want to know what they are. The ones I know are heavy enough, thank you very much."

She'd never considered that he held secrets. "Does Kelley know about these secrets?"

He shook his head. "They don't concern her. What I think Hunter needs to figure out is which ones concern you."

"Maybe I need to figure out which secrets concern me."

He crossed the kitchen and took her into his arms. He offered comfort, but it wasn't nearly as satisfying as what Hunter gave her.

"Don't kick him out of your life completely," Jack said. "He's one of the good guys."

Chapter 25

Judging by the number of women in the waiting room, Hunter had to assume that some serious love-making was going on in this town. Of course they didn't all have bulging bellies—but those who did looked as though they'd stuffed a basketball under their dresses or into their pants.

He'd seen pregnant women before, but he'd never given much thought to them. A lot of them walked funny. He'd actually assisted one woman as she'd tried to get out of the chair when her name was called. She'd given him an appreciative smile and said, "Twins."

Shit was what he'd thought. "Congratulations" was what he'd uttered.

He leaned toward Serena, who was busy playing a game she called "Character Hangman" with Riker in order to keep him occupied while they waited for her name to be called. Apparently the rules were that you could only use the names of characters from movies. He'd be lousy at that game. He'd never been a big moviegoer.

"How big do you get?" he asked.

She looked at him, her brow furrowed. "Pardon?"

He discreetly pointed a finger around the room. "How big do you get?"

She sighed. "With Riker, I got pretty big."

"So where are all the other fathers?"

"They don't usually come for the check-ups unless it's to hear the heartbeat or there's a problem."

"What kind of problem?"

"Mom?"

"Just a minute, sweetie."

"But it's your turn."

"Riker, I'm talking." She turned back to Hunter. "Sometimes a woman gets too big, too fast. Sometimes she doesn't get big at all. Sometimes something is wrong with the baby and the father needs to be here to offer support to the mother."

"And you were thinking of going through this by yourself?"

"Women do it all the time. Teenage girls do it."

"Yeah, well . . ." What more could he say to that?

"We need to talk sometime about whether or not you want to be in the delivery room. You'd have to take classes."

"For what?"

"To assist."

"What are we paying the doctor for?"

"To deliver the baby. You'd monitor my breathing

and be present in the delivery room to hold the baby when she's born."

"I'll let you know."

Although he already knew the answer. He'd be reporting back to work in another week, and he wouldn't be here to take classes. With any luck he might be back before the baby was born . . . then again, maybe not. But he didn't want to tell her that here because he figured they'd end up in a big discussion and he didn't need a roomful of women to witness it.

He'd been surprised when she'd phoned to tell him that she had this appointment and he might have an opportunity to hear the baby's heartbeat. She didn't seem as angry with him as before, but neither did she seem comfortable with him. She wanted him to trust her. How could he convince her that he already did—more than he'd ever trusted anyone?

"Mrs. Fletcher?"

It took him a minute to realize that the nurse standing at the open door was calling Serena. He'd never heard anyone call her that except for the minister right after he'd pronounced them man and wife.

She and Riker both stood, and she placed her hand on Riker's shoulder to guide him toward the door. She looked back at Hunter. "Come on."

The women he passed winked at him with approval, smiled at Riker. Then he was behind the closed door, standing in a corridor.

"So today is the day to hear the heartbeat, is it?" the nurse asked.

"Yes, it is," Serena said.

The nurse pointed to a bench along a wall. "If you gentlemen will wait on that bench, I need to get some information from Mrs. Fletcher."

Hunter sat and Riker joined him.

"This is like being in time out," said Riker.

"What's time out?"

"When I don't do what I'm told and I have to sit somewhere until Mom's not mad at me."

"Ah."

"It's no fun."

"No, I don't imagine it is."

"I thought when you married my mom that you'd be my dad."

Hunter didn't know what to say to that. *I'd like to be* hovered on the tip of his tongue, but he didn't want the kid to think that Serena was in any way responsible for this current situation.

"Your mom and I are still working some of the details out."

"Is it because you don't like me?"

"No, shit, no."

Riker's eyes got big and round. "We're not supposed to say shit."

Hunter grimaced. "Right. I'm not used to being around kids."

"Is that why you don't live with us anymore?"

Nah, kid, it's because your mom can't quite get past the fact that I have trust issues.

"Your mom just needs a little time, that's all."

"She cries at night."

He didn't like hearing that.

"Maybe you ought to send her some flowers."

Hunter grinned. Romance advice from a nine-year-old. What the heck, though. Maybe he had a point.

He winked at the kid. "I think I'll do that."

The nurse came around the corner, Serena with her. "All right, gentlemen, this way."

Serena narrowed her eyes slightly as she regarded them. "Why do you two look like you're up to something?"

"We're not," Hunter said. Riker was shaking his head so hard he was surprised it didn't fly off. "Just a little guy talk."

The nurse led them into an examination room. "If you gentlemen will just stand back over in the corner, the doctor will be in shortly."

Serena sat on the table while Hunter and Riker retreated to the corner like two boys caught scuffling on the playground.

"This is the worst part," Serena said. "Just sitting here, waiting."

Hunter felt a small hand slide up against his, and he closed his fingers around it.

"Don't look so worried, Riker. Nothing bad is going to happen," Serena said.

"I know."

"So this doctor is good?" Hunter asked.

"Of course Dr. Terrance is good. I wouldn't be using her if she wasn't."

Right. Of course she was. He just wasn't thinking. He'd never been in an OB/GYN's office. It was definitely designed for a woman. There were sketches of women and their body parts hanging on the door that could stunt a man's sex drive. Then he noticed the poster of the fetus's developmental stages that was on the wall beside Serena. He eased over to it.

"What's that?" Riker asked, following along since Hunter hadn't relinquished his hold on the kid's hand.

"That's how the baby grows," Serena said. Reaching out, she touched two different pictures. "The baby is somewhere between these two, I think."

Hunter glanced over at her stomach. If he didn't know she was pregnant, he wouldn't know she was pregnant. He looked back at the poster. He'd never given any real thought to the development of a child.

At some point, this little curled up creature was going to be a nine-year-old kid wondering why his dad wasn't living with his mom.

The door opened, and Hunter jerked back, banging a trash can and elbowing a container holding pamphlets to the floor. Riker laughed, Serena smiled, and the doctor said, "Nervous, Daddy?"

Daddy. The word hit him harder than he'd ever been hit in his life.

"No, I was just startled, that's all." He bent down and scooped up the pamphlets that gave instructions on how to examine a breast. That was something he didn't need lessons on.

"And you must be the big brother," he heard the doctor say as he placed the holder back on the counter and nudged the trash can back into place.

"Yep," Riker said.

"Do you want a brother or a sister?" the doctor asked.

Riker shrugged. "Doesn't matter as long as it's healthy."

"That sounds like something your mother taught you," Dr. Terrance said.

"Is it going to be healthy?" Hunter asked.

The doctor shifted her attention to Hunter, her smile warm and sincere. "It should be. Why don't we listen to the heartbeat and see?"

She helped Serena lie down. While the doctor got her instrument, Serena eased her pants down until her stomach was visible.

"Why don't you guys get on either side of the table and hold her hand?" Dr. Terrance said.

"Is it gonna hurt?" Riker asked as he quickly went to his mother's side and took her hand.

"Not at all," the doctor said.

Hunter moved to the other side of the table, but he hesitated to take Serena's hand. Her doctor obviously thought they were a happy little family, joyously awaiting the arrival of this baby. He felt like he'd felt for most of his life—trying to appear to fit into a situation in which he didn't really belong.

Serena wrapped her hand around his, and he shifted his gaze to her brown eyes. She looked so damned vulnerable lying there. But serene as well. Holding his gaze.

Then the room filled with sound.

"There it is," the doctor said.

Hunter watched as Serena smiled and tears pooled at the corners of her eyes. He'd expected a steady *thump, thump, thump.* Instead, he heard a rapid *swoosh, swoosh, swoosh.*

"Awesome," Riker said.

Awesome indeed. Until this moment, it had all seemed abstract. But here was the reality of it. His kid's heart pumping blood fast and furiously. He shifted his gaze to the poster on the wall, to the beaming boy on the other side of the table, to the eyes of the woman who was squeezing his hand.

"What do you think, Mr. Fletcher?" the doctor asked.

Holding Serena's gaze, he said, "I'd die to keep them safe."

Sitting in the front seat of the minivan as Hunter drove through town, Serena couldn't seem to get the look on Hunter's face as the heartbeat had filled the room out of her mind. Awe. Disbelief. She'd thought he was going to crush the bones in her hand, he'd been holding on so tightly.

Of course, Dr. Terrance had looked equally disbelieving when Hunter had said that he'd die to keep them safe. Only Serena knew he meant what he said.

"Mom, can we stop at Bert's?"

She glanced over at Hunter. "Do you have time for some ice cream?"

"Sure."

"It's a couple of blocks up. On the right. The place with the cow in front."

"Got it."

Hunter pulled into the parking lot, the van idling. Riker opened the side door. "Come on."

Serena opened her door. "Riker, wait there for just a second." She turned to Hunter. He'd never been a chatterbox, but he seemed particularly silent now. "Are you all right?"

He looked over at her. "It just seems more real." His gaze dipped to her stomach. "It's probably always seemed real to you. I mean, the kid's inside you—"

"Wait until she starts to kick," she said, trying to lighten what had somehow become a way too serious mood.

"She? It's a girl?"

"I don't know. Sometimes I refer to the baby as a she, sometimes as a he. I don't like to think of the baby as an it."

"So when will she start to kick?"

"Probably another month or two."

"I won't be here."

She thought she detected disappointment in his answer. Her heart suddenly began to beat as rapidly as the baby's. She was going to be alone again. She was going to go through all this alone. And he was going to be in danger. She wanted to beg him not to go.

"Mom? Mom? Come on. Let's get some ice cream."

She forced herself to focus her attention on Riker. "All right. Let's go inside."

Bert's Dairy Barn had carton after carton after carton of flavors to choose from. Riker always got two scoops of chocolate in a sugar cone. Serena always got a strawberry sundae. She stood there, watching Hunter look the selections over and wondered if he'd ever been inside an ice cream parlor. Finally he said, "A banana split."

"Riker, why don't you go find us a booth?" Serena suggested.

The parlor was small enough that he was never out of her sight as he selected a corner booth.

"When do you leave?" Serena asked, while the attendant behind the counter was working on the banana split.

"A few more days. I'll give you what details I can before I go. A phone number for someone to call who can get in touch with me if you need something."

What she needed was for him to stay, to be here with her. A strange thing to realize she needed when she had forced him to move out of the house. Married but separated. She hated it.

"I'm going to go sit with Riker. You can join us when your banana split is ready."

He nodded. She started to walk off.

"Serena?"

She stopped and looked back at him.

"Thanks for letting me be at the doctor's with you today."

Ah, God, she thought her heart might break. "You're the baby's father. I'm not going to deny you that."

She walked to the booth. "Scoot over, Riker, so I can sit by you."

He looked up at her, a little guiltily, she thought.

"You should sit by Dad."

She sat on the bench, nudged him over, and put her arm around him.

Hunter joined them, slid onto the bench opposite them. "This was a good idea, Riker."

"Me and Mom come here a lot."

Hunter gave her what she could only describe as a teasing grin. "You're supposed to have a pickle with your ice cream, aren't you?"

She grimaced. "No, that's an old wives' tale."

"Do you have any strange cravings?"

Nodding, she scooped up some ice cream, slipped it into her mouth.

"What?"

"I have a recipe for some stir and set cookies." She shook her head. He wouldn't know what she was talking about. "They don't have to be baked. You prepare them and you drop them by teaspoons onto a platter and they're ready to be eaten. They have oats in them. I make a bowl . . . and sit and eat the whole bowl."

"What are we talking here . . . cereal bowl?"

She held out her hands. "Mixing bowl."

His eyes widened slightly. "What other strange things do you do? Riker says you cry at night."

His smile was gone, his voice held no teasing.

"All pregnant women cry. It's hormones gone wild time." She patted Riker's hand. "Sweetie, I'll get moody, but I'm fine."

"Jason's mom cries."

"There, see?"

"She lets him ride his bike to the Sack 'n Go. All alone."

The Sack 'n Go was a gas station–convenience store at the edge of their neighborhood, a few blocks down from where they lived. The store had a help-yourself machine that made a frosty drink the boys liked.

"So can I ride my bike there?"

"No."

"Why?"

"You're too young."

"But I'm older than Jason."

"Doesn't matter. I don't want you riding your bike where I can't see you."

"I'm not a baby."

She could feel Hunter's gaze on her, knew he was probably thinking that she was overprotective. But psychos were out there, even in a small town. She wasn't willing to risk it. "We'll discuss it when we get home."

"But, Mom—"

"Riker."

He threw himself against the back of the booth. "A dad who lived with us would let me go."

She released a deep sigh. Yes, a dad might. How would she let a man help her raise a child who had been hers exclusively for so long?

Hunter slid a napkin toward Riker and set his

cherry on it. "Riker, I want you to look at that cherry. Don't take your eyes off it. No matter what I say. Understand?"

Riker nodded. Serena stared at him. What was he doing?

"How many people are in this building?" Hunter asked.

Riker lifted his head.

"Don't look," Hunter commanded.

Riker squeezed his eyes shut. "Five?"

"Twelve. When we were coming through the door, how many people were coming out?"

"One?"

"Very good. What did he look like?"

"Tall. Skinny. He had a beard."

"He was a she—a woman. So your one was a lucky guess."

"What difference does it make?"

"You always need to be aware of your surroundings. Your mom is right about convenience stores. You always look before you go into one. They get held up a lot. So you want to make sure nothing bad is going down before you go in."

Riker's eyes got big. "Is that what you do?"

"Yep. If I were an artist, without looking around, I could draw an accurate picture of everyone who's in here right now."

"Could you really?" Serena asked.

He nodded. "Yep."

"I thought you would think I was being over-protective," she confessed.

"I do think that. You just need to teach him to pay attention to what's going on around him so he avoids trouble." He tapped his plastic spoon against the plastic dish. "You have to trust him, Serena."

Low blow. It wasn't the same, wasn't the same at all.

He hated the damned motel, wanted to be at his cabin on the lake. Needed to be there in order to get his head back to where it had to be before he went out on his next assignment. Because right now his head was in places it had never been before.

He was stretched out on the bed in the darkness of the ratty hotel, unable to get the sound of the baby's heartbeat out of his head. His baby. He didn't even know if he'd be here when it was born. Hell, he could be dead.

It had never really mattered to him before. The possibility of death, going into dangerous places. He'd always had an edge. A man with nothing to lose. It had made him dangerous.

He'd never meant anything to anyone, no one had ever meant anything to him. Until now. Now everything mattered. Everyone mattered.

• • •

Serena walked down the stairs. It was after ten, Riker was asleep, everything was quiet. She couldn't seem to stop thinking about the fact that Hunter would be leaving in a few days. She should get the nursery decorated before he left. Buy the furniture. So he'd at least have an idea of where his baby would be sleeping.

She reached the bottom of the stairs, picked up the phone, set it back down. It was late and he could be asleep. After they'd finished with their ice cream, he'd simply brought her home, told her to call if she needed anything.

What she needed was someone who would hold her hand when this baby was born. Someone who would run to Bert's late at night when she was craving a sundae. Someone who would help her guide Riker into becoming the fine young man she was certain he'd become—if only she had the courage to give him wings.

She was terrified of losing him, terrified of losing this baby. She was surprised that she wasn't terrified of her own shadow.

The chime of the doorbell had her heart thudding. She lived next door to the police chief. She really didn't have anything to fear. Still, she quietly crossed the living room and peered into the peephole. And didn't know this much gladness existed.

She opened the door. "Hi."

"We need to talk," Hunter said.

She nodded. Yes, they did. "Come on in."

He looked good as he stepped into her house, carrying the scent of spicy soap with him. He'd just showered. She could tell. Shaved as well. And the clothes he was wearing weren't the ones he'd had on this afternoon.

She closed the door, locked it out of habit, and turned to him. "Can I get you something to drink?"

"No. How are you feeling?"

"Fine." She shrugged. "Craving a sundae actually."

"Do you want me to go get you one?"

She smiled. "Bert's closes at ten."

"Grocery stores don't."

"Maybe later. You wanted to talk."

"Yeah. You probably want to sit down for this."

Oh, God, it was bad news. He was leaving sooner than he'd planned. She wasn't ready for this, and she suddenly realized that she would probably never be ready for this. She walked into the living room and sat on the couch.

He sat beside her, and although she hadn't known him long, she couldn't recall him ever looking as grave.

"There are things I can't tell you, Serena, I wish to God that I could, but I can't."

Her stomach dropped. She didn't need to hear this. "Hunter—"

"I'd been undercover, gathering information for a couple of months. I don't know if there was an innocent leak in intelligence or someone sold me out, but I ended up getting captured. I had information that needed to be protected. The army sent a team in to get me out. All hell broke loose and your husband died as a result."

She felt the tears sting her eyes. "I don't blame you for Steve's death, Hunter. What I have a problem with is that you don't trust me."

She saw him reach for her hand, then halt and return his hand on his thigh, as though he feared she wouldn't welcome his touch. "You asked me once about my childhood. My father was a drunk who beat the holy crap out of my mother. One night he locked me in the closet and all I could hear were her screams. Until she stopped screaming."

"Oh, my God. Hunter—"

He held up a hand when she started to reach for him, as though he thought he'd shatter if she touched him. She could see the muscles in his throat working as he swallowed. "She died. I was eight. He was involved in drugs and so much other crap that they were able to stack the charges against him. He got the death penalty. He died by lethal injection when I was eighteen." He shook his head.

"He just went to sleep while my mother died in agony."

"I am so sorry."

He twisted around and faced her. "I'm not telling you this because I want your sympathy. I just need you to understand that I grew up going from house to house and place to place and there were never yellow curtains. I think I fell for you that first night. I have never not been able to get a woman out of my system—and when I realized who you were, I knew that if I told you that your husband died rescuing me, you'd never look at me the same. Because I know what it is to look at someone who is responsible for another person's death.

"It's not something that's easy to move beyond. Especially when you loved the person who died.

"I am so sorry that your husband was the one who had to make the sacrifice for me, that you and Riker had to make the sacrifice. I listened to my baby's heartbeat today because Steve Hamilton and I had a few minutes of waiting in the shadows for everything to clear so we could get out and he told me where to find paradise. What I have with you is bittersweet, because I know I wouldn't have any of it if he was alive. And I know I won't have a future with you if you can't forgive me."

"It's not about forgiveness, it's about trust."

"I'm trusting you now, Serena. I'm telling you as

much as I'm allowed to tell you. I took an oath. There are certain things I can't tell you, that I'll never be able to tell you. But I'm not going to spend the rest of my life living in a cheap motel so I can be near our child, simply because you don't trust me not to touch you if you don't want me touching you."

He got up and walked to the door. "Everything changed for me today. I've always fought for my country, but it's never been this personal. I wish you could forgive me for everything I've done wrong. If I could go back in time I would. I'd take that bullet for him."

And with that he was gone, leaving her stunned and aching and lost.

She didn't wish that Steve wasn't there, but neither did she not want Hunter to be there. The guilt wouldn't leave her alone. From the beginning she'd felt guilty because she loved the way Hunter made love to her. She was grateful that Hunter was in her life. And then she felt guilty for being grateful.

"You're a mess, Serena Hamilton," she whispered.

And the reality hit her hard and swift. She wasn't Serena Hamilton anymore. She was Serena Fletcher.

Chapter 26

Serena scrubbed the toilets, the bathtubs, the sinks, the floors in both bathrooms. Then she moved on to the kitchen.

She'd always considered herself a good housekeeper. But she didn't think her house had ever shined like it was shining today. Her thought processes seemed to work best when she was busy, when she had something to occupy her hands while decisions occupied her mind. She cleaned when she needed to make a decision.

How in the world had she ended up where she was right now?

Married to a man who wasn't living with her.

What was wrong with this picture?

She stilled, staring at the stainless steel sink. If she scrubbed it any more or any harder, she was going to scratch it, wear it out, reduce its shine.

Just like she'd diminished the shine on her relationship with Hunter.

From the beginning, she'd analyzed her actions

where he was concerned, tried to categorize them, tried to justify them—something she'd done with no other relationship in her life.

She'd been afraid to feel, to trust her heart, to let him in. To trust him to stay. Steve, her mother, and even Jack in a way, had left her. She'd been looking for an excuse to hold Hunter at bay, to shield her heart, and she'd jumped on the flimsiest of reasons.

He hadn't trusted her enough to tell her about his part in Steve's death.

Without trust, there could be no love.

The truth was she didn't trust her heart, her instincts, herself.

Because she'd never had to work at a relationship. She didn't have a road map. She'd feared failure and so she'd ensured it.

She wanted a life with Hunter. She loved him. For his honesty, and his integrity. For the burdens he carried alone. She wanted to share those with him. But she had to accept that some she couldn't share. But those that she could—she would.

She wanted his warmth and kindness and the manner in which he guided Riker.

She wanted Hunter. Needed him. For whatever time they would have.

The back door to the kitchen banged open, and she nearly came out of her skin.

"Mom, can I ride my bike over to the Sack 'n Go

with Jason? Please, I'll be careful. I'll pay attention to everything."

"Riker—"

"Please, Mom. I'm not a baby."

No, he wasn't. He was growing up and she had to learn to let go.

"All right." She crossed over to the counter where she'd set her purse earlier and took out five dollars. Much more than he'd need, but she had to begin trusting him sometime, just as she had to begin trusting Hunter. "Get me a candy bar, will you? And get something for yourself."

"Thanks, Mom."

He was out of the kitchen, the door slamming in his wake before she blinked, and she heard him yelling, "Jason, I can go!"

She didn't have a choice now. She returned to the sink and started scrubbing it, to keep her hands and mind occupied until he returned. Then she'd call Hunter, invite him over for supper. Invite him back into her life, into her bed, into their home.

The Roach Motel, as Hunter was coming to think of it, didn't have a refrigerator in the room. If he hadn't stayed in worse places in his day, he'd be more than a little unhappy with his current accommodations. But they were temporary. Tomorrow he was going to head back to Austin. He could drive in from there if anything came up that he was needed for. Staying here wasn't accomplishing anything except to make everyone miserable.

He was finishing up his morning jog, considered jogging by Serena's and stopping at the house for some water—then decided against it. He watched a solitary car pull away from the convenience store and decided that he'd just grab a bottle of cold water from there.

He went inside, acknowledged the young kid behind the counter, wondered when he'd started thinking of everyone under twenty-five as a young kid, and walked to the back of the store where the cooler was. He grabbed the water, then studied the array of snacks on the aisle across from the cooler. He could use something to tide him over until lunch. And he'd discovered that whoever cared for the vending machine at the motel wasn't too concerned with following the expiration date recommendations.

He heard the door open, and automatically looked up and over the shelving. The customer went straight to the counter. Probably to pay for gas. But he was sure a twitchy fellow.

Hunter started to put his grocery items down, realized Serena's worries were making him paranoid, and with a shake of his head, started to head for the counter.

Until he heard an unnatural high-pitched voice.

"That's all I've got, dude."

He crouched low and crept around the display until he could see the clerk at the counter with his hands raised, the guy in front of it waving a gun, reaching around into the cash register. Okay, this was going to get dicey.

He'd just decided how best to creep up on the guy when the door opened, the bell above it tinkled, and his blood turned to ice.

Everything happened in the blink of an eye.

The boys walked in, froze, the gunman turned.

"Hey, asshole!" Hunter yelled.

The gunman pivoted back around. An explosion.

Hunter and the bullet sailed through the air.

The bullet struck first.

Serena heard the sirens. Her heart did its usual thud against her chest. She stepped out onto the front porch—she told herself that she simply wanted to watch Riker ride his bike home from his first independent excursion to Sack 'n Go.

She wasn't panicking. She wasn't worried. She couldn't see the Sack 'n Go from here because it was up the block and over a street. Not a busy street. It wasn't a busy street and the boys didn't have to cross it. They just had to follow the sidewalk.

It sounded like a full scale emergency happening in that direction, though. She thought she could hear police sirens and fire trucks and ambulances. She didn't think Hopeful had that many emergency vehicles. She crossed her hands protectively over her stomach and tried to calm her pounding heart.

The boys should have been coming back by now. She wondered if they'd decided to drink their drinks there. That was probably safer than cycling one-handed. She should get her keys, lock up the house, and just walk down the block to make sure.

And embarrass Riker to death.

She heard a distant door close and looked to see Kelley crossing over onto her lawn. She smiled. "The boys should be heading back any moment, don't you think?"

But something in Kelley's eyes as she neared made Serena think they weren't going to be heading back.

"Oh, my God!" She flew off the steps and started running down the walk.

"No, Serena!" Kelley caught up with her and wrapped her arms around her. "The boys are fine. They're not hurt. Jack just called."

"The sirens?"

"There was an incident at the Sack 'n Go."

"An incident?"

"A shooting. Jack wants me to drive you to the hospital."

"Riker—"

"Is fine. He's with Jack."

"Jason—"

"Is fine."

Serena knew something wasn't fine, because Kelley was gripping her arms as though she thought Serena was contemplating a prison break. "I'll get my purse."

"Serena, Hunter was there, in the convenience store."

She knew what was coming, before the words were uttered, another nightmare that she didn't know if she could survive.

"Hunter was shot."

Serena tore into the emergency room reception area, surprising herself with her calm and determination. She walked up to the desk. "I'm Serena Fletcher. My husband was brought in."

My husband, my husband, my husband. The man living in the motel, the man who is always there when I need him, the man who doesn't know I love him—

"Mom! Mom!"

She swung around, dropped to her knees, and took Riker into her arms. "Oh, baby."

"He saved us, Mom, he saved us. Me and Jason didn't look before we went into the store. He told me to always look, and we didn't. We just walked in, and the guy had a gun and turned to shoot us. He was going to shoot us, Mom. But Hunter yelled and the guy turned back and the guy fired and Hunter got shot. It's not like on TV, Mom, it's not like on TV."

"I know, Riker, I know." She rocked him back and forth.

"Serena?"

She heard Jack's voice, felt his comforting touch, but it wasn't Jack she wanted, wasn't Jack she needed. "Where is he?"

"Surgery. Come on. I've got us some chairs over here."

He helped her to her feet, awkward as she was, trying to keep her arms around Riker. "How bad?"

"I don't know. Upper chest. Shoulder. I'm guessing that it missed anything important."

She allowed him to lead her to the chairs. "What happened?"

"Pretty much what Riker said. Sit here."

She sat in an unforgiving, hard chair and drew Riker onto her lap. He nestled his head within the crook of her shoulder and stuck his thumb into his mouth. He hadn't sucked on his thumb since he was four.

"Can you find something out, get some information?" she asked.

"Yeah, let me go ask if they know anything more."

The hospital was small. Deliveries, broken arms, heart attacks. Would they even know what to do with a bullet wound?

She glanced over and realized that Kelley was holding Jason. She'd been barely aware of her following her in, of her coming to sit nearby. "How is Jason?"

"Shaken up. I should probably take the boys home."

"I'm not going home," Riker said around his thumb. "Not until my dad's okay."

He peered up at her, defiance in his eyes. "You said he could be my dad."

"I know I did."

"What if he dies?"

She wouldn't be able to bear it. "He won't," she whispered, holding him more firmly. "I'd never forgive him. And he wants me to forgive him."

The minutes ticked by as though time were on vacation: leisurely, slowly, in no hurry to get anywhere. Jack sat beside her, hunched over, elbows on his thighs. Kelley had taken Jason home, had offered to take Riker, but he'd been adamant that he wanted to stay.

"He probably saved our boys, Serena. The guy at the convenience store"—he shook his head—"he was high on something. He would have fired without caring that he was killing children."

"Did Hunter kill him?"

"No, knocked him out cold, though, before he lost consciousness. We've got the guy down at the jail. You don't expect things like that to happen in a town like this."

No, you didn't expect them, but still they were always possible.

"I don't want to lose him, Jack."

"I don't think it's going to come to that."

But she knew it very well could. Not because of a bullet, but because she'd failed to recognize what she had before it was too late.

Hunter awoke from the darkness, aware of a dull ache in his left shoulder and his right hand wrapped around something warm and soft. The light in the room was pale, blinds on the window closed. He hated blinds. Hated anything that confined him.

He felt more than he heard the movement. He turned toward it.

An angel smiled at him. "Hi."

He thought he spoke but he couldn't be sure, he didn't hear the words.

With tenderness, she combed his hair off his brow.

"Do you want some ice chips?" she asked quietly.

He thought he shook his head, but the movement seemed sluggish and he couldn't be sure it had happened. "Beer."

She laughed softly. "You can't have a beer, silly. You're on a morphine drip." She lifted his hand, a hand that was holding something. "When you want more morphine, you push this button. Do you want me to push it for you?"

"No morphine. No drugs."

She angled her head and looked at him with what he thought could be described as fondness. "Then you shouldn't get shot."

"Shot?"

Images began flashing through his mind like an obscene slide show.

A crazed junkie.

A terrified clerk.

Innocent boys.

"Boys," he rasped.

"They're fine. A little shook up, but fine." She pressed her palm to his cheek and turned his head. "Riker is over there sleeping in the chair. Can you see him?"

With a blanket draped over him, the kid was curled up in the chair the way a dog might be.

"Safe," he murmured.

"Safe," she repeated. "He didn't want to leave you." She turned his head until he was looking at her again. "Neither did I." Tears coursed down her face.

"Don't cry."

She laid her damp cheek against his bristly one. "I was so scared. I don't think I've ever been this scared." She leaned back slightly. "I was so afraid that you were going to die, and you'd never know how much I love you. I love you so much, Hunter. You asked me to forgive you and there's nothing to forgive. I was confusing you with your job. You have to keep secrets. I can live with that. I trust you. And you can trust me. And you're going to drift off to sleep and not remember anything that I've said, but that's okay because I'm going to tell you again when you wake up."

He could feel the darkness calling him back, but she was wrong. He wasn't going to forget what she said. She loved him. For the first time in his life he was going to take light into the darkness with him.

Chapter 27

She loved the way he trailed his hot mouth along her throat, seeking out the sensitive spot just below her ear, nipping her tender flesh, before swirling his tongue along the outer shell, ending the journey with a gentle nibbling of her lobe and endearments murmured in a voice raspy with yearning.

"Sweet, sweet, Serena."

She combed her fingers up into his hair. "Hunter."

They'd come to the beach house, just the two of them, because it was relatively neutral territory. There were things they needed to discuss, a future they needed to plan.

But once she'd carried her suitcase and his duffle bag into the main bedroom, she hadn't seen any reason not to begin their discussion here. And no reason why it had to begin with words.

His movements were somewhat hampered by his healing shoulder, so she'd taken the initiative, been the seductress, slowly removing her clothes, then his, taking great care with his wound because the stub-

born man wouldn't take anything stronger than
Tylenol, as though he were afraid he'd spill the na-
tion's secrets if he was too doped up.

With his left hand on her waist, he held her in
place while his right hand roamed along her ribs,
until he cradled her breast.

"You're bigger."

"Because I'm pregnant."

He grinned. "I'm liking this pregnant thing."

"They won't stay big."

"As long as they stay mine, I don't care."

"Oh, Hunter." She wound her arms around his
neck, blanketing his mouth, welcoming the thrust-
ing and swirling of his tongue.

She drew back from the kiss, took his hand, and
led him to the bed. "Lie down," she ordered.

He didn't need to put pressure on that shoulder by
supporting himself. This evening she would be the
one in control. She lay down against his right side,
her body half covering his, her hand taking long
sweeping strokes up and down the length of his body.

"Thought we were coming out here to talk," he
said.

"We will."

She lowered her mouth and flicked her tongue
across his turgid nipple, relishing the shuddering of
his body beneath her. "I've missed you."

He threaded his fingers through her hair, closing

his hand on the back of her head. "I've missed you, too."

She peppered his chest with kisses while her hands stroked and explored his broad shoulders, his flat stomach. Hers had begun to round out. Before long, no matter how much she wanted to, she wouldn't be able to lie beneath him.

But they would have years to make up for the nights when she couldn't.

She tiptoed her fingers down his thigh and up, outside his thigh and inside. Down and up, lower and higher. There was so much strength in every aspect of his body. And tonight it was hers to do with as she pleased.

Boldly, she straddled him, dipped her head, and kissed him. Deeply, provocatively. She loved the taste of him, the feel of him between her thighs. In this position, she gave his hands easier access to her and he took advantage, to knead her breasts, to caress, to stroke. To stoke the fires that he alone could build.

She eased down, and he was waiting for her. She held his gaze as she sheathed him to the hilt.

"I've missed this," he rasped.

"Me, too."

She kissed him and rocked against him, rocked against him, and kissed him. All the while his hands fondled. He may have been wounded, but he wasn't weak. She could sense the power building within him, could feel the climax building within her.

When it arrived, it was stronger, more powerful than any that had come before it. And as she soared, she carried him with her, his name mingling with hers as they cried out in unison.

Hunter held her close, nestled against his side. In the far off distance, he could hear the surf and the breeze. A foghorn sounded. He thought he would be content to remain as he was for the remainder of his life.

But tomorrow Morgan was going to bring Riker out there. And in a few months, they'd have another child. And he decided he'd find contentment in being with them as well.

Serena was lazily trailing her finger over his chest. If he didn't need to keep his shoulder still to lessen its ache and help it heal, he'd be trailing his free hand over her as well.

"When will you be leaving?" she asked quietly, and he heard the hesitancy in her voice.

"I'm not."

She rose up on an elbow, her eyes meeting his. "What?"

"I sent in my resignation." Recovering from the bullet he'd taken had prevented him from going on the mission he'd been preparing for. If there was ever a time to resign, it was now, before he got caught up in the middle of another assignment.

A lovely smile of pleasure spread across her face. "Why?"

"I've never had a reason not to go, and now you've given me three reasons to stay. Besides, I'm thirty-four. The thrill of dodging bullets is waning. I followed the path I did because I always wanted to be Rambo. Now I just want to be your husband and a dad to your kids."

"Our kids."

"I thought only goats had kids."

"It's a hang-up I got over. I love you."

His heart swelled so much that he thought it might bruise his wound. "Same goes."

Shaking her head, she kissed him. "No, no, no, my smooth talker." She held his gaze. "When you mean the words, you have to say them."

He didn't think anything in his life had ever been as difficult or as important. Swallowing hard, he held her gaze. "I love you, Serena."

Tears pooled in her eyes and she buried her face against his neck.

"Don't cry, babe."

"I almost lost you."

"Yeah, but now you're stuck with me."

She raised her head. "What will you do for a living?"

"I've never had much to spend my money on. I invested some. Lost some on tech stocks, but I think it'll come back around. I can get into some sort of security business. But I was also thinking of opening up a small gym with a self-defense school. What do you think?"

"In Hopeful?"

"You bet."

"What about your cabin?"

"We can use it on the weekends. Maybe we'll re-tire there."

"That won't be for years."

"I like the sound of that. Years and years with you."

She lowered her sweet mouth to his, and he knew that he'd soon be hearing other sounds that he liked—her moans, cries, and whimpers.

Epilogue

They named her Mary Fiona Fletcher in honor of Serena's mother. Hunter was in the delivery room when she was born. It was the first time in his life that he'd ever felt tears sting his eyes. He had a feeling that it wasn't going to be the last.

She was currently nestled on his shoulder, asleep, while he stood near the beach house waiting for the fireworks to start. They'd invited their family and friends to join them there to celebrate the Fourth of July.

"I don't know if Riker should be around the fireworks that Jack is setting up," Serena said.

All right, he thought. Some things were never going to change. Her protectiveness being one of them—constant. With his free arm, Hunter drew her up against his side. "He'll be fine."

"It's just that you see these reports—"

"Jack will keep an eye out. He won't let the boys do anything dangerous."

"What do you think of this woman that Dad brought?"

Eloise Miller. From what Hunter had been able to determine, she and Serena's mother had been friends.

"I like her, but I can run a background check on her if you'd like." He'd set up a security business that involved running background checks. He knew how to get information out of places that most people didn't even know existed.

Serena glowered at him. "You don't have to do that. I just . . . well, I think they might be sleeping together."

"Good for him."

"You men, you always stick together."

He saw a shadow running away from the water's edge, and then Riker was at his side.

"We've got everything set up, but Uncle Jack doesn't want us near when he starts lighting them."

Hunter gave Serena an I-told-you-so look, to which she only rolled her eyes. The baby started to fuss.

"Here, I'll take her," Serena said.

Once in her mother's arms, Fiona immediately quieted. It always amazed Hunter to watch the two of them, the ease with which Serena took care of their children.

A whistling sound filled the air, and red, white, and blue stars burst out over the water.

"That's awesome!" Riker yelled.

Another whistle. Another burst of color.

"This is great, isn't it, Dad?" Riker asked. "I think it's the best Fourth of July ever."

Hunter drew his wife and daughter against his side and wrapped his other arm around Riker's shoulders. "Yes, son, it is. Tonight is all about celebrating dreams coming true."

Serena smiled up at him. "You never struck me as someone who believed in dreams."

"I wasn't," he said quietly. "And then I met you."